A LOT OF NERVE

A LOT OF NERVE

IAN MCCULLOCH

THISTLE
PUBLISHING

This first edition published in 2018 by:

Thistle Publishing
36 Great Smith Street
London
SW1P 3BU

www.thistlepublishing.co.uk

CHAPTER ONE
DOWN THE PUB

There's a grubby little back street down behind Farringdon Road that hasn't changed in sixty years. An old dilapidated pub stands on one corner, a proper boozer, most of its clientele old men in flat caps escaped from Smithfield Market across the road.

I was sitting in a corner of that pub now, cradling a pint of foul tasting bitter. There were four or five other sad looking punters in there, about what you'd expect for three o'clock on a Wednesday afternoon. By the state of them they'd been there since the market had shut its doors that morning. The sun had made an appearance outside and the shafts of light streaming through the windows picked up the dust eddies swirling around. It looked quite atmospheric in a down beat sort of way.

I took a sip from my almost undrinkable drink. Everything about the pub was exactly the same as it had been the previous Wednesday. Which was just what I was hoping for.

I'd had an appointment the week before with a hoodlum named Finch, and having an hour or so to kill dropped into the pub for a quick one. The Leg of Lamb it was called, and it didn't look very inviting. But it served its purpose, and what happened a few minutes or so after I arrived turned out to be very interesting.

As I'd taken my drink to a table, a small fat man had come in. He'd looked furtively around and walked up to the bar. Getting himself a drink he took it to a table a little bit over from me. What really stood out was how nervous he was. He was twitching as he sat there, hands constantly on the move, making little gestures and fiddling with things. Every few seconds he would get a handkerchief out of his pocket and wipe the sweat off his completely bald head. The guy was scared stiff of something.

My interest was immediately piqued. I had an instinct about these things, it was how I made my living. I sensed an opportunity.

A little bit later two other men came in and sat at the fat man's table. They were very well dressed, good suits, expensive shoes, nice haircuts, but they also had a look about them, a look I knew very well. They looked like someone's heavies, someone's bit of muscle. They exchanged a few words and then the fat man pushed some sheets of paper across the table. One of the goons looked at them, presumably approved of what he saw, and then passed back a bulging brown envelope. I recognised that sort of envelope as well. It depended on the denomination of bank notes being used, but I reckoned there was probably about ten grand inside. All three men glanced around as the envelope changed hands. I looked down and concentrated on my beer which, to be honest, in no way deserved that sort of attention.

There were some more words muttered that I couldn't hear, and then the two men got up. One of them said something about next week and then they left. The fat man followed them out. I would have loved nothing better than to have gone after them there and then and seen if I could get some sort of handle on what was going on, but my appointment took priority; Finch would cut my ears off if I was late.

I went up to the barman as I left. He looked mean and disinterested. He was wiping a glass with a dirty old cloth that clearly hadn't seen a wash in months.

"Afternoon," I said.

He nodded. Almost imperceptibly.

"Busy?"

He gave me a look. He wasn't sure if I was taking the piss or not.

"Some."

"Worked here long?"

"Yep."

"Enjoy it?"

He paused, then shrugged.

I pointed towards the door.

"Do you know those blokes?" I asked.

"Didn't see no blokes," he said. "Didn't see you neither."

I stared at him for a moment, pushed my unfinished beer towards him, and left.

So here I was, a week later, hoping that the meeting I'd witnessed wasn't a one-off and that they'd be back. I was trying a different beer this time, but it was as bad as the first one. I didn't know anything about running a pub, but you would have thought serving a decent pint of beer would have been a basic consideration. No wonder the place was empty. Which made it a great place for a meet though.

I shifted uncomfortably on my wooden seat. There were some armchairs dotted around that looked a touch more comfortable, but where I was sitting gave me the perfect vantage point to see what was going on. It was as I crossed my legs for the hundredth time that the fat man came in. He brought himself a drink, a scotch it looked like, and sat down at the same table as he had last week. I felt a shot of adrenalin running through me at the prospect of another deal going down.

Right on cue, the other two men arrived and sat down as well. The same transaction took place and the money changed hands. At least I hoped it was money. It was the only reason I was here.

They all left together and, giving it a minute, I followed them out. I'd given a bit of thought about who to go after. I'd made a basic assumption that they'd be going separate ways, and I'd swung backwards and forwards trying to decide who would be the best to pursue. In the end I'd decided on the two goons, partly because they were probably the most dangerous and it would be good to get them sussed out, and partly because it fitted in with the rough plan that I had mapped out for next week.

I left the pub not a moment too soon. The goons had got into a rather nice Bentley that was parked outside and were just driving off. The fat man was walking in the other direction.

Damn! It hadn't occurred to me that they would have a car; nobody drove in central London anymore, it cost a bloody fortune. I noticed there was a parking ticket under one of the windscreen wipers. Small beer for them I supposed. Business expenses.

I was really, really lucky then, something that gave me a nice, warm feeling, a good portent for what lay ahead. A vacant taxi came past. I hailed it down, jumped in and said, "Follow that car!"

The absurdity of what I said hit me at about the same moment the cabbie turned round and stared at me.

"You serious?" he asked.

I nodded. "Yeah. Step on it."

He grinned, turned round and gunned the motor.

"Twenty-five years I've been doing this, and no one's said that to me before. Guess I can die happy now."

If he was expecting a mad chase, with squealing tyres and running red lights, he was to be disappointed. The Bentley proceeded at a very sedate pace, making it easy to keep in sight, even around London's infuriating one-way systems. The entire chase only lasted about twenty-five minutes, the time it took us to drive through Holborn, up Shaftesbury Avenue and on into Mayfair.

The Bentley turned into a small side street full of very exclusive looking town houses just off South Audley Street. I told the cabbie to stop at the junction with the main road and we watched the Bentley park up.

"Want me to cover your back while you rush 'em?"

"Funny," I said. I gave him a tenner and got out.

"You forgot your violin case," he said.

The two goons had gone into a house halfway up the street. I walked casually past, but there was no indication that it was anything other than a private house. I did a couple of laps of the street, just strolling up and down, and on one of the passes I nipped over quickly to look at the front door. No nameplates, no doorbells, no nothing.

I hung about at the end of the street for a couple of hours, getting thoroughly brassed off. Not only did nothing happen with regard to the house, nothing happened in the street either. It was possibly the most boring stretch of road in the whole world.

Eventually I gave it up as a bad job and went back to the office. I'd hoped that I would find out a bit more about what was going on, but it wasn't the end of the world, with a fair wind my plan for next week would still work.

I call it an office, but it was just two rooms above a newsagents near Notting Hill Gate tube station. It had its own entrance, next to the shop doorway, and after climbing up a narrow winding staircase, you found yourself in a cramped little office with two desks and a couple of battered old filing cabinets. A door at the back of the office led through to another room where there were two old armchairs and everything needed to make a strong cup of tea.

"Afternoon, dear."

My assistant. Although whether she was my assistant, my secretary, my general factotum, or even, god forbid, my partner, was up for debate. What she was was my aunt. Aunt Mimi. She was sitting at her desk in an old flowery dress that could once have been somebody's curtains, and a shabby headscarf that was trying to disguise the fact that she hadn't bothered to take her curlers out when she got up that morning.

"Wotcher," I plonked myself down at the other desk. "Get me a cuppa will you?"

"Get your own tea, you lazy sod."

She gave me a smirk and shuffled off into the other room. I could hear the kettle being switched on and cups being rattled.

She was a treasure. There was no other way of putting it. She wasn't really my aunt, she used to live in the flat above us when I was little, but I always used to call her auntie. She hadn't done very much with her life, a bit of charring here and there, and she'd worked in Woolworth's off and on, but that all changed when her husband died a few years back. He left her a little bit of cash and she started to dabble on the horses. Turned out she had a real flair for numbers and bookkeeping, and she ended up running an enormous syndicate for all her mates and they regularly took the bookies to the cleaners. Made a tidy profit apparently.

We'd sort of kept in touch over the years and it just seemed like a natural turn of events when she started to give me hand running my books. Despite looking like a dotty old bag who couldn't remember where she'd put her pension book, she was extremely bright, worked hard, and never asked awkward questions about all the slightly suspect and irregular things that running my businesses involved. It had taken me a long time to find someone trustworthy enough to deal with all my untrustworthy stuff, and she now worked full time for me.

The office served as respectable front for the other somewhat nefarious activities that I got up to. I owned at least a dozen assorted companies, I couldn't tell you how many exactly because I tried very hard not to get involved. They were all legit, all above board, and they all made very healthy losses that came in handy for channelling the money that came in from sources that I preferred remained anonymous to both the police and the Inland Revenue. I liked to think that I wasn't exactly a crook in the accepted sense of the word, but I did get involved in deals that ran the definition of dishonest very close. I thought of myself as an entrepreneur, and in truth I was a middleman as much as anything else. I moved things on for people, or I facilitated people getting together who would otherwise never meet. I had a nose for an opportunity, a very large brass neck and the ability to think on my feet. And the thing I never ever did was ask questions. So I never asked where stuff had come from or what people were up to. So far it had all worked out pretty nicely for me.

And Mimi ran my world. In her own understated, slightly unorthodox way, she was probably the most efficient operator I've ever come across. She was also not the most honest person I'd ever come across either. She was clearly creaming off a portion of my profits, but so far I had chosen not to confront her with it. If she kept it within reason, good luck to her. As long as it didn't get to the stage where she was taking so much that it noticed, I was happy.

She came back in with a big mug of tea, set it down and went back to her desk. I watched her, fascinated. Who knew that behind that lived-in old face lay a mind like a computer.

"Oh, Finchy called you, dear," she suddenly announced.

Half my tea ended up on my desk.

"What?"

"Finch. Called you about four o'clock. Didn't sound too happy."

"Why didn't he call me?"

I pulled out my phone. Damn. I'd put it on mute when I was in the pub and forgotten to switch it back on. There were two missed calls from Finch. Damn, damn, damn.

I rang him.

"Where've you been, you tosser?"

"Sorry, Mr Finch, I've been in a meeting all afternoon."

"Well, get your sorry arse round here now."

The phone went dead.

Mimi was looking at me with a surprising amount of concern on her face.

"Trouble?"

"Everything to do with Finch is trouble, but I can't think of anything I've done wrong. Anyway, hold the fort. If you don't hear from me by Friday, call the cavalry."

She blew me a kiss as I left. I think she called me 'ducks'.

Finch used a pub down Canning Town way, the Rat and Ferret, as his headquarters. It took a long time to get there, and as I sat in the back of the cab I stewed over what might have happened that had got him in such a temper.

I'd first come across him about four years ago. Somebody had come to me with a load of medical supplies that they hadn't been able to shift, and I'd fixed them up with a buyer. I hadn't known it was Finch behind it then, but he'd obviously been pleased with the way I'd handled things, because he'd kept a steady stream of work coming my way ever since. It wasn't what I wanted. If I'd known it was Finch I would have run a mile. He had a reputation. Not a good one.

The last deal I'd done for him was just a couple of weeks ago. I'd shifted fifty cases of supposedly vintage wine for him. It had all gone smoothly enough I thought. He'd even given me a case, which I'd thrown away because it tasted crap.

The Rat and Ferret looked like it had once been a bunker in the Maginot Line. A square concrete block with just two tiny barred and shuttered windows, the only outward sign that it was anything other than somebody's defence against German invasion was the small, faded sign above the door that said that it was indeed the Rat and Ferret.

It was as forbidding inside as it was outside, only worse. There were about six people in there and they all stopped what they were doing and gave me a long hard look as I walked in. There was no natural light in the place and the two bare bulbs in the ceiling struggled against the dark. The stench of stale beer and urine was overpowering.

I walked through the eerie silence to the bar. The barman was sitting on a stool by the wall, and though he was looking hard at me, made no attempt to acknowledge my presence.

"Mr Finch is expecting me," I said. I walked over to the table where I knew he liked to hold court and sat down on a hard, upright chair. Out of the corner of my eye I saw the barman disappear. I waited uncomfortably for about ten minutes before Finch arrived, appearing through a small side door accompanied by two heavies. They were big, hard blokes. No mucking about here then, I thought. None of the people in the pub took any notice.

"That wine," barked Finch once he'd sat down. "It's rubbish."

"I know, you gave me some."

Finch was smoking a huge cigar, eying me carefully, while I, perched on my uncomfortable chair in front of him, tried not to look like a naughty schoolboy. He was fat, sweating like a pig, and looking very disagreeable.

"Well, what are you going to do about it?"

"There's no problem. There's no connection to you. If there's any comeback it will be to me, and I can handle that."

"No, no," he growled. "I've got another hundred cases that I can't shift. I sold a load to someone else, and they've brought them all back. I need you to get rid of them for me."

"I don't think I can," I said. "My buyers definitely won't want any more, especially if they've tasted the last lot, and there's nowhere else I can shift it. If it was kosher I might have a chance, but this stuff is unsalable. We were lucky that I managed to sell the load that I did."

Finch looked at me for a beat. The pub suddenly got very cold and still.

"I don't think you understand," he said calmly. "I wasn't asking for your views, I was asking what you're going to do about our problem."

"It's nothing to do with me," I said stubbornly. "I'm just the middleman. And I did a good job for you. It wasn't easy getting rid of that rubbish."

"And now you're getting rid of the rest of it for me. You're my wine distributor and I've got a lot of wine that needs distributing. I would say that's your problem, not mine, wouldn't you?"

"But. ..." I said.

Finch raised an eyebrow, and I subsided. He wasn't someone you argued with and lived. 'But' wasn't a word that should ever come up in a conversation with him.

"Good," he said. "Glad that's settled. And don't take forever about it. I've got a good few bob tied up in that wine."

I got up to go.

"I still don't see that it's my problem."

"Don't push it, Jones. You've done a lot of good work for me in the past. I trust you and I pay you well. But don't think that gives you any sort of say in what goes on here. You've got no privileges. Kapeesh?"

I nodded. I did understand. Very well. I left the pub trying to keep my cool as best as I could, but inside I was seething. One day, I thought, one day.

CHAPTER TWO
FINCH

What are they like these people? Every little pipsqueak comes in here thinks he's got something to say, think they can tell me how to run my business. They don't know what day it is. What is this, a bleeding democracy?

Look at that Jones. Thinks he's a really smooth operator. Walks around in his flashy suit with all his airs and graces, thinks he can tell me what to do. And off he goes with his tail between his legs like a right loser. What a tosser. Really thinks he's mister big bollox. Comes in here and tells me it's not his problem. I could almost laugh it's so comical.

Well, he's on borrowed time now. As long as he's useful I'll keep sticking work his way, but the second he cocks something up, I'll chop his nuts off. This wine job, if he doesn't manage to shift it, that'll be the end of him.

Now I come to think about it, I hope he doesn't sell that wine. Stuck up little bleeder.

CHAPTER THREE
BACK DOWN THE PUB

The next morning I rang the guy I'd sold the wine to.

"You've got a cheek," he said. "That's the worst bit of plonk I've ever put my laughing gear around. I should come over and give you a bath in it."

"Sorry about that, Tweezer," I said. "I had no idea. I really thought it was the real deal. We were all done over with that one. Did it give you any problems though?"

"Naah, not really. A couple of blokes tried to get a bit uppity but we dealt with them. Most of it went to little corner shops, the ones with post offices and newsagents. They wouldn't know a decent bit of wine if it got up and bit them on the bum."

"I'm really pleased to hear that. So you can take a few more cases then?"

There was the sound of laughter from the other end of the phone.

"Not a chance mate. I might get away with it once, but I don't want to get a reputation for doing dodgy gear. You got much more of it?"

"Another hundred cases."

There was more laughter down the phone.

"Blimey you have got a problem. Well good luck with that one, but it ain't coming nowhere near me I can tell you that for nothing."

"Don't suppose you know of anyone else who might be interested. At a discount of course, and something in it for yourself."

"Naah, don't think so. But I'll have a think. If I have any bright ideas I'll get in touch."

"Okay, thanks Tweezer."

I hung up. This was going to be a real issue. I had a feeling it wasn't going to end well.

The wine was still on my mind when I went for the meet the following Wednesday. I'd made a lot of calls without getting a sniff of interest. I was thinking that I was going to have to buy the stupid stuff myself if I didn't want Finch hanging me up on a hook in a meat freezer somewhere, but it was going to cost me somewhere around fifty grand less my commission, and I didn't want to have to do that particularly.

I tried to get my mind back on the matter in hand. I was back in Mayfair looking for the goons' Bentley. I walked up and down their street but there was no sign of it. Damn! This wasn't a good start. I walked back to the junction with the main road and looked around. This really was an expensive area, beautifully manicured houses full of, I presumed, Arabs and Russians. It was still really quiet. Perhaps nobody really lived there.

I let out a big breath, starting to feel a bit dispirited, when I saw it, parked about half a mile up the main road. The bastards couldn't find a parking spot I laughed to myself. That'll teach them to try and drive in London.

I walked quickly up to the car, had a quick look round, then bent down and slit two of the tyres with a penknife that I had ready and waiting in my pocket. Quickly I made my getaway. They weren't going to use that car in a hurry. Obviously they might have another one, or they could cab it, but it should give me enough time to do what I wanted to do.

I hailed a cab and headed out to the Leg of Lamb. I cradled the briefcase I had with me nervously. It contained fifty thousand pounds in mixed bundles of twenty's and fifty's and a selection of envelopes. Too right I was nervous.

I made it to the pub before the fat man, so I found a doorway nearby and settled down to wait. Right on time he appeared round a corner, labouring his way up the street and, as before, looking like he'd just seen a ghost. He really was a state. Fat, bald, covered in sweat, his suit was a size too small, his tie was all over the place and didn't match anything, and he just generally didn't look like he fitted in with the world in any shape or form.

Just as he was about to walk into the pub, I reached out and grabbed his arm.

"Change of plan, pal," I said quietly.

"Eh?"

I was a bit worried that he might have a heart attack. He looked like I imagined someone having a heart attack would look like.

"Change of plan," I said again. "I'm your new meet and we need to meet somewhere else."

"What? What? What do you mean?"

"Like I say. Things are changing a bit. We're meeting somewhere else. Do you know where The Duchess of Bedford is?"

The fat man shook his head.

"Okay, I'll show you. It's only a couple of streets away."

"No, wait. What's going on? This isn't right. Leave me alone."

I gripped the man's arm again. This time much harder, and I leaned into him to speak softly into his ear.

"Listen pal. I'm not making a suggestion, and I'm not looking for a debate. I'm telling you what's going to happen. We're going to The Duchess and we're going to go now. Okay?"

I squeezed his arm a bit harder. He sort of nodded and we started walking. He looked to be having trouble putting one foot in front of the other.

The Duchess was only a couple of streets away, so it was convenient but far enough away from the Lamb to avoid everyone bumping into each other. It was newly converted into a gastro pub and its location meant it got pretty busy in the evenings. I was hoping that on a Wednesday afternoon it might be a bit quieter. We went in and stood blinking for a few moments as our eyes got used to the dim surroundings after the bright sunlight outside. I was grateful for that, I needed somewhere dark, and it wasn't too crowded which was also a bonus. There were people there, but it was a big place and there were plenty of empty tables. We found a little table out of the way in the corner and sat down.

A waitress came over and plonked down a couple of menus. She asked us what we wanted to drink. A waitress in a pub – unbelievable. I was very old fashioned about some things, and pubs were one of them. You should go up to the bar to buy your drinks and pay for them there and then. End of story. I wasn't all that happy about pubs that sold food either. A pub was for drinking. A pie with your pint was just about acceptable, but nothing much else. I bet the waitress was going to want a tip.

"Pint of bitter," I said.

"I don't think we do that," she said.

I looked over at the bar. I couldn't see any pumps.

"What beer do you have?"

"Beer? Yes, we have that."

She looked over at Fatboy.

"Scotch," he said, stuttering over the S. I wasn't sure if he had a lisp or it was nerves.

The waitress went, leaving me wondering what sort of drink I was going to get. I looked at the menu. It was very fancy, written in such a stylised way that it was almost illegible. You could still get a pie I noticed, but it was going to cost you a week's wages.

"Look here, what's going on?" Fatboy suddenly blurted out.

"Nothing to worry about," I said. "Just a slight change of plans. I've taken over from the other chaps. We'll meet up here every week and everything else carries on as normal. Oh, except that we won't be paying you as much."

"What?"

His face was a real picture, surprised, indignant, angry. I wiped some of his spittle off my sleeve.

"How much is it you get at the moment," I asked. He was so taken aback by the question that he actually told me. This was all going easier than I thought.

"You know how much, ten thousand pounds," he said.

"Right,' I said. "Well from now on it's going to be five thousand."

He was just about to explode at me when the waitress came back with our drinks. Mine was a bottle of American lager. I gave her a tenner and told her to keep the change.

"It's thirteen pounds," she said. "You can start a tab if you give me a credit card."

I started to say something but thought better of it. I dug some pound coins out of my pocket and gave them to her.

"Don't you want something to eat?" she said. I shook my head and she left, muttering to herself.

I picked my briefcase up and put it on my lap. Using the lid as a shield I put two bundles of fifty-pound notes into an envelope.

"We'll give you the ten grand this time," I said to Fatboy. "As a gesture of good faith. But from next week it will have to be five."

"That's not fair," he said.

"Life's like that. It's not fair at all. This is all a matter of supply and demand, and demand for what you're giving us has fallen off. But you're still getting a good price. I would be happy with that if I were you." I tried to look at him threateningly, but I felt more like laughing truth be told.

"No," he said. "I'm not doing it. I won't.'

I leant over to him and spoke quietly, trying to put as much menace into my voice as I could.

"Listen to me, you haven't got any choice about this. You're in for the duration, and I think you know that. I have a friend who'll come round and start carving slices off you if you don't cooperate."

Fatboy didn't say anything. I could see behind his eyes that there was plenty he wanted to say, but he just didn't have the courage.

"Okay?" I said.

He nodded.

"Okay. Well, let's get on with this."

I put the envelope on the table, and looked at him. He hesitated for a minute, but then put his hand in his pocket, took out several sheets of paper and slid them across the table to me. I passed the envelope over. He tore open the top and flicked a thumb across the notes.

"Okay." I said. "This is all good. See you next week. Same time, but here."

He glared at me, downed his scotch, and stomped out. I bet when he got home he went through all the things that he would have said to me if only he'd had the nerve. I bet he really told me what's what.

I looked at the sheets of paper; four of them. They were covered in intricate zigzag graphs and pie charts, and what looked like complicated scientific equations. None of it made any sense whatsoever. There were no headings to give me any sort of clue, although there was a reference printed at the bottom of the page: Dstl FCU/4276/wcy 4. The other three pages had the same reference but ended 5, 6 and 7. I assumed I was looking at an extract from some sort of report. Shame I couldn't see the first page. Shrugging mentally I took my phone out of my pocket and took pictures of them all. This was very interesting though. I had no idea what it was about, but if someone was happy to pay ten grand for these bits of paper it must be something pretty damn amazing.

I waved to the waitress as I went out. She didn't wave back.

I wandered back to the Lamb. I realised I hadn't touched my American lager and I laughed to myself. I was turning into an old fart.

The same barman was there when I walked in, wiping the same glass with the same dirty tea towel. I walked up to the bar and he nodded warily at me. I asked for a pint of the bitter that I hadn't tried yet. I took a sip as he handed it over. It was just about all I could do not to make a face as the whatever it was went down my throat. Whatever it was wasn't beer.

Then I had a thought.

"Want to buy some wine?" I asked.

The barman shrugged. It was what he did best.

"Maybe."

"I've got a few crates of some really nice vintage stuff that I could do you for a good price."

"Yeah?"

"Yeah."

We looked at each other some more. He really was hard work. And hard work to look at as well. He had a horribly pocked marked face, a big hooter with ugly red veins all over it, and a few straggly strands of hair plastered over the top of his bald dome. His personal hygiene, or lack of it, just didn't bear thinking about.

He put the glass down and leant over the bar towards me.

"If I put the business your way I'd want a nice little earner."

"Of course," I nodded. "How much?"

"Hundred sovs."

I nodded again. Don't suppose he'd ever had a hundred pounds in his life.

"Sure," I said. "Sounds reasonable. How much do you think you might want of the stuff?"

"Bloke who owns this pub has got a dozen more places in the West End. Could be a tidy order if the stuff's okay. And if the price is right. Why don't you bring some in for us to try?"

"Ok," I said. "Sounds good. When's the best time?"

"Monday evenings. He's always in then."

"Okay, that works. By the way, what's your name?"

"Terry. Terry the Glove."

"Terry the Glove? How'd you get a name like that?"

"My business ain't it."

"Okay, Tel, fair enough. I'm Jones." I tipped my pint to him and walked over to Fatboy's usual table. Hopefully my luck was changing with the wine. It would mean I could never go into a pub in the West End again, but if it got Finch off my back that was a small sacrifice.

I hadn't been sat for more than a couple of minutes before the goons rushed in, looking a bit sweaty and very harassed. They stood in front of my table, gawped a bit, and then stared frenziedly round the rest of the pub.

"Gawd, he's going to kill us," said one of them. They turned to go out.

"You're late," I said quietly.

The effect that had on the two blokes was amazing. It was like they'd been hit by a stun gun. They both froze in their tracks. Slowly they turned round and stared at me.

"I've been sat here for an hour," I said, "Not very professional of you."

They both spoke at the same time.

"Who the fuck are you?"

"Where's Darby?"

Aah! Darby. That was a useful bit of leverage they'd just given me.

"Have a seat, gentlemen, and let's get on with this."

They didn't move, just stood there staring suspiciously at me. This was good too. I had them sussed out now, they were just muscle, not a brain between the pair of them. They didn't have a clue what to do confronted with something different. Not that it didn't make them any less dangerous of course.

I patted the table and, very slowly, they eased into the two seats opposite me. I noticed one of them sliding one side of his suit jacket back. All the better to get at his gun I assumed. More useful knowledge.

"What's going on?" the other one said.

"No problem chaps," I said cheerily. "It's just that Darby's had a bit of an accident at work. He won't be around for a while. So they've asked me to take over."

The two goons looked at each other.

"What are you talking about?" said the one who seemed to be in charge. The one who hadn't made it obvious that he had a gun. "What do you mean they've asked you to take over? There's nobody else in on this, it's just him."

"Yeah," parroted the other one. "Just him. It's just him and us."

I had to think fast here.

"Don't be daft," I said. " This isn't anything that anyone can do on their own. You should know that. He needs some help, like we all do. And now he's indisposed you'll have to deal with me for a while. No problem, it's all cushtie."

They looked at each other again. They were really big blokes, difficult to tell if there was any fat on them under their suits, but I guessed there probably wasn't much. They had close-cropped, well-manicured hair, and those big, square, clean cut faces where you can never really tell what people are thinking, mostly because they aren't thinking. I reminded myself not to get too overconfident, I still had no idea what was going on. It would be very easy to get in too deep without realising it.

"Look," said the almost chatty one. He leant forward over the table and his mate followed his lead. Out of the corner of my eye I could see the ugly barman taking an interest in what was going on. That was something I'd have to deal with later as well. "I don't know what your game is," the goon went on. "But piss off out of it, and don't let me see you sticking your nose into our business again. Got it?"

I looked at him calmly.

"Okay, if that's what you want, but I've got your papers."

A glimmer of something passed over the chatty one's face, but he held it together pretty well.

"Show me," he said.

"Show me the money."

"No. You first."

"Not a chance. You first."

There was an impasse, and we all stared at each for a couple of minutes. They started to look uncomfortable under my gaze. I had my cool, calm persona on, something I had perfected over the years, and something I used a lot in my line of work where haggling and bartering were the stock-in-trade. Never, never show any sign of weakness. Don't show any sign of friendship, don't ever show any gratitude, don't ever plead, always stay in charge, and don't ever, ever fill a silence.

Eventually their resolve crumbled. The chatty one took an envelope out of his pocket and passed it over. Just as Darby had done I slit the top and rifled my thumb across the notes inside. That was just about as close to ten thousand pounds as I could imagine. Satisfied, I took the papers out of my pocket and passed them across.

I think they were quite surprised it was the real deal.

"Right then," the first goon said. The two of them looked at each other waiting for a lead. Eventually they started to get up.

"Wait," I said. "There are a couple of other little changes we're going to make. Firstly, we're going to meet here at four o'clock from now on. And more importantly the price is going up. It's going to cost you twenty thousand from now on."

"Why you…" the heavy with the gun leant across the table and went to make a grab for me, but the other goon just managed to restrain him in time.

"What are you talking about?"

"Well, we've realised what a saleable commodity we've got here. There are plenty of other buyers interested, and they're willing to pay a lot more than you are. But we like dealing with you, so we're happy to continue with our little arrangement, but it needs to be a bit more equitable. Okay?"

"Listen, you little toerag," the guy was starting to lose it a bit more and his voice was rising. "I don't know what you're talking about, but you can go screw yourself. We ain't paying you any more money. If you don't stop playing silly buggers, we'll blow the whistle on you and Darby, then you'll be in trouble."

I smiled.

"Well, Darby isn't around any more, so I don't suppose he'll care. And I'm just the middleman. I do as I'm told. You aren't going to be able to blow the whistle on the people who tell me what to do, because you don't know who they are. And if you blow the whistle on me, they're going to be very unhappy. I wouldn't want to be in your shoes when they find out."

The goons looked at each other. A bit non-plussed. One of them shrugged.

"Well, our boss isn't going to be very happy either. You're going to want to watch your back when we tell him."

I smiled again. I'd won.

"You tell him what happened today. And you tell him it's twenty grand next week. Take it or leave it, it's up to him. Now get lost, I've got things to do."

A muscle twitched next to the chatty goon's eye, but he did nothing. He had a fair bit of control over himself I thought, because I knew exactly what he wanted to do to me.

He got up.

"You want to watch yourself," he said. He knocked my pint of beer on the floor with the back of his hand, and the pair of them left.

The barman came over with a mop.

"Got a nice bit of business going on here have you?"

I grabbed him by the arm.

"If I ever find you've said anything to anyone about this, or got involved in any way, I'm going to come and find you and cut your nose off. Understand?"

He sort of nodded and shrugged at the same time and shuffled off. I let out a big breath, and let the tension seep out of my body.

A really strange thing happened as I left the pub. Two blokes bumped into me, well, one of the blokes bumped into me, and then the second bloke was sort of all over me as well. We were all mixed up together in a big melee just for a fraction of a second, and then they were gone, walking quickly away up the street. I instantly felt for my wallet, because that's what it felt like had happened, they were pickpockets, but it was still there. I looked inside, everything was intact. Weird, I was sure that wasn't an accident, that it was choreographed, but god knows why. I turned and looked after them, but they'd gone.

It was when I was sitting in a taxi back to the office that I noticed my phone wasn't there. Damn, was that what they were after? They must have been very good because I hadn't felt a hand in my pocket. I immediately got the cab to turn round and went back to the pub. I was sure those blokes had it, but I felt I had to check the pub first. And, lo and behold, there it was, on the floor under the table we'd been sitting at. I checked it out, but it seemed okay, undamaged.

Terry the barman was looking over at me enquiringly.

"Lost my phone for a moment," I said. "Didn't see anyone put it under that table did you?"

"Didn't see no table," he said.

Miserable bugger.

Mimi plonked a pile of papers on my desk for signing when I got back. They were tax and accounting things that I left entirely up to her. I could be signing my life away for all I knew.

"Good day, dear?" she asked.

"You know, it was a pretty good day actually," I said. "Worked out all right in the end, but it was a bit edgy for a while."

"Want a cup of tea? A nice strong one will sort you out."

"Nah, think I'll go for a coffee."

She shrugged and went back to her desk.

"Escobar in the two-thirty at Haydock tomorrow," she shouted at my back. "I would risk a couple of bob on it."

I didn't live too far from the office, just a few streets away, perhaps a ten, fifteen-minute walk in the heart of Notting Hill. If someone really wanted to find me though, there were two places they could look. The first was a pub called The Spotted Horse, a big old Victorian monstrosity in Ladbroke Grove where I'd be one or two evenings a week, and the second was a coffee shop called Ray's, just around the corner from the office and where I went if I needed a break from Mimi's tea. It was a little independent place, about as far removed from the big chains that proliferated everywhere as you could imagine. It was dimly lit, had a few comfortable saggy old sofas dotted around, and brewed excellent coffee.

"Usual?" said Kostas behind the counter as I walked in.

"Please." I plonked down on a sofa in the corner. I could feel a spring pushing into the small of my back, but I didn't mind, it was as comforting as the rest of the place.

Kostas put my drink down in front of me. It was big, black and very strong. I took a sip, and felt the rush as it went down my throat.

"Okay?"

I nodded. "Mmm."

I was miles away, thinking about scientific equations and wine and a million other things when I became vaguely aware that someone had sat down on the sofa next to me. He was a big, ugly bloke, and I had a feeling I'd seen him before.

"I've got a message from Mr Finch."

Aah. It was one of the heavies from Finch's pub.

I looked at him evenly, although inside my heart had started thumping.

"He's a bit disappointed you haven't got rid of all that wine yet."

I started to protest, to say that I hadn't had enough time, that it wasn't my fault that he'd ended up with so much rubbish, that it was going to be really difficult, but I stopped myself. This wasn't what this was about. This wasn't about listening to me come up with excuses, this was about putting the frighteners on me, making sure I got the message.

"Yeah?" I said.

"Yeah. Very disappointed. He was expecting you to have come through by now. He wanted me to let you know that time's running out. He said it would be best to leave it to your imagination what's going to happen to you if time does run out."

That familiar old image of meat hooks and freezers flashed through my mind.

"Tell Mr Finch it's all in hand," I told him. "It'll all be sorted out by the end of the week."

The guy looked hard at me.

"Well don't disappoint him." He got up and left. God, he was a big bloke.

I subsided back onto the sofa. When I was through with this I promised myself I'd never go near another gangster again.

"Friend of yours?" said Kostas.

"An acquaintance," I said. "Soon to be an ex-acquaintance with any luck."

Kostas laughed. I didn't have it in me to laugh along with him.

CHAPTER FOUR
TERRY THE GLOVE

Could be a nice little earner in this for me. Hundred sovs would come in right handy at the moment, and who knows I might be able to squeeze a bit more out of it if the deal goes down.

Suppose I should go and clear up those empty glasses in a minute. It's not right I have to run this whole place on my own every day. Should at least be a pot man here to do all the fetching and carrying for me. S'not fair. They really take advantage of my better nature. They just don't realise how much they rely on me. So it's only fair if I even things out a bit. If I work me socks off and then they just pay me a pittance, who can blame me for taking a bit extra? It's only right.

How long have I got before I clock off – another hour. Hmm, it's been very quiet today, so can't take too much. Let's have a look. Blimey, there's hardly anything in the till, it's been even quieter than I thought. Oh well, just take a tenner then. At least that'll get me a couple of bevvies. Be nice to go down a proper boozer tonight, not like this doss house, what a hole. I don't know how they get away with running a place like this, no wonder we get so many losers in here. I've never tasted beer like it, absolute piss. Shocking.

Wonder what's going on with that flash bloke? What was his name, Smith or something? Something very dodgy going on there. Been watching that fat bloke meet up with those mean looking geezers for weeks, and then the flashy guy turns up instead. Very interesting. Perhaps I can muscle in on that as well. I'm doing all right with that hundred sovs so far, another hundred would be a right result. I'll have to put my mind to it. I'm a lot smarter than all those idiots, should be a piece of cake getting a cut from whatever's going down.

You know, I'm really on a roll here.

CHAPTER FIVE
OLD PALS ACT

I made a couple of phone calls when I woke up the next morning. The first was to a mate of mine who ran a wine shop in Chelsea, just off the King's Road.

"Hello, Spike," I said when he answered. "It's Jones."

"Oh gawd," he groaned down the other end of the phone. "Here come's trouble. Like a bad penny you are. I only hear from you when you've got a problem that you want to make my problem. Piss off, I'm busy."

I laughed. Spike and I went back years, we were old drinking buddies. He was a proper cockney, could really come out with the patter when he wanted to.

"Yeah, yeah, I know," I said. "Look, I just want to buy some wine. You got any Chateau Margaux, 2004?"

"Blimey, I have got a few bottles as it happens. Bit out of your league though isn't it? It's what my lot buy for really special occasions, and they've all got more money than sense. I can recommend some other stuff that's just as good but won't set you back nearly as much."

"Nah, it has to be that. How much?"

"Well it's normally £350 a bottle, but I'll do you a twenty per cent discount if you buy a case."

"What? How much? You're kidding?"

"No I'm not. That's how much it goes for. You won't find it much cheaper anywhere else. It's officially a sought after wine. What do you want it for?"

"Present for a friend."

Spike laughed.

"Yeah, I know your game. Some scam going on. Should have gone for something cheaper."

"Yeah, yeah, I know. Wish I could now. Listen I was going to buy a few bottles, but not at that price. I'll come over later and pick one up, but could you put a few more to one side in case I need them?"

"Sure. For you, anything. And I'll do you the bottle wholesale. Can't say fairer than that, can I."

"Spike, you're a star. I'll be over at lunchtime."

"See ya."

The next call was to a guy called Paradine who I'd done some work with a few years ago. He was something scientific, worked in a laboratory somewhere, and the only person in the world that I knew who might be able to throw some light on my enigmatic papers. I'd spent a bit of time the night before looking at the pictures on my phone, but it didn't do me any good, the more I studied them the less sense they made. It wasn't something that a bit of common sense and some inspired intuition was ever going to solve.

"Hello Jones, good to hear from you. How are you?"

It made a nice change to have someone seem pleased to hear from me. I remembered that I'd made him a nice bit of dosh when we'd done the previous bit of business together, so he obviously had some warm, fuzzy feelings about me.

I told him I had this scientific thing that I needed interpreting and he was more than happy to meet up. I guess he thought there was a good chance that he could earn a few bob on the side. I was hoping I would too. We arranged to meet in a little café in South Kensington that we'd used as a meeting place before. I knew he worked somewhere round there although I couldn't quite remember what it was he did.

I caught a cab over to Spike's wine shop first. Just off the busy part of King's Road, it was in a perfect location. I loved the King's Road. I wished I'd ended up living there instead of Notting Hill. The King's Road had always had a special feel about it, sort of classy and homely at the same time, loads of good places to go to and loads of good things to do. Notting Hill had been gentrified but it didn't seem to fit so well with the area. There was lots of money there now, but it didn't feel like it belonged somehow. It was an uncomfortable fit with the roots of the place. It didn't have the charm that that part of Chelsea did. I would have loved to have been around the King's Road in the sixties, to have gone to the Chelsea Drugstore, perhaps bumped into the Rolling Stones.

Anyway, Spike had this tiny little shop which fitted the character of the area perfectly. He'd spent a lot of money doing it up, so it was all polished wood and tasteful fittings, the sort of place that people who were spending a lot of money liked to come. They liked their surroundings to be right, and they liked to be chatted up too. Spike had that down to a tee – it was all first names and how were the kids, and I've kept a bottle back especially for you because I know this is exactly the sort of wine you like. I wasn't even sure Spike was his real name, I always suspected he adopted it because it had the perfect ring for the persona he was putting on.

"What do you want this for?"

Spike had plonked the bottle down on the counter, and I was comparing the label to a picture of one of Finch's bottles to make sure it was the same. As far as I could see it was identical. I decided I'd be honest with Spike. Who knows, maybe he might be able to help.

"Well," I said. "I've got to shift a load. And it might not taste as good as this bottle."

"Aha! I knew it. Dodgy plonk. How do you think you're going to get away with that? They're going to come looking for you as soon they taste it aren't they?"

"Well, I suppose the key is disappearing pretty quickly once the deal is done."

"Jonesy, you're an idiot. There must be a better way of making a living isn't there?"

He looked really young, Spike, although he wasn't any more. He had this mop of floppy blond hair that hung down to his eyes, he was very skinny, and he had this very lively, bouncy manner about him that came from all the pills he took. It all contrived to make him appear a lot younger than he was. That helped with his older clientele as well, they liked that. As they did his cheeky chappy cockney spiel.

"You can't help I suppose? It's cheap."

"Yeah, I bet it is. But no, I can't help. How much have you got?"

"About a hundred cases."

By the time Spike stopped laughing, he had tears running down his cheeks. I was struggling to see the humour myself and I could feel myself starting to get a bit tetchy.

"Yeah, well, thanks for your help, I don't think."

He laughed a bit more, slapped me on the back and wrapped my wine in some fancy gift-wrap.

"Two hundred quid," he said, "And I'm losing money on the deal."

"You're a pal," I said. I gave him the money, nodded my thanks and left.

"Bottom's up!" I heard him call as I shut the door behind me.

The café where I was meeting Paradine was about half an hour away, and I decided to walk it. It's a very pleasant stroll along the

King's Road, and I hoped it might clear my head a bit. I needed some inspiration as far as this wine was concerned. Even if I could do some sort of deal with the people at the Leg of Lamb, I still had a feeling that I was going to have to stump up a fair bit myself.

The café hadn't changed a bit. Very down to earth, basic, catering for the working man, it was full of taxi drivers. I think it must have been a dairy once as all the walls were covered in white tiles. Surrounded by a lot of upmarket shops it was a complete anachronism, and given the price of property around there amazing that it was still going. Paradine was already inside, tucking into an enormous bacon sandwich that had ketchup oozing out of the sides. I ordered a mug of tea at the counter and joined him at his table. He was a really nice guy, very ordinary, with absolutely no side to him. I got the feeling he would do just about anything for anybody. What you saw was what you got. He'd aged a bit since I'd last seen him, got a bit greyer around the temples, a bit more jowly, but he looked okay.

We exchanged all the usual pleasantries. He looked genuinely pleased to see me. Eventually I got round to showing him the copies of the papers that I'd got Mimi to print out for me.

"What's this then?" he said.

"I was hoping you could tell me. I haven't a clue."

"Where did you get them?"

I pulled a face at him.

"Come on Michael, you know I can't tell you that."

"Oh, yeah, sorry. I just thought it might help me work out what it was if I could put it in some sort of context. Sorry."

"Nah, you're ok. But I can't give you any more detail myself. I haven't got any context either. All I can tell you is that they changed hands for a lot of money. Either I'm missing something or these are very valuable pieces of paper."

"Oh right, well let's have a look." He pulled a pair of glasses out of his pocket and bent his head over the paper. I left him to it and drifted off. Whenever I came across someone like Paradine I always got sort of introspective, started comparing my life to theirs.

Paradine was a very clever bloke, he'd proven that when we'd worked together before. Presumably he'd worked hard at school, probably gone to University, and done everything that his parents had wanted him to. I'd been no good at school. I was bright enough, but I couldn't bear people telling me what to do, so I got out as early as I legally could, although, in truth, I'd hardly turned up for a year before that. I quickly discovered that I did have a talent, despite everything my teachers had told me. I was streetwise. I could think on my feet, I had a bit of chat and I could make myself look the part, whatever that part might be. I had tried a couple of regular jobs but they didn't last long, although in neither case was it my decision that I should leave. So the street became my domain. I could see opportunities wherever I looked. And I could see where people had problems that I could sort out for them. And I discovered that the pies that I started sticking my fingers into were actually very lucrative. And so that was what I did. I worked the street and lived off my wits. And it led to the life I had now. I was very well off and I had all the trappings that that brings, expensive apartment, expensive car, expensive everything else. I went to nice restaurants, went to nice places, and never had to worry about how much I was spending.

I pictured Paradine going off to work at the same place every day and then going back to his wife and two point four kids in suburbia somewhere. Could I live that life? There was a little bit of me that wanted to sometimes. But at the same time I knew that I wouldn't last five minutes if I did. There would be the sniff of a deal, the opportunity to take a risk, and I'd be off again, leaving everybody behind.

"You happy, Michael?"

"Eh?" Paradine looked up, surprised. "Of course, you know I'm always pleased to help you out."

"No, I mean you. Your life, the way your life has turned out? Are you happy?"

He shrugged.

"Suppose so," he said. "I don't think much about it."

"Sure. You married?"

"Oh yes. Fifteen years now. And a couple of kids, boy and a girl."

I nodded. It didn't make me feel any better.

"Anyway, what about this thing? Any ideas?"

Paradine shook his head.

"Not really. It looks like someone's produced a report on some tests they've carried out. Looks like they're trying out new ways of doing something, trying different combinations of things, mixing different things together and seeing what comes out of it. But there's no clue what they are. Usually on a graph you'd have the indices or the variables, but on this there's nothing. It's completely meaningless without knowing what the measurements are. Presumably the people interpreting this would have all that information separately. And the rest of the stuff, all the equations, is a bit beyond me as well. Nothing I can hang my hat on at all."

Paradine could see I was looking a bit crestfallen, so he tried to cheer me up.

"Leave it with me," he said. "I'm sure I can work it out given a bit of time."

"I don't know," I said doubtfully. "These aren't really something I should let out of my sight. They really are very valuable."

"Don't worry, I'll look after them. I can do a bit of research on some of these formulae once I get back to the lab."

Reluctantly I agreed.

"Promise me you won't let them out of your sight," I said. "This really is extremely sensitive. It's got to be completely confidential, not a word about it to anyone else. You do understand don't you, this is dynamite. You've got to take this seriously."

Paradine laughed.

"Course. You shouldn't worry so much. I'll be the absolute soul of discretion."

I sat drinking my tea after he left. I had this nasty little nagging feeling in the pit of my stomach that I'd done the wrong thing.

I also thought I'd done the wrong thing when I went back to the Leg of Lamb on Monday. The owner of the pub was a weasily little guy who I instantly decided I didn't trust an inch. He was standing at the end of the bar and he had a bunch of mates with him. When I went over after the girl behind the bar had pointed him out, they all turned round and laughed.

"You the geezer with the wine?" the weasel asked. The pub was deader than it was on Wednesday afternoons. If all his pubs were this busy he wouldn't be buying much wine.

"Yeah. My name's Jones."

There was an uncomfortable pause as they all looked at me.

"That it there then?" The weasel pointed at the carrier bag I was carrying.

"Yeah."

"Give us a taster then."

"I'd like to find out what sort of deal we might be able to do first. This is expensive stuff, I don't want to waste it."

This drew a few more sniggers from the weasel's mates. I really didn't want to do business with these idiots. I was very tempted to just walk away, but there was some satisfaction in knowing that I was going to sell them crap.

"Well," said the weasel. "What do you want to know?"

"For starters, a name would be nice so I know who I'm doing business with. Secondly, if we do end up doing business what sort of quantities you might be interested in, and thirdly, I'd rather have our conversation away from these giggling clowns."

A couple of them bristled at that, but the weasel restrained them with a look. He really was in charge. The ones who didn't react probably hadn't understood what I'd said.

"All right," said the weasel. "There's a quiet table over there. Mary, bring us a couple of wine glasses if you can find any."

He led us over to Darby's table. Spooky, I thought. I might as well set up an office here.

"My name's Walton," he said. "Eric Walton. But everyone calls me John Boy."

"John Boy?" I echoed. "Why's that?"

"Are you serious? You ever watch television?"

"Not much," I admitted.

"Hah! Well let's leave it as sign of everyone's affection, shall we. Anyway, let's have a taster of your plonk."

A bit non-plussed I got the bottle out of my bag.

"Well, it's certainly not plonk," I said. I showed him the label. "It's Chateau Margaux, 2004. This is about as good as you can get in wine terms."

I took a corkscrew out of the bag and pulled the cork. I poured a couple of inches into the two glasses that the girl had brought over.

"Of course, it would better if we could let it breathe a bit first, but it'll give you an idea how good it is."

This is where I was hoping Spike hadn't let me down. The trouble was with wine that you never really knew if was good or bad until you tasted it.

Walton knocked back half of it in one gulp and smacked his lips.

"You know, that's not half bad," he said.

I took a sip myself. It was decent, which was a huge relief.

"Know much about wine do you?" I asked.

"Course. I'm in the trade aren't I. Got to know all about wine. And beer."

I thought back to the awful bitter I'd had to endure there. Yeah, right.

"Your man said you own about a dozen pubs."

"Yeah, but I wouldn't buy this stuff for those. I have another market that would be interested in some good stuff. How much have you got?"

"About a hundred cases."

He raised his eyebrows.

"Wow. I thought you'd be talking about a couple of crates. You do mean business. How much you selling them for."

"If you went to a decent wine-seller, he'd charge you three hundred and fifty quid a bottle. I'm prepared to sell it to you for two and a half thousand pounds a case of twelve."

I'd sold the last lot for a thousand pounds a case, so I had a fair bit of room for manoeuvre.

"Quarter of a mill, eh? That's a lot of money." I perked up at this. Was he seriously considering buying the lot? My luck was in tonight. I mentally crossed everything I could think of.

"Where did you get it from?" he asked.

"None of your business," I said. "You know that. You buy it as it is, no questions asked."

"It's not red hot, is it? I don't want plod jumping down my neck the second I open a bottle do I? I can't be doing with that."

"No, you're ok. It's not on anyone's wanted list, it's just that someone needs the cash and wants to get rid of it very quickly."

In fact, I had no idea where it had come from. Finch had brewed it in his shed down the bottom of his garden by the taste of it. And strained it through a pair of his old sweaty socks.

"I'll give you fifteen hundred nicker a crate for it. For all of it."

I wanted to leap up and hug him. I wanted to bite his hand off, but I managed to restrain myself.

"Two grand."

"No, you don't understand. I'm not bargaining, I don't do any of that negotiating stuff. I'm a businessman. You've got some stuff that you're desperate to get rid off. I don't care one way or the other whether I buy it or not. So that makes it a buyers market, and as I'm the buyer that means I set the price."

He sat back with a very smug look on his face. He'd struck a mean bargain.

"I can't sell it for that," I said. "I'll lose a fortune on it. It's not worth my while. Eighteen hundred."

"Nope. Fifteen hundred. Take it or leave it." He swigged back the rest of his glass and poured himself another decent measure. "Not a bad bit of plonk. I'll have to hold back a couple of bottles for myself. Now, what do you say?"

"You're a hard man, Mr Walton," I said. "But this is your lucky day. You're taking advantage of me, but like you say, business is business I suppose. Okay, One hundred cases at fifteen hundred quid a case. Cash."

He nodded.

"Course. How soon can I get it?"

"Shouldn't take too long. I can sort out delivery times tomorrow. How long will it take you to get the cash?"

"About a week I should think. Here's my number. Give me a call in a couple of days and we'll sort out the details then."

He gave me a card. It said: **'John Boy' Walton, Licensed Victualler**, and then a phone number. I slipped it in my pocket and stood up to go.

"I hope I can trust you," I said. "I've got some big players behind this. They wouldn't take too kindly to being mucked around."

"Yeah well, I've got a big player behind me as well. Probably bigger than yours, so don't you muck about either."

We smiled at each other. We both thought we'd got a win, so we were both happy. He thrust out a hand and I shook it. It was like touching a bit of dead meat.

"Shalom," he said.

CHAPTER SIX
PARADINE

What was it Sandra told me to bring home? Oh god, I can't remember. She's going to kill me. Seeing Jones again has put everything out of my mind, I'm all in a tizzy now. What was it? What was it? Milk? Bread? Coffee? I'm going to be in such trouble if I come home empty handed. Perhaps I should buy her some flowers then. No, she'll just think I've done something wrong and I'm feeling guilty. Like last time. Come on, think, think.

I bet Jones doesn't have problems like this. I bet he does just what he wants all the time, doesn't worry about anybody or anything. It's other people who do the worrying not him. Would be nice to do something with him again though. That was great what we did before. What was nice was that I knew stuff that he didn't, he needed me. I was cleverer than him. And he made me feel clever. He made me feel very special. He made me feel like he needed me.

Come on, think. I was leaving the house. I was late. I was finishing off my toast as I was walking out of the door. I hadn't had time to finish my coffee. And Sandra yelled at me just as I was closing the door. Bring some something home with you, we've run out. Trouble was, Belinda was shouting something down from upstairs, and Brian had some music blaring from the other room, it was all so confusing. Could hardly hear myself think.

No wonder I've forgotten whatever it was. Bet Jones doesn't have that problem. Bet it's all neat and ordered in his world. Expect he has people to do things for him. Someone to clean and cook and sort his clothes out. And do other things for him too I bet. Things you don't get done when you've been married for twelve years.

Still, he hasn't got kids has he. They're such a blessing. They bring such joy to our lives. Which isn't to say they're not a trial a lot of the time, because they are. A real trial. All I ever do is worry about them. Can't wait until they grow up and leave home. Oh not really I suppose. They're my kids, I have to love them.

I bet Jones would love a Brian and Belinda of his own.

Sugar! Thank Christ for that. Sugar. Oh well, a stop off in Waitrose on the way home will be nice.

You know I'm going to try really hard to work out what those test results are for Jones. I'm really going to make an effort for him. I'll bet he'll be so grateful for that.

CHAPTER SEVEN
A PROFITABLE DAY

I phoned Finch the next day to tell him the good news, but he didn't seem all that pleased. I said it would take about a week to do the deal, and he had a good moan about that. He didn't seem very impressed that I'd managed to up the price either. This was definitely the last bit of business I was going to do for that chump, even if it meant I might have to lie low for a while afterwards. Change my phone number, lose the office, that sort of thing. Just not be around when people wanted to get hold of me, until eventually they'd forget I existed.

But with one problem out of the way, I started worrying about Paradine. My gut was telling me that I shouldn't have let him have the papers, and after a couple of days stewing about it, and not having heard anything, I rang him.

"No news as such," he said after I'd asked him what was happening. "But I'm really hoping that I'm going to get some good news soon. There's a couple of people who've said they're quite optimistic about making some sense of it."

"What?" I exploded down the phone. If we'd been face to face my hands would have been round his neck. "What people? I bloody well told you not to talk to anyone about it. You bloody idiot!"

"Calm down, don't get so excited. There's nothing to worry about. These are all people I can trust, good people. They're colleagues. They're not going to do anything stupid."

I tried to get myself under control. I very rarely lost my temper, it was a sign of weakness, but I felt like the top of my head was going to blow off. I knew I should always trust my instincts, and I was as angry at myself as I was with Paradine.

"How many people?"

"Ooh, six or seven."

"Six or seven?"

"Yes."

"And what, they all came over to your lab to have a look at the papers?"

"Of course not. They work all over the country. I faxed the sheet out to each of them. But don't worry, I made it very clear that this was something very secret, they weren't supposed to talk to anyone about it"

"Like you weren't supposed to talk to anyone about it?" My voice was very calm and level now, but even I could hear the menace in it."

"Ah, I see what you mean, but even so, these are the most trustworthy people. They're not going to let me down."

"Paradine, you're a bloody idiot. You'll call every one of your 'colleagues' and you'll get them to send you back the sheets, and you'll tell them that if they breathe a word about it to anyone else, you've got a friend who's going to come round and rip their arms out of their sockets. Now, have you got that? And I want that done now. Now!" I slammed the phone down before I said anything I'd regret. Jesus Christ, what a plank.

I stewed for ages about what to do about Paradine. One of my biggest principles in this business was that I never let other people have information that could ever be used against me. I didn't ever write anything down. I was very, very careful. Always. And now for the first time in my life I'd been an idiot, and there were priceless bits of paper floating around the universe totally outside my control.

I wandered into the office to take my mind off it all. Mimi had made up an envelope with five thousand pounds in it ready to take to that day's meet with Darby. It got me wondering if she'd actually banked the suitcase of money I'd given her last week or whether she'd just taken it home. Her face when she'd opened it was a real picture. I decided I was going to have a browse through the bank statements when I had a little more time to myself.

I was a bit worried that the new arrangements might not work, but Darby dutifully turned up at the new pub, looking even more hangdog than ever. I got the impression that he'd spent the entire week rehearsing what he was going to say to me, because he burst out talking as soon as we sat down.

"Look," he said. "This isn't fair, I'd agreed a deal, you can't come along a few weeks later and say the deal's changed. That's not right, I'm going to …"

"Mr Darby," I interrupted. He instantly subsided. I think it was almost a relief to him because he was too scared to say what he really wanted to say. "What's your first name? We might as well get to know each other a bit better if we're going to be doing business together."

"Well," he muttered, "It's Reginald, but I don't …"

"Reginald. Good," I said. "You mentioned the original deal. Who was that with again?"

"Not saying." He was mumbling now and getting very sweaty. "None of this is right. None of it. It's not right."

I was very curious to get Darby's story and understand a bit more about what was going on, but I was conscious I was going to have to leave to meet the goons shortly, so this was going to have to wait for another time. I needed to get to the next pub very early to make sure they weren't getting up to anything. I didn't anticipate there being any problems in getting him to reveal all at a later date though.

"Okay, okay Reginald. No problem. Anyway, here's the five grand, if you'll let me have the sheets now."

I held out the envelope with the money in it and watched the cloud pass over his face. A small muscle beside his left eye started to twitch. He said something, but it was so low and so mumbled that I couldn't hear it.

"Sorry, Reginald. I couldn't quite hear what you said."

"Supposed to be ten," he said through clenched teeth.

"Look Reginald, we've been though all that. We agreed on five. Now let's get on with it, I've got other more important things to do." My tone had stiffened now, and I passed the envelope over to him.

He took it. Meekly. And with a sweaty hand passed the pieces of paper over to me. Mentally I breathed a huge sigh of relief. I looked at the papers. They seemed identical to the ones I'd already seen, so I pulled out my phone and compared them to the pictures I'd taken. There were actually a lot of small differences, which made sense I guess, remembering what Paradine had told me about trying new combinations of things to see if they worked.

"Thank you, Reginald," I said. "And don't worry about things so much. Just enjoy the money and get on with your life. Spend some of that lovely cash, eh?"

As I left the pub I looked back at Darby. He was staring morosely at the envelope in front of him, a perfect picture of abject misery and frustration.

It had turned into a beautiful day. There had been a lot of cloud around earlier but now the sun had come out. London can be a very beautiful place sometimes. Not always, it's often the ugliest place in the world, but occasionally it can take your breath away. A late spring day, everything coming into bloom, people sitting outside eating and drinking, it was just magical. It made you feel like you could do anything. Unfortunately on this beautiful day, I was heading to the world's worst pub to meet two very unpleasant characters who were as likely to break my arms as smell the roses.

I'd been trying to think of a few contingencies in case they decided they weren't too happy with me. I had considered bringing some muscle of my own for support, but had eventually decided against it. I didn't want things getting any more complicated than they already were. I'd decided I was going to watch them arrive from a safe distance and see if they brought any more backup with them. If it was just the two of them I was confident I could deal with them. I wasn't any Mohammed Ali or anything but I could hold my own. I'd done it before so I knew what had to be done in those situations. And I think people underestimated me a lot of the time, I was tougher than I looked.

But what I did do was to phone Mimi and tell her that if I hadn't texted her 'ok' by five o'clock, she was to get hold of Spook and Beaky, two muscular friends of mine, and send them round to the house in Mayfair to come and find me. I gave her the address. I'd spent a lot of time teaching her how to text, as she hadn't owned a phone before she came to work for me. Every time she did text me she put 'dear' on the end.

I found a doorway and waited. Right on time, the Bentley pulled up, eased into a Disabled Parking Bay, and the two goons out. They walked into the pub and I waited another five minutes, to see if all was quiet. It was. I followed them into the pub.

"Afternoon, gentlemen."

I sat down on the other side of the table to them, but they instantly moved round to sit on either side of me. It was very threatening, but not altogether surprising, I was expecting a show of strength.

"Listen, you prat." The chatty goon had leaned right in on me and was almost whispering in my ear. "Our boss isn't happy with what's going on. He's asked me to make you an offer."

I looked at him and nodded.

"He says, no we aren't going to pay you twenty grand. But what he'll do, as a gesture of good faith, is let you give us the test results and he'll let you walk away without having anything broken. Now that sounds like a fair deal, doesn't it? So what do you say?"

At this point the second goon also leaned in on me and put a hand inside his jacket. I was thinking that perhaps I had miscalculated being able to deal with them.

"Can I get you gentlemen anything to drink?" A voice suddenly made everyone sit up. It was Terry, the pockmarked barman, standing at our table. Well, well, well, perhaps I did have some backup after all.

"Afternoon, Terry," I said cheerfully. "Three scotches please, we'll have three scotches. Large ones. Scotch all right for you gentlemen?"

The two goons pulled back away from me and tried to look normal.

Terry came back with the drinks after a few minutes. The three of us had sat in silence while he was away.

"Oh by the way," Terry said to me as he put the drinks down. "Mr Walton said to remind you that you've got a meeting with him later. Said to me to let him know if for any reason you might not be able to make it."

He turned and went back to the bar with a leery smile on his face.

I took a big gulp of my scotch. It burned as it went down but it did me good.

"Look," I said. "You can lay off this hard stuff. It's not going to work with me. All you're going to do is start a war, and I don't think any of us wants that. This is business. Either you pay the going rate or you piss off. If you think you can come in here and start threatening me and think that we're all going to roll over, then you ought to go back to school and start your education again. Don't waste your time or mine with all this macho stuff, it's pathetic. Now do we have a deal? If we don't, you can just walk away now."

They both stared at me. If looks could kill I would have been a dead man twenty times over. The chatty goon took an envelope out of his pocket and tossed it on the table. I slit it open. Four bundles instead of two.

"No monkey business?" I said. They glared at me. I passed over the sheets.

"Listen fartface," the chief goon said. "You might have something we need now, but that's not going to last forever. One day, when this is all over, you're going to come home and find us waiting for you. I can promise you that. And I hope your neighbours don't mind the sound of screaming."

That vision of the meat hooks sprang into my head again.

They got up. The second goon snarled in my face as they left. He'd had fish for lunch and it wasn't good fish. I finished my scotch and went up to the bar.

"Thanks, Terry," I said. "Does this cover it for the drinks?"

I gave him two fifty-pound notes.

"Just about," he said.

I nodded to him and went to leave, my heart still beating louder than my footsteps.

There was a bit of park about a five-minute walk from the pub. Just a left over sliver from some forgotten something or other lost amongst all the noise and commotion that was Smithfield Market at its worst. A calm little retreat where you could get away from everything. Except this was obviously where everybody came when the sun finally made an appearance. I used to use it for meets occasionally when I needed somewhere secluded, but now it was absolutely heaving. Londoners did like the sun. There wasn't a patch of grass without somebody on it trying to get bits of their pale white bodies to turn red.

I managed to find a bench in the shade that had just one little old lady sitting on it. I subsided thankfully down and texted Mimi. "Ok!"

I tried to get my head round where I stood in all of this.

In basic terms I was now doing a weekly business where I was making fifteen thousand pounds profit by basically turning up to two pubs for a couple of hours one afternoon a week. It wasn't pleasant dealing with the goons, but as long as I watched my back I would be all right. So I couldn't see any reason to stop. It might not last very long for any number of reasons. The biggest threat to the whole thing was the goons trying to get hold of Darby directly. There must have been some sort of original approach by one side or the other in the first place, so they must have known where to get hold of him. I was surprised they hadn't done that already, but I concluded they weren't over-blessed with brains. But they might think of that soon.

The other thing to think about was the test results themselves. What was obvious was that the papers were extremely valuable. If the goons, or whoever they worked for, could pay twenty grand for them they were obviously selling them on for a lot more. If I could only work out what they were I might be able to eliminate the goons completely and start making some real money.

All in all, things weren't going too badly considering.

As I got up to go, the old lady said, "You look like the cat that's swallowed the cream."

I smiled.

"Yeah, suppose I am really."

"Smug git," she said.

CHAPTER EIGHT
DARBY

I don't like him, I don't like him at all. As if I didn't have enough to deal with already without him coming along and sticking his nose in where it's not wanted and telling me what I'm going to do.

And now they've cut back on what they're paying me. I could see that coming a mile off mind you. This isn't really blackmail they said, and to prove it we'll pay you, pay you handsomely. Don't think of it like blackmail, it's just a business deal. You give us some harmless information and we'll give you a lot of money. But of course, they said, you don't really have any choice, because if you don't help us we'll have to tell your wife what you've been up to. But it's not blackmail, it just us being public spirited. If you want to go around doing naughty things that's up to you. But forget about all that, this is just a business deal.

But it's not being naughty, it really isn't. It's a lovely thing, a good thing, the first thing that's ever made me truly happy in my whole life. It's beautiful. But Agnes isn't going to understand that. She doesn't understand anything. She doesn't want me to be happy. I think she really wants me to be unhappy the way she goes on. Perhaps I should just tell her, get these blokes off my back once and for all. Perhaps I should tell her. No I can't. I couldn't do it, we've been together for so long. It just doesn't bear thinking about. No, no, what would happen to us. It would be terrible. I just wouldn't know what to do.

And I don't even know what it is I'm giving them. They don't tell anybody what's going on. All a lot of gobbledy-gook as far as I'm concerned. God knows what bullies like them want it for. It's madness.

Still, even though it's not ten any more, five thousand pounds a week is still a lot of money.

It's still enough for me to spend on her, to keep her happy. Her.

CHAPTER NINE
TWO UNPLEASANT SURPRISES

Eventually I rang Paradine again. I'd given myself a few days, enough time to calm down I thought. The problem was I needed him, there wasn't anybody else I knew that could even remotely do what he could do for me. I had the new papers to show him, and I figured as long as he could convince me that he'd got all of the others back and minimised any chance of them being talked about at large, I was happy to go forward with him. But he'd bloody better not step out of line again.

I called his number. After a couple of rings it was answered and a man's voice I didn't recognise said, "Who is this?"

Damn. I immediately hung up. Christ, that didn't sound right. The voice had an ominously official tone to it. Something was wrong. Very, very wrong.

I really wished I'd hadn't used my mobile to make the call, that was stupid. Whoever it was who answered had my number now and could easily track me down. I hoped against hope there was a harmless explanation for this, but I had a nasty feeling it was going to be bad news. Christ, that was two mistakes I'd made now, what was happening to me? And they were both to do with that idiot Paradine. Well, that settled it for me, he's out.

* * *

I spent all day thinking about it and worrying. The most frustrating thing was that I couldn't think of any way of finding out if there was a problem or not without phoning Paradine again. And I definitely didn't want to do that. As it happened, my frustrations were resolved pretty quickly. And, as I suspected, it was bad news.

My doorbell rang about eight-thirty that night. I was in my living room, sipping a brandy and thinking about switching on the TV to take my mind off things.

I crept quietly to the front door and looked through the peephole. A couple stood outside, a man and a woman. I could only see him clearly, and he had plod written all over him.

I opened the door.

"Mr Jones?" This was the woman.

I nodded.

"I'm Detective Inspector Hernandez from the Metropolitan Police. And this is Detective Sergeant Monk." They both held out their warrant cards, but at an angle so that I couldn't see them properly.

I nodded.

"May we come in?"

"What's it all about?" I said.

"I'm sure you'd prefer it if we talked inside rather than letting your neighbours find out what's going on in your life." The female copper was very assertive, very dominating. Not somebody I would want to cross I thought.

I asked to see their warrant cards again, and I examined them closely. As far as I could tell they looked genuine enough, but I was no expert. I opened the door and gestured them inside. My gut feeling was that they were police and not some lowlifes coming to get me, but I was certainly going to tread carefully with them either way. My mind raced trying to think what the police could want me for. I couldn't think of anything, unless that dodgy wine was going to crop up and bite me on the arse again.

"Take a seat," I said.

They both sat on the big, main sofa, and I chose a seat opposite them, one that was considerably nearer the front door.

They were a right pair. Monk was middle aged, wearing a crumpled old suit that was a size too big for him, and had that look behind his eyes that said he would rather be anywhere else in the world than here at this moment. He looked like a real timeserving copper, doing the bare minimum, doing it by the book, and counting down the days until he could pick up his pension. She, on the other hand, was tall, slim, long black hair, wearing a white shirt under a jet-black, fitted trouser suit, and very much in charge. I couldn't take my eyes off her. I wonder what poor old Monk thought of it all. She was young enough to be his daughter, already outranked him, and he probably went home and had dreams about her every night.

We sat and stared at each for a while. I was very good at not breaking silences. It was something you learned very quickly when you were negotiating. The woman spoke first.

"When did you last see Michael Paradine?"

Oh God, not him again. What's the idiot been up to now?

"I'm not sure," I said calmly. "Last week? Tuesday or Wednesday? Why, what's he done?"

"Where did you last see him?"

"Why do you want to know?"

"Just answer the question. Where did you last see him?"

"In a café in South Kensington."

"And that place was called?"

"Dora's."

"And the purpose of that meeting?"

"No purpose. We were just meeting up for a cup of tea."

"And when had you last seen him before that?"

"Years ago. I hadn't seen him for years. I can't remember when."

"Isn't that a bit strange, you meeting up with him for a cup of tea when you hadn't seen him for years? That would make it appear that there must have been some purpose to the meeting."

"Well, it might appear strange to you because you know what he's been up to. It's not strange to me because I was just having a cup of tea with an old friend. If you were to fill me in on what he's supposed to have done, we might start getting somewhere."

The pair of them sort of settled back in the sofa. Both sets of eyes bored into me. I was good at this, but I was starting to feel a tad uncomfortable inside.

It was Monk who spoke this time. The first time he'd said anything.

"Paradine's dead. We have every reason to believe he was murdered."

Everything started to go black, my head swam. I don't think I have ever felt as shocked as I did then. I tried to pull myself together. Hernandez leant forward, her eyes piercing.

"You're looking pale, Mr Jones. Something you want to tell us?"

"Are you sure?" I managed to get out. "There must be some mistake."

"Really? A mistake? Why would you say that?"

"Well, he's just an ordinary guy, why would anybody want to murder him? It doesn't make sense."

"Well, we're hoping you might be able to throw some light on that." She looked over at Monk.

"According to Paradine's phone records, you phoned him just over a week ago, again a few days later and again this morning, when you hung up as soon I answered. There's no record of you having contacted him at any time over the previous three years. So within a week of calling him after not having spoken to him for some considerable time, he is found dead. Murdered. That's an incredible coincidence, wouldn't you say?"

I just stared at them. I didn't know what to say.

"Let's stop playing about here," said Hernandez. "Let's start by you telling us what the purpose of the meeting was."

I shook my head, everything was still spinning.

"There wasn't any reason," I said, trying to keep everything under control. "We were just hooking up again. We were good friends years ago and I just fancied seeing him again."

"And can you think of any reason why anybody would want to have him killed?"

I shook my head again.

"I don't really know much about his life any more. But I doubt it, he was just an ordinary family guy doing an ordinary job. And he was a nice guy, I can't believe for a moment he had any enemies. It just doesn't make sense."

"What was his job?"

"I'm not sure. I think he worked in a laboratory or something."

"You don't seem to know much about him considering you were such good friends?"

"I told you, we were good friends a long time ago, but I hadn't seen him for years. I'd lost touch with what he was doing with himself."

"And you didn't ask him what he was up to when you caught up with him after not having seen him for years?"

Christ, I thought, she was good. Really good. She knew what she was doing. I was going to have to be really careful here. Minimum of detail and concentrate on not contradicting myself.

"No," I said. "That's not really me. I find all that stuff a bit boring."

I thought I almost caught the beginning of a smile, but it instantly disappeared.

"No," she said. "Of course not. Tell me Mr Jones, what do you do for a living?"

"I'm a business man. I own a few companies."

"Oh, really? What sort of companies?"

"Well. ..." I paused, I had to think. "... I own a dry-cleaning business."

I was pretty sure Mimi had told me that once.

She raised an eyebrow.

"Really? Is it a successful business?"

"Well, it pays the rent."

She raised an eyebrow again and pointedly looked around the room.

To be fair, it was quite special. I'd spent a lot of money having the whole flat done up when I'd bought it. I'd employed a very expensive interior designer and she hadn't stinted in spending my money on the most exclusive furniture and fittings money could buy. The place looked spectacular, certainly not your average, run-of-the-mill living room.

I shrugged.

"Well, can you tell us anything else about Mr Paradine that might be relevant to this case?"

I shook my head.

"Afraid not. Like I said, I hardly knew him now." I suddenly had a thought. "How was he killed?"

"We were hoping you might be able to tell us."

I kept my mouth shut.

They both got up, still staring at me. I got the feeling very strongly that my reaction to finding out about Paradine's death had got me off the hook. My reaction had clearly been genuine and had been obvious to them both, even Monk.

"This certainly won't be the last time you'll hear from us," said Hernandez. She handed me a card. "You contacting him shortly before he gets killed would certainly lead us to believe that there's more to your connection than you're telling us. We'll be in touch again. Please don't leave London without letting us know. And if you think of anything that might help us in this case you can call me on this number."

I looked down at the card. It said: **Detective Inspector Hernandez, Metropolitan Police**, and then a phone number.

"You Mexican?" I queried.

She looked at me for a beat.

"Long story," she said. "Don't leave town."

I sat down and poured myself another brandy after they'd gone. Poor old Paradine, he didn't deserve what had happened. Whatever had happened. The only thing of significance that I could think of was something that hadn't been mentioned – the papers. I was sure that if the police had found them on him or at his house they would have asked me about them. If the police hadn't found them, then the people who'd killed him had, and that had to be the reason for the murder. The thought made my blood run cold.

Actually there was one more thing of significance I could think of I realised. I was really looking forward to hearing the story behind Hernandez' Mexican connection.

I spent a good part of the next day in the office catching up on a few things and brooding about Paradine. It wasn't an emotion I was used to, but I did feel sort of guilty about his death. I was a great believer in people being responsible for themselves, making their own decisions, standing on their own two feet, not looking to other people to do things for them. I didn't have much sympathy with needy people. But Paradine. He was such a nice bloke. A nice ordinary bloke. He didn't deserve what had happened to him, and it was my fault he'd got involved. If I hadn't come along with those stupid test results he'd still be here, still leading his boring, mundane life, but still alive.

I'd already decided that I was going to help Paradine's widow in some way, give her a big chunk of money that would see her and the kids though for the foreseeable future. What I couldn't decide was how to go about it. I was conscious of how it would look to the police if I suddenly pitched up and gave her a wad of money. I tried to work out how I would react if I really didn't know what was going on, if he really was just a casual friend I hadn't seen for years? Would I go and see his wife? Would I just ignore what had happened? What would a normal person do?

I had no idea.

Mimi had some stuff for me to sign, which I did without reading, and she gave me an update on a few things that I didn't really listen to. As I was sat there, pondering all my options, I had a thought.

"Can you give me a list of all the companies I own," I asked. "Give me a brief summary of what they do, how many people they employ, that sort of thing."

She looked at me a bit askew.

"What on earth for?"

"Just in case somebody starts asking me questions about them," I said. "It would be handy if I had some of the answers."

"Are you checking up on me, dear?"

"Of course not. It's just I had the police round last night, and they started asking."

"What? What did they want?"

"Friend of mine was in an accident. Wanted to know if I knew anything about it."

She let out a big sigh of relief.

"Thank goodness for that," she said.

"Feeling guilty?"

"Absolutely I am, ducks. And so should you be. We could hang for some of the stuff that we've got going through our books."

I laughed.

"Yeah, you're right. Doesn't bear thinking about."

"But I haven't got a list, or anything like it." She frowned. "I'll have to put it together from scratch. It'll take me ages. You've got twenty-seven separate business you know."

Good god, I thought, I won't be able to remember them all even if I do have a list.

I went for a drink down the Spotted Horse after I left the office, had a couple of pints and then left for home.

Unfortunately, I didn't actually leave.

Just as I was walking out of the door, two men came in. Very neatly they walked either side of me, took hold of me by the elbows, shuffled me backwards and plonked me down on a saggy old sofa. They sat down on either side of me, still holding me by the elbows. It was all very smoothly done. Very quietly and very effectively, they'd completely immobilised me. It was just about as professional thing as I had ever seen. These guys were the real deal.

"So this is our middle man," said the one on my left. He was quite young, had unfashionably long fair hair, and was very, very upper class.

"Well, well, well," said the other. He had the same sort of look and the same sort of plummy accent, the only difference between him and the other one was that his hair was dark. "A middle man, eh? I don't think I like middle men."

The two of them burst out laughing. I wasn't sure what the joke was, but I wasn't finding it very funny.

"This is by way of being an official warning," said the first one, getting serious all of a sudden. "You're interfering with something you shouldn't be. This is something that you shouldn't be involved with. Understand? So, no hard feelings, but this is the end of it. No more middle man."

"I don't know what you're talking about."

"Oh, I think you do. You've managed to insert yourself very cleverly in between the exchange of certain pieces of paper and some rather large amounts of money. Very nicely done, if I might say so, but your little run has come to an end. Like I say, no hard feelings, no repercussions, but time to move along, as they say."

"Nothing to be seen here," said the other man, and they both burst out laughing again.

"Who are you two clowns?" I asked.

"Clowns? That's not very nice," said the one on the left. He seemed to be the senior of the two. "I'm not going to tell you who we are, other than to say we're official. Properly official. You've got yourself mixed up in something very serious, and what's important now, is that you get out of it and stay out of it. Disappear. Got it?"

"And if I don't? If I don't take you clowns seriously?"

"Then you might well find yourself thrown in the Tower of London, with someone throwing away the key." Predictably, this caused them to burst out laughing again.

They got up.

"Friendly warning," said the first one. "But don't let's see you again. That would be very unwelcome. And then we'd have to stop being friends."

They both smiled at me.

"Mind how you go," said the second one. He slapped the other one on the back and they left, laughing happily to themselves.

I sat there stunned.

Official? Now what was going on?

CHAPTER TEN
D.I. HERNANDEZ

ook at all that paperwork, there must be more than twenty files sat there that I'm supposed to go through. And then they say, why aren't you out catching thieves? It's unbelievable. They say we're not supposed to sit at our desks, but I get so much paperwork I could spend my whole working week sat here. This isn't why I became a copper. This isn't why I worked my way through University and Training College and put up with all the abuse and the snide remarks because I was a woman and I was educated. I want to get out there and make a difference. But I can't because I'm snowed under by all this rubbish.

Look at this one. From that idiot Monk. He questioned three people about that burglary in Kilburn and he's written forty pages about it. Makes it look like he did a full day's work, when it took him twenty minutes and he spent the rest of the day down the pub. And all the next day in the office writing about it. Hark at this: 'I was proceeding in a westerly direction down Kilburn High Road, when I noticed a person of male description, well known to me as someone with known criminal tendencies, coming in the other direction.' What a load of bloody rubbish.

I should be out investigating that murder of, what's his name, Paradine. That was gruesome, really gruesome. He'd taken a lot of punishment before they'd finally killed him. So what was that all about? Torture for the sake of it? Possibly. Revenge for something he'd done? Unlikely, he sounded a saint from the way everyone talked about him. Even that Jones said so. Trying to get some information out of him? More like it. But he'd held out for a long time judging by the state of his body. Poor bloke. And we've no idea if he did hold out. Whatever way it ended he'd had to go through a lot of pain first.

And that Jones knows more about this than he's saying. There's no doubt he was shocked when he heard the news, that was genuine enough. But he and Paradine were definitely up to something together. I'll stake my career on it. I think we'll pop over and see him again tomorrow. Try and catch him in his apartment again. I'll look forward to that.

Why are all the good looking ones bloody crooks?

CHAPTER ELEVEN
THE RETURN OF THE WINE

The wine handover was arranged for the next day, Thursday. I was still fretting over Paradine and what I should be doing about him, but life had to go on.

There was a bit of waste ground up by Scrubs Lane that I used a lot for that sort of thing. It was the perfect spot, a bit out of the way, secluded, and there really wasn't anywhere for someone to hide to do any spying. Or to do the dirty on me. There were also a lot of exits. I wasn't going to be penned in anytime soon.

I'd cabbed round to Finch's warehouse. The lorry was already loaded up and ready to go, with the driver sat in the cab looking bored and disinterested. Bugger. He'd driven some stuff for me before, and he was a nightmare. I presumed Finch didn't pay him much otherwise I don't know how he put up with him.

"Door," he said.

I looked at him quizzically. He gestured towards the main doors of the warehouse.

"Expect me to magically waft through them, do you?"

I stared at him, controlling my temper beautifully. There was no point in having a go at berks like this. Complete waste of time.

"I need to check the load first," I said. He shrugged.

I went round the back, opened up the doors and climbed inside. It was a bit of a squeeze, but I could just about get round and count the cases. The hundred were all there. I opened up three or four at random; they all contained the dreaded Chateau Margaux, 2004. I would have liked to check them all because I had a bad feeling about Finch, but I just didn't have the time. I was going to have to take it on trust. But for the last time, I told myself.

It was about a thirty-minute drive to the waste ground. I'd heard a rumour that some crappy football club was going to buy it and build some super new stadium there that they'd never fill. That was a shame because there weren't many places like that left any more. It wasn't all that long ago that London was filled with open spaces, bombsites everywhere, but not any more.

A bit of a drizzle had started to fall by the time we arrived. It was grey and miserable, exactly matching my mood. Walton was already there, leaning against the side of his own lorry. He had two heavies with him, which I didn't like the look of.

"Morning," he said as I got out. I turned my collar up against the rain and nodded to him.

"John Boy."

"Let's have a look at the goodies," he said. He was rubbing his hands together, looking like he was really excited.

I opened up the back and the two heavies started shifting the crates over to their own lorry. As they did they opened each one and made sure they were full.

"Got the money," I said.

Walton took some big bundles of cash out of his coat and waved them in front of me.

"When I've got the merchandise," he said. I didn't like the way this was going. I usually had a lot more control over things. I knew the driver, who was still in his cab reading the Daily Mirror, wasn't going to be much help in times of trouble.

"Well, no funny business," I said. "Don't forget I know where to find you. The guy who owns this stuff doesn't like being mucked about. He can get very nasty."

"Don't worry, don't worry, we're all good. I need to do the deal as much as you do."

"Yeah? What do you want it for?"

"It's a present for someone."

"That's very generous of you."

"Well, not exactly a present, I'm going to want my money back. But there's a guy I want to get in with, want to do some work for. I figured if I present him with this lot, and at a very good price, he'll be well impressed, let me into his organisation. He can put a lot of business my way."

The last crate had just been loaded onto Walton's lorry and one of his heavies gave him the thumbs up. Walton handed me the cash and I quickly counted it. It was a skill I had learned over the years. To my immense surprise it was all there.

I looked up, conscious that Walton was smiling at me.

"You're a real mug," he said. "A real mug. This is a steal. I would have given you double that if you'd been able to negotiate properly. Not very good at this sort of business, are you?"

"I was desperate," I said. I said it with a straight face, but it wasn't easy.

"Yeah, sure. But I get the feeling you ain't very good at this. Anyway, ciao. Be happy."

He turned to go.

"Wait," I called. "What's the name of this guy you're trying to get in with?"

He tapped the side of his nose.

"That's for me to know and you to wonder. See ya."

I watched them drive off, then walked over to Happy, who was still reading the Mirror, completely unaware that life was going on around him. He was moving his lips as he read.

I gave him the money.

"A hundred and fifty grand," I said. "And I'm texting Finch now to tell him how much to expect. I'll catch the train back."

I was very damp by now, but I thought a walk might clear my head a bit. It was good to have got the wine business out of the way, but I needed to think about what was happening with all the other stuff. Paradine's murder, the cops, and now these two new blokes turning up. It was all getting a bit heavy.

At least I wouldn't have to see Finch again any time soon.

"What the bloody hell are you playing at, you stupid little piece of dirt?"

I was once again sitting in Finch's travesty of a pub. His two minders were standing behind him with their arms folded, and if Finch had been any angrier, I swear his head would have exploded. He'd rung me about eleven o'clock the next morning, and the message was very curt.

"Get your stupid arse round here now." The phone went dead. This was getting awfully familiar.

Dutifully I traipsed over to his place, desperately trying to imagine what had gone wrong now. The only thing I could think of was that Happy had done a runner with the money. But that was the way we always did business, I gave the money to one of his monkeys and Finch gave me my cut later. He couldn't blame me for the way his employees behaved. Perhaps he just wanted to give me my commission personally so he could express his undying gratitude. Yeah, sure.

He was steaming when I got there, he was already sitting at his table. There was smoke coming out of his ears.

"Well?" he said.

I tried my best to look innocent, even though I was.

"What?" I said, shrugging my shoulders. "If there's something wrong I don't know what it is. What's happened?"

"What's happened?" he exploded. "What's happened? I'll tell you what's happened, you little toerag. The bloody wine's turned up again. That's what's bloody happened."

"The wine?" I repeated stupidly. I was so taken by surprise I didn't know what to say.

"Yes, the wine, you prat."

"But how, what's happened? I did the deal ok, I got a bloody good price for it as it happened. Your driver should have given you the money yesterday. And the guy I sold it to took it away. It's all over, done with. If you've got any more it must be different wine."

Finch simmered, staring at me from under enormous bushy eyebrows that desperately needed cutting. He was generally a really unprepossessing bloke to look at. His hair was greasy, his fingernails were dirty and he looked like he hadn't changed his clothes in months. I suppose if you're that wealthy and powerful you don't have to worry about personal hygiene if you don't want to. Nobody was going to tell Finch that he smelled, that's for sure.

"Tell me that you didn't do this to wind me up, because if you did this on purpose I'm going to cut your ears off."

I sighed wearily. I tried to put a lot of emphasis into the sigh.

"Mr Finch, you're the last person I would try to wind up. Seriously do you think I look that stupid."

Finch sort of growled. I think that was his natural means of communication, but he forced himself to speak English whenever he was confronted by a human being.

"Maybe I'll just break your arms then. Just in case you think you can play silly buggers with me."

He was still trying to sound threatening, but I could tell he was easing off. With any luck I was in the clear over what awful thing was going on with this stupid wine.

"I still don't understand," I said, trying to speak in a calm, even tone. "Are you saying you've got the wine back?"

"That's exactly what I'm saying."

"But how? What happened?"

"Some stupid little prick called Walton turned up here last night and tried to sell it to me. Stupid little tosser. Brought it straight here to my gaff. Unbelievable."

My mouth opened but nothing came out. I tried a few more times, but I couldn't speak. There just weren't any words.

"Prat offered to sell it to me for a hundred grand."

"But I sold it to him for a hundred and fifty!"

"I know, Danny had already given me the cash."

"I don't understand."

"This Walton geezer has been weaselling around me for years, trying to get in on the organisation. Small time little nobody. Been trying to get me involved in deals or bankroll him for ages. It was all stupid stuff, nothing I would touch with a barge pole. So he gets the offer from you, thinks he's pulled a masterstroke because you're a mug, pays over the odds, brings it over to me and offers it to me at a knockdown price. He thinks it's genuine stuff at a fantastic price, and he reckons I'm going to be so grateful I'm going to start bunging lots of work his way. Because he's such a good operator."

"Good god, this is unbelievable. But it still isn't a problem, why don't you just tell him to sling his hook?"

"Well, I have. In a manner of speaking."

I went cold. The meat fridge image sparked into my brain.

"You don't mean ..."

Finch nodded.

"He won't be bothering me again, you can be sure of that. And you've lost one mug that you won't be able to sell any more rubbish to."

I swallowed.

"Wasn't that a bit extreme," I ventured slowly. "Couldn't you have just told him to get lost? You've got your money, a nice profit, and he's stuck with a load of dodgy wine."

"Nah. He was really getting on my nerves. He wouldn't take the hint. He was too stupid to realise. He had to be dealt with. People need to see that they can't muck around with me. Turning up and trying to sell me my own wine. I'd be a laughing stock if I let him get away with that."

"I suppose," I said doubtfully. "Do you know he didn't even try the wine, just took it at face value that it was what it said it was."

"Then that just goes to show. What a complete and utter loser. The world's a better place without him."

I tried to get that positive thought into my brain, but it wasn't having any of it. But then I brightened.

"At least that's the end of it," I said. "You've made a nice bit of coin, just dump the wine and we'll all move on."

"No. I don't think you understand. You can be very slow at times. You've got to sell the wine again."

"What? Why?"

"Because that's what you do. I told you to sell the wine for me, and lo and behold, I've still got it. So get rid of it for me. And I shall expect at least as much as you got for it from Walton."

My mouth opened and closed a few times. I must have looked like a fish to Finch. I tried to pull myself together.

"Look," I said. "I'm not sure I'm understanding this. I do a good job for you, always have done. I got rid of the first lot of dodgy wine for you when no one else could. Then you make me get rid of a second lot although there's no reason on earth why I should. But I did get rid of it, and at a bloody good price. Now you're saying I've got to sell it again, and at a bloody unrealistic price. It's not my responsibility. If you want to sell it, sell it. If not, dump it, you've made your money. It's nothing to do with me any more."

A small smile came over Finch's face. A chilling smile. Now I came to think about it I don't think I'd ever seen him smile before.

"You don't get it do you?" he said, leaning back and clasping his hands over his ample stomach. "Well, just because I'm a really nice guy, I'll explain it to you in very simple terms so an ignoramus like you can understand. First, what I do is sell things. At a profit. It's as simple as that. And it's made me a very wealthy man. What hasn't made me a very wealthy man is having something handed to me on a plate for nothing, and then me just throwing it away. Not even if I've made some money out of it already. The opportunity to get some double dipper out of something like this is like a Birthday and a Christmas all wrapped up in one. It's very simple really, I'm sure you can understand that?"

"Of course," I said. "Of course. But I don't understand why I have to do it."

"Ah," he said. "Right. Point number two. You. You've been getting right on my nerves lately. Right on my nerves. Given me the right hump, you have. Too flash for my liking, too full of yourself. I said just that the other day, didn't I, PJ?"

He turned round to look at one of his heavies, who clearly had not listened to one word of the conversation, and was now staring at Finch with obvious signs of panic on his face. He took a flier on his response.

"Yes, Boss," he said.

Finch turned back to me and nodded.

I had gone cold. Cold as ice, but I could still feel a bead of sweat running down my back.

"Then I'm out of here," I said. "You'll never see me again."

"No, no, no." Finch almost laughed. "It's me who decides if you disappear or not. But I'm a fair man. If I do, what shall we call them, bad things to people, it's because the people who get bad things done to them deserve it. And you haven't actually done anything to deserve having something bad being done to you. Yet. You've just been a prat. But what I said to myself was, if you didn't get rid of that wine for a decent price, then I would have to deal with you."

"But I did get rid of it, and at a decent price."

"And now you've got to do it again. My promise to myself still stands. I'm giving you a chance because you've done some good work for me in the past. I wouldn't do anything to you just because I don't like you, but if you let me down, then that's a whole different ball game. I've got my reputation to think about. I can't let people see me letting people who let me down get away with it, can I?"

He had this smug look on his face. Smug and evil. I knew there was nothing I could say or do to get out of this.

"I've asked Smiley John to take a personal interest in this," he said. "Now piss off."

Smiley John was Finch's henchman, the guy who did all the really dirty work for him. He didn't smile much.

"What about my commission," I asked.

"Get lost."

As I left I exchanged glances with PJ. I think he'd seen his life flash in front of him for a second when he'd heard his name called out, and I thought I saw a momentary glint of sympathy in his eyes. It was gone almost before it appeared.

CHAPTER TWELVE
'JOHN BOY' WALTON

Dear god, I'm frightened. I don't think I've ever been so frightened in my life. This is terrifying. And I've pissed my bloody trousers. This is the worst thing that's ever happened to me.

All I did was ask him if he wanted to buy some wine. Then he blew his top. Thought he was going to strangle me right there in the pub. And I was really nice about it as well. I know my place. Lots of sirs, and yes Mr Finch's. Nothing there to get upset about. And I offered him a bloody good price. Cutting my own throat selling it that cheap, but I thought it would stand me in good stead. Thought he would see that I was giving him a good deal. Perhaps he got insulted by that, but I don't know why he should.

God, I wish I could stop shivering. Why am I so frightened? He's only trying to give me a good scare.

Maybe he didn't like the wine. But what was not to like? What was it called? Some French stuff. Margot somebody or other. Perhaps he doesn't like that sort of wine. But there's still no need to do this to me. He could have just said he wasn't interested.

But no, his bloody great bodyguards start doing me in, thumping seven bells out of me until I pass out. And here I am. Tied up, bloody great bag or something over my head so I can't see, and I've pissed my trousers. I'm thirsty, I'm frightened and I can't breath properly. All I want to know is why. I know he's just trying to scare me and he'll let me out in a bit, but I just don't know why. If he didn't want me to come and see him again that's no problem. I don't know why it has to be done this way.

I hope he lets me out soon, I think I'm going to piss myself again.

Why is it so cold in here? And why does it smell of meat?

CHAPTER THIRTEEN
THE PLOT THICKENS

The next few days were just generally dispiriting. I called everybody I knew trying to offload the wine, but even at a huge discount nobody was interested. I think word must have got round about how awful it was.

I'd gradually come to the conclusion that I was going to have to buy it myself. A hundred and fifty grand was a lot of money, but it wasn't the end of the world. The profit I was making out of the other business would go some way towards it I figured. I planned on storing the wine in my lock up and selling it off piecemeal as and I when I could. There wasn't any rush, it wasn't as though it was going to go off or anything, it was already off. Perhaps I could use it for Birthday and Christmas presents for the next fifty years.

I hadn't heard from any of Finch's heavies since I'd last seen him, so that was a bonus. I needed to think of some sort of solution to get him out of my hair forever, and I mentally gave myself a week to think of one.

It was one evening later that week that things started to ramp up a bit. It was about eight o'clock. I'd done a few things around the apartment, gone through the pile of mail that had built up, thrown away ninety-eight per cent of that mail because it was junk, and just settled down on the sofa with a drink.

It seemed like it was the first time for ages that I'd had a bit of time to catch up with myself. I always had a lot of things going on, I was always busy, always had a lot on my plate, but what with the secrets business and the wine catastrophe, everything seemed to have ratcheted up a few notches. I suppose it was because I still didn't understand what it was all about. I liked to be in control. All the time. Knowledge is power, and I was feeling very uneducated at that moment.

The two murders had really affected me. I wasn't that concerned about John Boy if I was being perfectly honest, if in fact he had been murdered, but the news about Paradine's death had shaken me to the core. More than I would have thought possible.

The widow and what to do about her had been on my mind a good bit, but it seemed sensible to give it a few more weeks more until all the fuss had died down before I did anything.

I was just trying to decide whether I should nip down the pub for a quick one or spend the evening googling complex chemical equations when the front doorbell rang.

It was the female detective again, on her own this time.

We stared at each other across my threshold.

"Mr Jones."

"Detective… I'm sorry, I can't remember your name. It was long."

"Hernandez. May I come in?"

"Have you got a warrant?"

"Do I need one?"

"Depends what you want."

"Well it's not a social call."

We both smiled. There'd been a bit of electricity behind that bit of banter. I gestured her in and she sat on the big sofa again.

"I thought you people always went round in pairs, you know, joined at the hip. You must be a bit lost without that Neanderthal behind you."

She didn't bite.

"Your flat is looking immaculate again. Your wife must work very hard keeping it looking so nice all the time."

Aha. Showing a bit of personal interest.

"I'm not married. Single. I have a lovely old Polish lady who comes in and does for me three times a week."

"I hope she enjoys it as much as you seem to do."

Actually, this was going rather well. I was definitely on home territory with this sort of thing.

"So where is Sergeant … Monk, was it? Have you worn him out?'

A glimmer of another smile at that one.

"I expect he's down the pub. It's where he does his best work."

It was my turn to smile at that.

"So, as pleasant as it is to see you relaxing on my sofa again, what can I do for you?"

She didn't say anything for a bit, just looked at me. Then she pointed at my drink and said, "I could do with one of those."

That did surprise me.

"You never saw Dixon of Dock Green drink on duty," I said.

"Ah, but I'm not on duty. That's why I'm on my own."

"You said this wasn't a social call," I said, turning round to look at her while I made her a drink. I handed her a glass of brandy. I never asked people what they wanted to drink, I just made the decision for them. It put me in control immediately.

"It's not a social call, so don't start getting ideas, but it is unofficial."

I looked at her enquiringly.

"I need to know more about your relationship with Paradine."

"I though you said this wasn't official?"

"It isn't. I'm doing this off my own bat. But it's important to me to find out what's going on. His murder was gruesome if you didn't already know. As it happens I don't think you did it, but you definitely know more about what happened than you're letting on. I want you to fill me in on a few more details."

I realised I was staring at her and not really concentrating on what she was saying. That was a recipe for disaster, especially as I didn't have any sort of story prepared for why I had met up with Paradine. I was going to have to think quickly.

I shrugged.

"There's nothing more to tell you than you already know."

"Why did you phone him after so many years?"

"Well…" think, think. "…we were quite close once."

"So why hadn't you seen him for so long?"

"Well, you know how it is. Relationships. They come and go. No rhyme or reason to them a lot of the time."

"So why get in touch now?"

"No reason really, I just wanted to talk to him. He was always a good listener."

I was all too aware how limp that sounded.

She snorted. And then smiled.

"Not much of an alibi really, is it?"

I smiled back.

"No." I said. "But perhaps that proves my innocence."

We both laughed.

"I was thinking that I wanted to do something for Paradine's wife and kids," I said. "Make sure they're looked after, that they're going to be all right."

"That's very philanthropic of you."

"Well, he was a good friend once. I wouldn't want to think they were suffering any financial hardship or anything."

"Feeling guilty are you?'

"No, nothing like that. It just seems the right thing to do."

"Do it then."

"Well, to be honest, I was a bit worried how that would look to you lot. A sure sign of guilt."

She was silent for a while. I didn't break the silence.

"Okay. I'll level with you," she said eventually. "It doesn't really matter any more. The truth is I've been pulled off the case."

"Really? Too big for you?"

She gave me a look.

"No. We're off it completely. We've been told to close the case. Told by someone in government apparently, I'm too junior to be told by exactly who. And they took all our files away."

My brain was racing. What was going on here? This was really getting heavy. I wondered if I should tell her about my being officially warned off.

"So why are you still asking questions?"

"I don't know really. I'm a bit too bloody-minded I suppose. Don't like being told what to do without someone telling me why. And I don't like the thought of someone getting away with a murder like that. Whatever the bigger picture is."

"But what reason would anybody in the Government have for closing the case?" Then a thought struck me. "Spies?"

She nodded.

"Yes. Well, sort of. It'll be intelligence work of some kind. That's usually why some department or other comes leaping in with their knickers in a twist. MI5 or MI6, someone's been treading on their toes. Or some bigwig politician involved in a scandal that they want keeping quiet."

I laughed.

"That'll be it. Paradine murdered because he was having a gay affair with the Chancellor of the Exchequer." I immediately felt bad about making a joke about Paradine's death. "No, that's not funny," I said. "He was a good man. He didn't deserve what happened to him."

She shook her head.

"Nobody deserves to die the way he died. The people who did this deserve to be punished." She looked at me very pointedly.

"Perhaps if you're a high-powered scientist you make enemies," I ventured tentatively. "I guess things can get pretty competitive when you're working on all that secret stuff."

"High-powered scientist?" She almost snorted. "He was a lab technician in a medical centre. He tested blood samples for a living."

"Really? I always thought he was a bit more important than that. I could have sworn he told me what he did, but it wasn't that."

"But you were too busy talking about you to listen, eh?"

I didn't know what to say to that.

"Think you've got me sussed, do you?" I said eventually.

"Well on the surface of it I think I have got you sussed, as you put it." She got up and walked round the room, having a good look at everything and then walked in to the open plan kitchen. "Everything in this place is top end, must have cost a fortune. You're not short of a few bob, that's for sure. Where do you get your money from? A dry-cleaners did you say?"

"Yeah, that's right." Damn, I still hadn't got that list of companies. I hoped she wasn't going to ask too many difficult questions. I wondered if I asked her out for dinner it might take her mind off things.

"I've been making a few enquiries about you," she said.

Damn, again.

"You run quite a few business it appears. And yes, one of them is a dry cleaners bizarrely enough. And do you know the interesting thing I discovered about all these businesses of yours? Hmm? Not one of those businesses makes any money. Not one of them. And yet here you are living the life of Riley. Now how do you account for that?'

I shrugged.

"I really don't care what you get up to," she went on. "It's clearly not kosher, and I suspect you're breaking every law under the sun, but I don't give a damn at the moment. All I care about is finding out who killed poor old Paradine, and then shoving it down those grey-suited idiots from Whitehall's throats."

She came and stood in front of me. I got up and faced her. She was perhaps two or three inches smaller than me.

"We can be friends, you know," she said.

"Yeah?" I said huskily.

"Yes. We can be on the same side. I think we can do a lot for each other. There are things I think you can do for me, and I know there are things I can do for you."

"I think I'd like to be friends," I said.

"Friends that tell each other things?"

"Maybe, but I don't think I've got much of interest to tell you."

"Well, why don't we see how it works out. I really could be a good friend, you know. It's always useful to have an ally in the police force, somebody who can get your back. I would have thought that would have been very handy for someone in your line of work, you know, the dry cleaning business."

I smiled and leaned my head into kiss her. Unfortunately she wasn't there any more, she'd instantly stepped back a few paces. Her eyes had a wonderfully challenging look in them.

"What about dinner then?" I suggested. "Talk about our new-found alliance and what we can do for each other."

"Perhaps," she smiled. "I'll think about it. What's your number?"

I gave her one of my cards with just the number on it.

"You really are a mystery man, aren't you?" She walked past me to the door. As she did she brushed against me. It was electrifying.

"I bet you give old Monk a heart-attack every day," I said.

"I've never been this close to Monk," she smiled. "So you're doing quite well considering."

As I let her out of the door I thought of something.

"Wait, you were going to tell me about your Mexican connection," I said.

She laughed. "I don't know you well enough yet. I never tell secrets on a second date."

When she'd gone, I sat back on the sofa and tried to bring my blood pressure down. It took some time.

"It's terrible, init?"

Kostas interrupted my thoughts at just about the moment I was coming to exactly that conclusion about what was going on in my life. I looked up in surprise.

"It's terrible." He gestured at the paper he was reading, The Sun. Splashed across the front page was the news that some TV celebrity I'd never heard of had walked out of some reality show in some jungle somewhere.

"How's that?" I said.

He slapped the paper with the back of his hand.

"It's terrible. They all ganged up on her, made her cry. Just because she wouldn't eat those bugs. It's not fair, they're all horrible people. She's lovely. My bet is they were all jealous. She's got more talent in her little finger than all the rest of them put together. She's going to be a big star, a big star. That'll show the rest of them."

"What does she do?" I asked.

"Do?" he said incredulously. "Do? She's the weather girl on the telly."

I nodded. Even from here I could see that the picture that filled almost the whole of the front page had put the emphasis on her enormous chest. Below that picture, right at the bottom, in really tiny words, it said: '35 people killed in suicide bombing in Iraq.'

"You're right," I said. "It's terrible."

Kostas went back to his paper and I went back to my coffee and my thoughts.

I'd woken up early, and instead of staying in bed for an hour or so going through emails and stuff on my phone like I usually did, I got up straight away. My head was buzzing with what Hernandez had told me last night, unfortunately it hadn't clarified anything, it had just left me more confused than ever.

I took a slow, circular walk to the office. I needed a bit of time to think about things. One of the things was Hernandez, she was still very much on my mind.

I was very good about keeping professional and private separate. Very disciplined. To be honest it had never been a problem before, but I sensed this could be. Could I trust a policeman? They were a different breed. And surely she was just in this for what she could get out of it, just as I was. I was sure she wouldn't have any hesitation about using me to get what she wanted, just as I wouldn't. But the stupid thing was I just couldn't stop thinking about her.

I was so deep in my thoughts that I didn't notice somebody standing in front of me. I jumped when he spoke.

"Wotcher Jonesy, how's your luck?"

It was Spike from the Wine Shop.

"Christ," I said. "Don't creep up on me like that, you'll give someone a heart attack."

"Thought you was looking a bit jumpy," he laughed. "Not like you. Got some worries have you?"

I shrugged.

"Nothing I can't handle. What brings you to this side of town? Not your usual manor, I would have thought."

"Not really that unusual, I've got customers all over the place. Old girl I know wanted a few cases of the good stuff delivered for some shindig she's throwing, so I've just dropped them off. Here, tell you what, she invited me along, don't fancy going do you? It's only round the corner from your gaff."

"What sort of shindig?"

"A soiree. Thirty-odd people in her mansion, top nosh served by waiters in tuxedos, great wine of course, and possibly the chance to meet some high-class totty. What do you say?"

"I don't know, I've got a lot on my plate at the moment. But when you say old girl, how old are we talking about?"

"Oh, probably around seventy or so."

"Seventy! You've got to be kidding me. You can keep that sort of totty, thanks."

"Nah, don't be stupid, what do you think I am? No, she's a rich old widow who likes to be surrounded by bright young things. It's what she does. And the bright young things are quite happy to do the surrounding because she treats them so well, no expense spared. I'll tell you what, I'll bet you'll be the second oldest there."

"Hmm. Well, I'll think about it. What sort of time?"

"Oh I'll probably head over about ten'ish. Don't suppose it'll start warming up much before then. Go on, come with me, we'll have a right laugh."

"I'll give you a bell." I turned to go, but Spike grabbed me the arm.

"As it happens, I'm pleased I bumped into you," he said. "I was thinking of giving you a call. Did you ever get rid of that wine you were on about the other week?"

He bent his head into his jacket to light a cigarette and let out a big breath of smoke. He held the cigarette cupped in his hand.

"It's a long story," I said. "I did get rid of it, and for a good price as well, considering, but it's come back and now I've got to do something with it all over again. The trouble is, it's absolute crap. I don't think it's even wine, just red-coloured vinegar or something, although I could probably get more for it if it was vinegar. Why, got any good ideas?"

"Well, funnily enough I might have."

I was all ears now, and I looked at him eagerly as we walked along behind the back of the market stalls.

"Yeah?"

"Yeah. To be frank, I could do with a bit of extra dosh at the moment, had a bit of bad luck with the gee-gees you might say. So I was thinking of ways that might earn me an extra copper or two, when, completely by chance, I stumbled across what could well be the answer to both our prayers."

I looked at him expectantly.

"Tell me more."

"Yeah. Well, it's a bit of a coincidence really, but the other day I was down at this wine wholesaler I use. It's a big warehouse near Lingfield. Sussex, you know. I happened to look at the bonded section as I was walking past, that's where they keep all the imported stuff until all the tax is paid on it. I couldn't believe my eyes, they had a big load of that Margaux you're trying to shift. I happened to overhear a couple of blokes talking about it, and it's a right cock-up apparently. Lot of mucked-up deals, it's been round the world a few times – I noticed some US import stickers on the bottles. And basically they think a lot of it has spoiled, and when they've sold off a few small quantities, at full price mind you, it's all been returned."

I was looking a bit bemused by now.

"Wake up Jonesy, I thought you were smarter than this. So here's my thinking. How about we buy the wine? You go down and buy it on your own, but then we return it and insist on our money back because it's rubbish, and I'll come with you then, as your partner. They'll give us our money back because I'm a very good customer and they know I'm kosher. And of course, what we do is give them your rubbish and keep theirs."

"And where does that get me?"

"Their rubbish is going to be a hundred times better than yours. How much did you sell yours for?"

"Fifteen hundred quid a case."

"Good grief. I buy a case for double that, about two hundred and fifty quid a bottle, maybe less depending on the deal. I reckon we could sell it for about two grand a case and be completely up front about the state of it. say it's buyer beware. To be honest there's going to be loads of people who would jump at it at that price. It would be a risk for them, but a good risk. They'll bite our hands off for it. What do you think?"

I was mentally doing the maths. That was two-hundred grand. Blimey. Was I interested? Not much.

"Sounds too good to be true. How come you weren't this helpful before?"

"I didn't need the money before. And I hadn't come across all that Margaux then. This is a bit of a once in a lifetime opportunity really."

"What about the warehouse when they discover what's in the bottles we're giving back to them?"

"They'll never find out, that's the beauty of it. If they manage to sell any of it again and it gets returned it's what they would have expected. It's poor quality wine. How are they ever going to work out it's poorer than it was before?"

"Blimey, you've got it all worked out haven't you? Foolproof?"

"As much as it can be, I guess. I certainly can't see any problems with it. All we need is a lot of confidence and a bit of chat. No problem there either as far as I can see."

I nodded.

"Ok, I'm in. When?"

He frowned suddenly.

"Well, the only problem is having the readies up front. Don't suppose you've got three hundred grand handy to buy the stuff?"

I laughed.

"Do me a favour."

"Well, perhaps we can be a bit clever. Buy it one day and return it the next before it hits whatever method we decide on to pay for with. It must be possible to do something like that."

"Yeah," I nodded. "I've done stuff like that in the past using my bank. As long as we do the transaction as late in the day as possible, and then get in there first thing the next day and get them to tear up whatever it is we use, then it's doable, very doable. Are you sure they'll play ball though?"

Spike nodded. "I do a lot of business there, a lot of business, none of that will be a problem. Trust me, it'll be sweet."

"And what about your cut?"

"No, no cut. Fifty per cent of the profits, we split it, straight down the middle."

Fair enough I thought, I wouldn't have asked for any less. At least there was going to be some profit in this one.

"You'll send me to the poor house you will," I pretended to moan. "But you've got me over a barrel here, don't suppose I've got much choice, you old crook."

"Spike smiled a happy smile and clapped me on the shoulder.

"What are old friends for," he laughed. "Anyway, got to go. Laters. See you tonight?"

I nodded.

As I watched him go, I felt so elated I actually texted Finch. "Buyer found for wine." I regretted it as soon as I'd pressed send. I hope being that confident wasn't going to come back and bite me.

CHAPTER FOURTEEN
SPIKE

Jeez, I hope I've done the right thing here. Trouble is Jonesey's a good mate, I really don't want to do the dirty on him. Thing is, I need the money so badly. I'm going to get killed if I don't cough up the readies soon. So it's worth the risk. I've got no other way of making some big money so quickly, and who knows, if it all works, then everybody wins, that'll be sweet.

So I had to over-egg it to Jones, had to sell it like it was a sure thing otherwise he wouldn't have bought into it. And you never know, it might work. Swapping Jonesey's muck for the real stuff won't be a problem, we can do that part of it okay. It's selling it on is going to be the issue. But maybe there are people out there who'd be prepared to take a risk on buying wine that might be off. Trouble is I don't know anybody. Not sure where I'm going to find anyone either. And even if I did, they're not going to pay anything like the money I promised Jones.

If only you could try each bottle so you'd know if it was any good or not. How nice would that be? What a dopey system where you pay a fortune for something but have no idea if it's any good or not. If you buy a bottle of beer you know it's going to taste like all the other hundred bottles you've drunk. But with wine, it could be fabulous one day, and awful the next. I blame the French. Found a new way to stick it to the English hundreds of years ago, and they're still doing it. Get rid of all their old rubbish on us. They know the English won't complain. It's like the Beaujolais they send us. Crap wine, not ready for drinking and we make a big song and dance over like it's a Chateau Lafitte. They must be laughing their socks off.

Still feel bad about Jonesy though. I'm going to have to have a few cases away and sell them retail. That way I should be able to raise the money I need. If I select the customers carefully I could get away with it, choose the ones who know sod all about wine, and if I can get them to buy a load for a party they're throwing, at a very attractive discount of course, then I really might get away with it. Nobody knows what they're drinking at parties. It's not like you're going to complain to your host that his wine is no good, is it?

So that might work. Just a shame about Jonesy. But I've got no choice. They've got me in a corner. I'll tell you what, that's the last time I ever play cards. Ever. And I still don't think that game was kosher. I play poker better than that. I'm sure it was a set up. And no wonder I bet big with a hand like that. It had to be a million to one that there was a better hand in the same deal. Bunch of crooks.

Shame about Jonesy though.

CHAPTER FIFTEEN
SECRETLY SERVICED

Mimi was hard at it when I got to the office, piles of papers on her desk.

"Morning," I said.

"Hello, dear," she said. "Everything all right?' She didn't have her curlers in this morning, just an old hair net. At least she had her teeth in today, she forgot sometimes.

"Fine," I said. "Everything okay with you?"

Mimi nodded.

"Payroll day, dear." she said. "Bit of a pain in the neck really. Did you know that the majority of the people who work for you still get paid in cash? Weekly?"

"Really? Can't you make them change to direct transfer or whatever it's called?"

"Not really. They'd probably all leave if they had to become official for the taxman. I'd be surprised if more than a handful of them have bank accounts anyway."

"How many people do I have working for me then?"

"Forty-two."

"Forty-two? You're joking."

"Certainly not. How many did you think there were?"

"I don't know, I hadn't thought about it really. Where did they all come from?"

"Mostly they came with the companies when you bought them. I've had to replace one or two occasionally."

She looked at me with a sort of 'aren't I wonderful' look. The trouble was she was wonderful.

"I'll make myself a cup of tea," I said. "I don't want to interrupt all this hard work."

I went into the back room and sat down on one of the two lumpy armchairs. I hadn't been sat for more than a couple of minutes when Mimi came in, closing the door behind her.

"I'm sorry to trouble you dear, but there's someone here to see you," she whispered. "Someone I haven't seen before. He wouldn't give me his name, but said to tell you it was official, said you'd know what that meant."

Something twitched in my stomach.

"Did you say I was here?"

"He said he'd seen you come in. But I said you might be too busy to see anyone."

"What's he look like?"

"Blond hair, fringe that needs cutting, slim, just a boy really."

I knew exactly who it was. One of the officials. Oh well, this was going to happen at some stage.

"Okay, show him in."

He appeared in the doorway.

"Mr Jones, the middle man. Good day to you." He absolutely radiated positivity and joie de vivre. Interestingly, it looked as if he was on his own.

Mimi was looking at me protectively, waiting for a signal. I nodded to her and she left. I wondered what she would do if she thought I was in trouble. Hit him over the head with one of her slippers perhaps.

"And you are?" I said as brusquely as I could.

I wasn't going to make this an easy ride for him, but I was quite surprised he didn't have his mate with him. Being on your own generally didn't work too well if you were trying to be heavy with someone. Unless he had the rest of his army waiting outside, of course.

He sat down in the vacant chair. For a fleeting moment he looked slightly put out at the amount of dust that came out of it, but he recovered himself well. The smile returned. He elegantly crossed his legs and twisted the signet ring that was on the little finger of his left hand.

"You can call me Lambert if you like. It's probably not my real name, but it will do for the time being."

"Well, if it's probably not your name, why don't I just call you a prat, and tell you not to come round here and start threatening me again. Okay?"

He continued to smile. In fact he looked like he was thoroughly enjoying himself.

"Mr Jones, Mr Jones," Lambert held up both of his hands, palms out, in a placatory gesture. "Please, please. I can understand you being, ah, slightly put out after our last little meeting, but circumstances have changed somewhat. And if you'll give me a chance to explain I think we can begin again on a completely different footing."

I leaned back on my sofa. I was steaming, but I was also trying hard to control myself. I had so much on my plate at the moment that I didn't need this ninny coming round and telling me what to do. Gradually I could feel my temper subsiding. Good. I needed to be in control for this.

"Mr Jones, as I said last time we met, I am official. I represent our government in a manner of speaking, the detail of which I don't particularly want to go into. Nevertheless, you can rest assured that the only thing of concern here is the well being of this great country of ours. Nothing else. Okay so far?"

Arrogant prat. I didn't acknowledge him, just kept staring, coldly.

"Suffice to say," he went on undeterred. "That when we met before, and we gave you that friendly warning, it was because you were treading on our toes. We were in the middle of something quite delicate, and, frankly, you were getting in the way."

"So?"

"So, we've actually had a little rethink, and rather than you disappearing, we would prefer it now if you were to actually take on a considerably larger part in the whole process. In conjunction with us of course. As a partnership you might say."

"Don't make me laugh," I snorted. "Why on earth would I want to do that?"

Lambert smiled happily.

"Why? Why would you indeed? Well, lets see now." He started ticking things off with his fingers as he spoke." For a start, there's loyalty, then there's patriotism, and then there's wanting to help out your country in its hour of need. That's three for a kick off. But mostly I suspect the main reason might be that you'll probably end up doing twenty years in prison if you don't."

"What?" I wasn't making any sense of this.

"Okay, perhaps it might be better if I did give you a bit of background. Help you see how giving us a helping hand might be preferable to a period of incarceration and hard labour. Sound a plan?"

I grimaced at him. I really didn't have a clue what he was on about, but it didn't sound like I was going to come out of this smelling of roses.

"What about some tea to lubricate the old vocal chords eh?"

I got up and filled the kettle. I was determined to make his drink as bitter as possible. He started speaking while I was up.

"You would probably know us as MI5," he began. "Of course we're not called that any more, but that label is still attached to us by the public at large, and under that label people understand, broadly speaking, what it is that we do. And what that is, of course, is security. Not just physical security, military and terrorism and all that nasty stuff, but economic as well."

I plonked Lambert's tea down in front of him, spilling it a little. He didn't bat an eyelid.

"Which is where you come in. You are, in fact, stealing secrets from a company called Integrated Electronics, one of the most prominent research and development companies that we have in this country. They receive an awful lot of government money in the nature of grants and subsidies and that sort of thing. They are working on a particularly exciting piece of research at the moment, something which, if successful, could revolutionise the way each and every one of us leads our lives. You are stealing data relating to that particular development.

"Of course, as we know, it's really your fat friend Darby doing the actual stealing. Some particularly sharp-eyed people at Integrated put us on to the fact that he was acting rather suspiciously, and we've had him under surveillance ever since. What we discovered, of course, was that he was selling the information to those two nasties that you have become acquainted with. They, in turn, led us to an organisation best described as, ah, criminal. A very bad bunch, up to all manner of evil things, fingers in all sorts of revolting pies, and very, very ruthless. Not afraid to do the dirty where necessary, if you know what I mean.

He paused and took a sip of his drink.

"Good tea, very good tea."

Damn, it was supposed to be undrinkable.

"But that unfortunately is where the trail goes cold, as dear old John Wayne might say. Clearly they're just the middlemen, as indeed were you my friend, but so far we haven't been able to come up with any inkling of whom their buyer might be. We even put one of our own people on the inside, but unfortunately we haven't heard from him for some time, so I'm afraid we are rather fearing the worst there. Which brings us neatly on to you."

I swallowed the remnants of my tea, still looking coolly at him.

"So, in complete contrast to last week's instruction to bugger off, we would now like you to do the opposite, and do all you can to get on the inside of this little mob. We want you to devise a scheme that that will get you accepted by them, and then when you're on the inside, find out what's going on."

He looked up, surprised, I think, that I hadn't said anything at that. Inside, my head was spinning.

"I can actually see what you're thinking," he said. "And the words, 'piss off' are writ large in your brain. So, let's pretend you did say that, and I'll now tell you why I'm not going to piss off and why you're going to help us."

Lambert reached into his pocket, took out his phone and pressed a couple of buttons. Suddenly there was the sound of my own voice. It was me talking to Darby in the pub. Lambert pressed another couple of buttons, and there was me talking again, this time to the goons. My blood ran cold, the bloody pub was bugged.

"Impressive isn't it? I'm sure I don't need to play you all the recordings we've got, suffice to say we've got just about all the conversations you've had regarding this business, plus we've got recordings of every phone call you've made over the last few weeks, so we've got a pretty good handle on all the other nefarious deeds you've been up to. Want to buy some wine?"

"Good god, how have you done that?"

"I suppose you'd call it an app really. We downloaded that app onto your phone without you realising it. And it's completely undetectable once it's on there. So we can activate your phone from our own phones, we can turn on its microphone for instance and then we can listen to and record whatever conversation is going on at that moment. Or we can dial into your phone calls, it becomes like a third-party call, although you'll be oblivious to the fact that we're there. Remarkable technology, isn't it?

"We've actually been keeping you company quite a lot over the last few weeks, although you won't have been aware of that at all. But what it means is we have a record of nearly every conversation you've had face to face with Darby, nearly every conversation you've had face to face with the two gangsters, and…the conversations you've had face to face with poor old Paradine."

Something must have passed across my face.

"Ah, we've finally hit home, have we? Such a shame about Paradine, a terrible waste. Anyway, what it does mean is that we have proof that you were stealing secrets pertaining to the security of this country, proof you were selling on these secrets, probably to a foreign entity, and we've proof that you were in collusion with a scientist who was subsequently murdered. And with all the circumstantial evidence around, you could certainly carry the can for that. So yes, we do think you'll help us out, and if you don't, then we'll decide whether to send you down for twenty years for treason or twenty years for murder. Or possibly for both."

Whoosh. I didn't have any answer to any of that. Done up like a kipper. How could I have been so stupid?

"Well why don't you just go in mob-handed, arrest them or whatever you do, and get them to tell you what's going on," I said, desperately trying to think of some way I could get out of this.

"Yes, that is an option of course, but all that does is stop these gangsters. We wouldn't find out who was behind it, which is obviously what we really want to know. Who their customer is."

"Well, why me? Why not send in another of your guys, somebody trained to do this sort of thing?"

"We've done that once, and there's a considerable chance that it hasn't worked. Think about it, if you're in that gang, you're going to be very suspicious of someone just turning up, they're going to smell a rat straight away. You on the other hand, are very believable, and that's because you're real. You might even have come across these people in the past, or they might possibly even have heard of you."

I was quickly running out of arguments.

"Why should I believe you?" I said. "Anybody can come in here and tell me a load of old malarkey like that."

"Fair point. I've a car and a driver outside. You can come with me now and we'll drive straight to our building, Thames House. Millbank. And you can meet my boss. And you won't like her, I can tell you that now. She's not nearly so personable as I am."

I didn't know what to say. It was like all the steam had been knocked out of me.

"Was it this gang who killed Paradine?"

"Yes. As far as we can make out, whoever they're selling the information to had got wind of the fact that he was passing round the stuff they were buying, and they wanted to find out where he'd got it from. Unsuccessfully as it turns out. And just for your information, we've got the police to drop the case and forget all about the murder, we didn't want them to get in the way and start arresting you or something."

I kept quiet. At least there was something I knew that they didn't.

"But when this is all over," Lambert went on, "We've absolutely no objection to you exerting your justice on the perpetrators, in fact, we might even be able to assist you, make sure that it never becomes a matter for public consumption, as it were."

"So what is this thing that's being developed?"

"I think it's probably best that you don't know at this stage. Might appear a bit suspicious if you're too genned up."

Lambert brightened up then, a smile appearing on his face.

"But finally," he said. "The good news. I'm very pleased to tell you that you will be handsomely rewarded for your efforts. On the successful completion of your mission, I have been authorised to pay you the princely sum of five hundred thousand pounds. It will take the form of used notes, and can be in the denominations of your choosing."

Bloody hell. I think he could see my surprise.

"Yes, we do use the carrot and stick approach a lot of the time. We're making you do it, don't make any mistake about that. You have no choice, but we're making sure you do a good job by rewarding you for all your hard work."

"And what constitutes a successful conclusion?"

"You find out who is buying the information from the gangsters, simple as that. As soon as you find out, you get out and, if necessary, disappear. We can help with that as well, if you need us to."

I grunted.

"By the way," he went on. "A word to the wise. What the clever people are doing these days, they're dumping their smart phones and buying cheap pay-as-you-go ones, the ones that make phone calls and do nothing else. They're absolutely foolproof, you can't do anything nefarious with those. And for good measure, the really clever people with lots to hide, change their pay-as-you-go's every couple of weeks or so and just dump the old ones."

A thought hit me.

"So those guys who bumped into me in the pub were your people?"

Lambert nodded.

"Takes ten minutes to download the new software, your phone does it itself. Of course we had to jailbreak it first, so you might find your warranty voided if you ever get a problem. I'd recommend getting a new one from Tesco's if I were you. They do a lovely plastic job for about thirty pounds."

He leant forward. I think he could hear my brain ticking.

"Have we got a deal?"

I didn't say anything for minute or two, but then I nodded. What choice did I have? He burst into one of his happy smiles and held out his hand. I looked at it for a beat and then shook it.

"Excellent," he said. "Welcome to the world of smoke and mirrors."

And what happened next was we did go to his office. Lambert did have a car and a driver waiting outside, he was actually based at Thames House on Millbank, and he did work for MI5, although nowadays it was called something like the Security Service. Snappy name I thought, must confuse the hell out of all those Russian spies who probably don't know whether they're coming or going now they're called something different.

Oh, and he was right about his boss as well, she was an absolute witch.

Lambert introduced her as his Director. There were no pleasantries, no small talk, nothing. She just there and stared at me while we stood the other side of her desk. Out of the corner of my eye it looked like Lambert was standing to attention. I slouched my shoulders just a bit more.

She looked like she was tiny. I would be surprised if her feet were touching the floor behind her desk. Fifties perhaps? She could have been in her sixties or seventies for all I could tell. Her hair was pulled up tight into a severe bun and her chin was hairy. She was just about as unpleasant a person to look at as you could get.

Eventually she let out a big sigh.

"Mr. ..." she consulted a piece of paper. "... Jones."

She looked over at Lambert. "Real name?" He nodded.

"Mr Jones. You have been allowed in here to verify that what you have been told is, in fact, correct. You will now forget everything you have seen today, you will forget that you actually came here, you will even forget that you have forgotten. You have signed the Official Secrets Act 1989, and if you so much as breath a word of this even to your dear old grandma on her deathbed, I shall make sure you hang from the neck until you're dead. Got it?"

I had indeed signed the Official Secrets Act. Thames House turned out to be a large imposing white stone building right on the banks of the river. Not exactly secret. It took about an hour and a half for me to properly get in. Half a dozen photos from all different angles, fingerprints, three sets of different forms all signed in triplicate, and, of course, the precious Official Secrets Act 1989. At the completion of it all they'd created a file on me two inches thick. The Security Guard, who had called me sir throughout the whole process as though it was hurting his throat to say it, directed me through a full-body scanner, and, eventually, I was in.

Lambert was waiting for me when it was all finished.

"Sorry about that," he said. "Can't be too careful, you know."

"Do you do the rectal searches personally?"

He snorted.

"You've got me now, haven't you?" I said. "That file's going to be here forever isn't it?"

He nodded.

"It will join the one we've already got. That one's considerably thicker."

And so we found ourselves in front of the gorgon and she was telling me in no uncertain terms how awful it would be if I ever opened my mouth about any of this.

"Clear?" she said, when she'd finished.

"Not really," I said. "Something to do with secret stuff is it? Perhaps you could run over it just one more time. I got a bit bored and stopped listening half way through." God knows what made me say that, but she had seriously got up my nose.

I actually thought she was going to leap over the desk and throttle me.

Lambert intervened quickly.

"Mr Jones like to have his jokes," he said. "Part of his charm." He laughed. Nervously.

"Well Mr Jones had better start taking things a bit more seriously. I don't think he realises how much trouble he's in. Now, get out of here, and educate him as to his responsibilities. And his manners."

She bent her head and started scribbling furiously onto a piece of paper in front of her. I was about to say something scathing to the top of her bun, when Lambert grabbed me by the arm and quickly hustled me out.

He exhaled a deep breath as we walked along the corridor.

"I thought that went well," I said.

"Really? On what basis?"

"Well, we managed to get out without either of us being turned into frogs."

Lambert gave me a lift back to the office. On the way I asked him how I was supposed to infiltrate the gang. His answer wasn't very encouraging. The basic idea was that I was to try and offer them something more than they were getting at the moment, to start bargaining with them and hope that an opportunity might present itself for me to find out a bit more about what was going on. Unfortunately, the something more was all very vague. As was the rest of the plan. The whole thing seemed to rely on me being able to think on my feet. Lambert also made it very clear that under no circumstances was I to contact him until the whole thing was over, he would get in touch with me.

"These people are very clever," he said. "Or more likely, the people running them are very clever. They will be being very, very careful and will be very, very suspicious. Your instructions are exactly the same as were given to our other agent. There can be no communication from you to us, none at all. These people are better at this than you, and you can bet your life that they will know what you're up to. You have to lead your life in a normal way, if you can call it normal, but you mustn't do anything that would arouse suspicion in any way whatsoever. So there can be no telephone calls to us, no messages, no nothing. It's too, too dangerous. I can guarantee if you try you will be found out, I guarantee it, it always happens. This isn't like spying in books. This is real life, and it's your life on the line. Got it?"

I nodded, he was scaring me witless now.

"Periodically I will contact you. We will make sure that it will be at times that are totally secure. But, for when it's all over, here's a telephone number to contact me. He called out a number and I tried to memorise it. It took a few goes, but eventually it stuck.

"And you don't ever, ever use that until the whole thing is over and you're out. Understand?"

"Got it."

I had a thought.

"Your agent, what was his name?"

Lambert shook his head.

"Nope. No details. In fact, it's a shame you know there was an agent at all. The less you know the safer for you … and for him. So no name, no description, nothing. Okay?"

"I guess that makes sense. It sort of leaves me feeling a bit vulnerable though."

"The way of the world, my old son, the way of the world. It's the nature of the beast."

I was still puzzling over what that was supposed to mean when he dropped me off outside the office. The only thing that I was sure about was that I was on my own. There wasn't going to be any back up, no seventh cavalry riding in at the last minute to save my scalp. God help me.

CHAPTER SIXTEEN
LAMBERT

I almost get tired of doing this. People are just so naïve. You tell them you're secret service, show them a great big building with lots of security and they do whatever you tell them. I don't know how we keep getting away with it.

And they don't ask questions, that's what makes me laugh. This Jones, we've got him completely bang to rights, there's no doubt about that, we've got enough to put him away for a couple of lifetimes. But why would we? He's nothing to us, it's no skin off our noses what he gets up to.

I ask you, how likely is it we're just going to grab somebody off the street and say we need you to do a mission for us? That's something that happens in books, not in real life. But they always fall for it. Every time. They just get on with whatever we tell them do. Amazing. I would say that this Jones is probably quite bright, makes his living out of his wits I shouldn't wonder. But I threaten him with a bit of exposure on some of the stuff he gets up to, and he comes as quietly as a lamb.

They're too good for us, I say, these nasty gangsters, they're too smart. We need somebody brave and clever like you to do our work for us. And he swallows it, just like they all do. Does he really think he can do better than we could? Not one of them ever thinks, how come they need me to do this when they're the professionals, when they're the ones with the training and the technology. What does he think we do all day? What a laugh. What a klutz.

But nobody questions it. They just go along with it all. I don't know how many times I've done this ... dozens. Not once has anyone ever worked it out. Never. That we need some poor sap to take the focus away from our own guy, make sure any suspicion and doubt falls on them instead of him. Feed them full of false information so they start asking really dumb questions.

No one ever gets it. That they're there to be expendable.

CHAPTER SEVENTEEN
WINE TIME

Mimi looked genuinely relieved to see me when I walked in.

"I was worried about you," she said. "Who was that? What was he going on about being official?"

"They've sworn me to secrecy," I said. "It's one of those things, if I tell you I'll have to kill you."

She looked a little put out.

"It's nothing to worry about. I've just got to do a little bit of work for them. And it is secret. Sorry to be so mysterious, but this actually is one of those things that you're probably better off not knowing. Simpler for everybody."

She still looked a little piqued.

"Well, you know best, I suppose. It's just that it doesn't make it very easy for me if I don't know what's going on."

"I know, and I appreciate that."

Sitting down at my desk, I took out my phone and googled Integrated Electronics. Wikipedia told me that: 'The Integrated Electronics Company, or IE, is a major UK-based industrial conglomerate involved in consumer and defence electronics, communications, and engineering.' I read down for a couple of pages, but it was basically just an endless list of all the things they made and who they sold them to. There weren't really any surprises. As a company they did what it said on the tin. Unsurprisingly there was no mention of what they might be developing of a secret nature. But that was a thought, so I googled that. A whole load of stuff come up about a new sort of radar system. Could be, I thought. Could be. Though what a bunch of gangsters would want with radar was beyond me.

Not enormously helpful, but a bit of extra knowledge was always useful. Giving up on it as a bad job, I went home.

A quiet evening in and an early night was what I had planned. But two invitations came in in quick succession to make me change my mind.

Firstly Spike rang, to see if I was going to his party. I hummed and hawed for a bit, but eventually I agreed. We arranged to meet in the Spotted Horse for a pint about nine.

I was just hanging up when the phone rang again. It was Inspector Hernandez.

"Is your invitation to dinner still on," she asked.

"Definitely."

"How about tonight?"

Damn. Why couldn't she have rung five minutes earlier? I could blow Spike out I suppose, but I wanted to keep on top of him about the wine.

"Ah," I said. "Not a good night for me tonight, I've got something on."

"Oh." Was that a tinge of disappointment I could hear. I don't suppose she had ever had anyone turn her down in her life before. "Well, never mind. Is your Polish lady coming round to do for you?"

I snorted down the phone. That was funny.

"No Anna does for me in the mornings. She leaves me in peace in the evenings."

"How very discrete of her. Another of your harem then?"

"No, no. I'm meeting up with an old mate of mine as it happens. His name's Spike. He called me two minutes before you did. I'm sure you can check my phone records to verify that."

She chuckled.

"Okay, I believe you. Another time."

"I'm free tomorrow."

"Yes, well, I'll think about it. Don't hold your breath."

She hung up. Damn, perhaps I'd made a mistake sticking with Spike. I hoped I hadn't blown my opportunity of getting to know her. In the back of my mind I thought there was a good chance that she could be useful to me. In the front of my mind I knew that wasn't the real reason.

So, feeling slightly annoyed, I went off to meet Spike and after a couple of pints in the pub we moved on to the party. The house was on Blenheim Crescent and I was seriously impressed. Most of the places in the street had been split up into flats and maisonettes, but the old girl owned all of her house, all four floors of it. It must have been worth millions. And it was immaculate inside, the furniture was all good quality antique stuff, everything was very expensive.

And the old girl herself was incredible, spectacular. She looked her age, but she was so full of life, so full of vitality and energy that it made you forget how old she was. She was a lot of fun and we got on well. She made it very clear that she wouldn't be unhappy if I didn't go home that night.

And I didn't go home. I didn't stay at the old girl's though, I went home with someone else. Her name was Jane Smythe-Bannister, which, for a while, I thought she was making up. She took me home to her lovely little apartment in Kensington and was very physical with me. We didn't talk very much because she didn't seem to have very much to say. She was twenty-two, sixteen years younger than me, lived off a three hundred thousand a year stipend from her father and went to parties. There didn't appear to be much else.

As I was getting dressed to leave in the morning, she asked me what I did for a living. I said I ran a dry cleaners.

"Oh," she said. "I thought you seemed very clean."

Spike and I had agreed to shift the wine early next week. Monday for me to fix up the deal for the wine, Tuesday for me to arrange a banker's draft and buy the good stuff, and Wednesday for Spike to take back the rubbish. So on the Friday I called into my bank to arrange a temporary overdraft and organise the banker's draft.

Fortunately this wasn't the first time I'd done something like this. There was a young lad who worked there who seemed to be as in charge as much as anyone else did these days, and he and I had done a lot of business together over the last year or so. They didn't appear to have managers in banks any more, just a lot of kids, so it wasn't really all that difficult to persuade one of them to do you a few favours every now and then. In return I was very generous to him. He received a lot of bonuses on a very regular basis.

I explained that I'd need the draft on the Tuesday, but if all went well I'd be bringing it back on the Wednesday untouched. None of that was a problem he said reassuringly.

After the bank I called in to Tescos. Lambert was right, they did a really ugly black and white pay-as-you-go phone for thirty-nine pounds. It was hideous and I bought it there and then.

I switched my smartphone off. My plan was to switch it on every hour or so to check my messages and use my new phone to make any calls. I tried calling Mimi on it and it worked perfectly. Funnily enough the sound quality seemed better than on my old one. I explained what I was doing.

"You're getting more mysterious by the minute, you are," she said.

Then I rang Finch. I said I'd got a plan to get rid of the wine. It might take a bit longer to put it all together, but it should result in a better price.

He seemed quite intrigued by the fact that I had a plan, although he didn't ask me what it was.

"Growing some brains then, eh?" he growled. "Think it all up yourself?"

"I've got a partner working with me on this one," I said.

"Well maybe I need to meet this partner. Especially if he turns out to be the clever one in the family."

"I'm not sure he wants to meet you." I was pushing it a bit now, but he did sound a bit more mellow than the last couple of times we'd talked.

He grunted.

"Well, I'll expect a good price then."

"I'll see what I can do." I hung up before he could ask for any more details. I could give him a good price and still have some left over.

The biggest surprise of the day came later that evening. I'd got into the rhythm of checking my smartphone every hour or so, switching it on, checking for any messages, and switching it back off again. About eight-thirty I did just that. There was a missed call with no message left. It was Hernandez' number. I called her back on the new phone.

"I saw I had a missed call from you," I said.

"Yeah. I didn't leave a message, I didn't want to disturb you. I thought you might have your Polish lady round."

"Nope, all on my jacksie. What can I do for you?"

"I was finishing up at the office. Thought I might take you up on your offer of dinner."

I felt my heart beat faster.

"Sure," I said. "I was just about to heat up a tin of soup, so that would save me the bother."

"You do that yourself? You don't have anybody to do it for you?"

"Funny. Where are you?"

"No, it's too late now, another time perhaps."

"That's a shame."

"Yeah, but listen, I did want to talk to you. I need you to open up about Paradine."

"I thought you'd been warned off."

"I have, which is why I'm keener than ever to find out what's going on. I know you know a lot more than you're telling me. You might as well spill the beans, I'm not going to let up until you do. We can be on the same side in this, you know I can be of help."

"Yeah, I think you could be," I said. "The trouble is, I signed the Official Secrets Act yesterday. They'll poke my eyes out with red hot pokers if I talk to anyone about it."

"You're kidding me."

"Nope. This is official government business now, and they've roped me in. They exerted a bit of pressure on me you might say, to get me to cooperate."

"They bloody must have. Are these the same people who warned us off the case?"

"Probably."

"What about Paradine?"

"I'm going to get the bastards who did it when this is all over."

"I can help you, you know. There are a lot of things a Police Inspector can do that an ordinary person can't."

"Yeah. Your help would be good I think. Give me a bit of time though. I haven't really figured out exactly what's going on myself yet. Bear with me for a few days?"

"Okay. But don't leave me out. Otherwise I'll be very unhappy."

"You got it."

"Wait," I said, just as she was about to hang up. "You were going to tell me about your Mexican connection."

She laughed. "It's not a very interesting story. It's actually Colombian, but the name comes from my husband. English mother, Colombian father. His father ran off when he was twelve."

Oh, oh. Husband. There wasn't a ring that I'd noticed though.

"What does he do, the husband. Policeman too?"

"I've no idea what he does. He ran off too. Like father like son. Haven't heard from him for three years."

She was wrong about it not being very interesting. It was. It was about the most interesting thing I'd heard in ages.

The wine exchange itself went like a dream. Spike gave me the address of the warehouse and I drove down there on the Monday morning. I hadn't driven my car for months, it just wasn't worth it in London, and I enjoyed the novelty of pootling down the motorway without having to worry that I was going to be late for somewhere. It was a cool, crisp day and it was nice to look at trees and fields rather than houses and traffic jams for a change.

I adopted the persona of an arrogant know-it-all when I got there, someone who couldn't be told anything. I could see the guy showing me around had me figured out as that straight away. He could sense some easy pickings.

The bonded section of the warehouse was really obvious, and I casually asked about the Margaux as we walked past. I tried to calculate how much was there; it looked like it was a hundred cases as near as dammit. He said it had just come in the week before, guaranteed top quality. It had been stored in the vineyard's own cellars since it had been bottled. You little liar, I thought.

We haggled over the price for a bit. Spike was right, they wanted just under three thousand quid per case for a hundred cases, but eventually the guy offered me a small discount and I said yes. I could see the pound signs light up behind the guy's eyes, he couldn't believe his luck.

"What you going to do with it all then?" he asked as we filled out the paperwork.

"I'm buying it as an investment," I said. "I plan to lay it down for a few years. Reckon I'll make a fortune on it the way wine prices are going."

"Very shrewd, very shrewd." I could see the guy was having difficulty not laughing.

We arranged that I'd be back the next day with a banker's draft.

My contact at the bank was as good as gold, and with the draft safely in my pocket, I drove a rented van back down to Lingfield on the Tuesday. The Warehouse closed at five-thirty and I arrived exactly at five–twenty-five, loaded up the wine and hot-footed it back to Spike's lock-up.

Once we'd unloaded it all, we opened up a few random bottles. We did eight altogether, all from different cases. Six were quite delicious and two were bordering on iffy, although, admittedly, not nearly as iffy as Finch's stuff.

"That's interesting," said Spike, almost to himself. "Maybe this might work after all."

"What?" I said, surprised. "What do you mean 'might' work?"

"Figure of speech, Jonesy. Figure of speech. Got a buyer all lined up. Might be able to squeeze a few more bob out him if we can get this many good bottles out of it."

I gave him a look. My instincts were twitching and I knew to trust my instincts.

We corked up the good bottles we'd opened and put them to one side. Spike said he'd use those as samples for the buyer.

We took the two spoiled bottles and drove over to Finch's place. Fortunately, he wasn't there.

After we loaded Finch's wine onto the van, we opened up six bottles from the six crates nearest us. Spike pulled a real face as he tried each one.

"Christ, you weren't joking were you?"

The wine got put back, and then we substituted the two bottles of spoiled wine for a couple of the unopened ones. Spike marked those two cases.

"Listen, mate, what are you trying to pull here?" Spike was in a belligerent mood, walking up and down in front of the open van and waving his arms around. "I sent my mate down here because I thought I could trust you. And what have you done? Trying to treat us like a couple of plonkers. What do you think, that I haven't been round the block? This is bleeding gnat's pee. Bleeding gnat's pee."

We'd arrived at the warehouse one minute after the place opened and Spike had immediately started raising the roof. The guy we'd been dealing with had bought the big boss down from the office. They kept eying each other warily.

"Try it, go on try it, you pair of bleeding swindlers."

They got a couple of plastic glasses and Spike swilled a mouthful of wine into each from the two opened bottles he'd marked. I could see the blokes didn't really need to taste it. They knew already. They each took a sip and frowned at each other.

"See? See?" said Spike. "You bunch of crooks. I opened eight bloody cases and eight bloody bottles and they're all as bad. Want to try them?"

The manager shook his head.

"This is unbelievable," Spike went on. "To think that you could stiff me like this. Me, after all the business I've done with you. Well I want my money back, and I want it now."

There was a beat, then the manager nodded at the guy who went off to get my banker's draft which, to my immense relief was still lying untouched in the manager's office. I stood back and admired Spike's performance. You know, he really was very, very good. When we've brought this to a successful conclusion we should do more work together I thought. We make a good team. And I can trust him.

And that was it. The wine was unloaded and with me clutching the precious banker's draft, Spike and I drove back up the M23 singing our heads off and feeling like pigs in clover.

I was back at the bank by ten thirty, watching the banker's draft being torn up in front of me. The whole transaction had cost me nothing other than the two hundred pounds in a brown envelope that I passed into a pair of grateful hands.

Spike dropped me off at the office.

"Nice to do business with you," I said. "How long do you reckon it will take you to shift it?"

"Shouldn't take too long. Week or so, maybe. I'll be in touch."

I got out of the van with a nice warm glow inside me. Things hadn't gone this well for ages.

CHAPTER EIGHTEEN
JANE

I'm so bored. So bored. I can hardly bring myself to get out of bed. And I've got so much to do, I don't have a minute to myself hardly. I've got to meet the girls for lunch at twelve, so I need to get my hair done first, and then my nails. And then I'm supposed to meet Daddy at Fortnum's, says he's got a surprise he wants to buy me. Yawn. And then there's Felicity's dinner party in the evening. So I suppose I'm going to have to go and buy a new outfit for that. So not a minute to myself, and it's all so boring. So boring.

I wonder if that Jones will ring me. Actually, I don't think he took my number now I come to think about it. And I didn't take his. Stupid. I suppose he was all a bit caught up in it all to think about things like that. Because I'm sure he would like to see me again. I'm sure he really liked me. He was very attentive. I like older men I've decided.

I wonder if I can find him. He wasn't the usual sort you find at Dorothea's. There was him and that other chap, the soppy one who kept coming over all cockney. The silly one. Not sure how they would know Dorothea really, or how they would get invited to one of her party's. But I suppose I can ask her. Perhaps I'll give her a ring later, I know she doesn't get up until the afternoon. Trouble is I'm so busy, don't know if I'll have the time.

I'm dying for a cup of tea, but it's such a long way to the kitchen.

CHAPTER NINETEEN
A COMFORTING HOT-DRINK

"Right, you mug, you're coming with us now."

I was standing inside the Lamb, confronted by the two goons and Darby. Darby was making soft mewing noises and the goons had guns in their hands that were pointed directly at me.

I'd already done the handover with Darby, and having got to the Lamb early gone over to have a word with Terry the barman.

"Ere," he said. "I've still not seen hide nor hair of Walton. What do you fink's happened?"

I shrugged.

"No idea. Do you have any idea who he might have been selling the wine to?"

He shook his head.

"Haven't a clue. I never had anything to do with him apart from him coming in and treating his mates to free drinks once a week. Just seems odd, that's all. He's got a manager who looks after his pubs for him, so he's been a couple of times, and he ain't seen him either. Says he's thinking about going to the police, but he's afraid of opening up any cans of worms."

I hadn't heard Terry speak so much before. I didn't know he had it in him.

"Why's that then?"

"Well, he ain't exactly legit, if you know what I mean."

"Yeah, I do. Thought when he bought the wine he might be biting off more than he could chew. It was like he was trying to get into the big league and didn't know what he was letting himself in for."

Terry nodded.

"Could be. He's a right ding-a-ling, doesn't know his arse from his elbow."

I laughed, and ordered a scotch.

"Thought you drank beer?"

"You can have too much of a good thing," I said.

"Still, we're doing all right though, ain't we?"

"What do you mean?"

"You know? You and me. Working together. On this sting you've got going on. I've got your back like. That's going good isn't it?"

"Yeah," I said. He was probably getting used to the money I was giving him every week. "You've been very useful. I've been very pleased to have you around."

"Maybe there's some more stuff we could do together, you know, in some of the other stuff you've got going on. Become partners like."

I stared at him. Partners. Good god. I didn't know what to say. Fortunately Darby came in at that point so I didn't need to say anything. Unfortunately the goons were with him.

And there we stood, everybody staring stupidly at each like we were frozen in some bizarre waxworks tableau.

"Lets go," said the first goon. "Now."

"Okay," I said. "I was coming to see your boss anyway. Got something I want to talk to him about. Let's go."

That actually caught the goons on the hop a bit. I think all they'd visualised was having to take me forcibly and they didn't quite know how to react to me telling them to get moving. I heard a strange noise and looked over. Darby was peeing his pants.

"We don't need to take him along," I said. "He's got nothing to do with what I want to talk about."

"Well, he's coming anyway. Boss wants a word with him as well, he ain't very happy with him."

I could see Darby start to sag a bit, but at that moment, Terry came over brandishing his broom like a cudgel. That made a couple of the regulars look up and notice that there were a couple of guns on display. The place started to wake up a bit.

"Ere. You two. Get out of my pub now. Go on, get out of it before I call the police." Fair play to old Terry, it took a lot of guts standing up to a couple of guns with just a broom for protection. Perhaps we should become partners, I thought.

I laid a hand on Terry's arm to restrain him. "It's all right, Terry, everything's fine. We're all friends here. There's just been a bit of a communication breakdown, that's all. But it's all sorted now. We're fine. In fact, we're all going to go off together now. Once these gentlemen put their hardware away, of course. But thanks again for your support, Terry. It's good to know you've got our backs in here."

I slipped him a fifty-pound note, and walked to the door. The two goons looked at each other in confusion, but eventually grabbed Darby by the arms and followed me out.

The ride in the Bentley wasn't a very pleasant experience. Squeezed between Darby and a goon in the back, I had the smell of urine on one side and gun pointed at me on the other. Darby was weeping softly.

"You don't need that," I said, pointing to the gun. "You're boss is going to get very upset if anything nasty happens to me."

I could see the goon thinking about that, but he kept the gun pointed at me anyway.

I had assumed we were going to the house in Mayfair, but after a while, instead of continuing west we dropped down into Soho, ending up in a seedy little backstreet just off Wardour Street. We pulled up outside an anonymous brick building. There was a sex shop on one side and a take-away kebab place on the other. We shuffled out of the car, the goons trying to keep close to me and carry Darby at the same time. Darby was still conscious, but he'd lost the means to make his limbs work.

We walked up some steps to an enormous black painted front door. One of the goons rapped hard on the front with his knuckles. A metal panel was slid open and a ghastly pale face stared back at us. Nobody said anything, but the panel was eventually slid shut and the door creaked open. We walked in.

It was a drinking club, pure and simple. The front door opened straight into a big oblong room. A bar ran down the entire length of the right hand side, and a dozen or so tables with chairs filled up the rest of it. A dartboard was fixed to a wall in the far corner. A faded sign above the bar claimed that the place was called The Albemarle. It was gloomy, dingy and not very inviting. I'd been to places like this before, they were somewhere to go if you wanted a drink out of hours, but I didn't think they existed any more. With the way the licensing hours had been extended, they'd really lost their reason for being.

There were a good few people in the place though. Quite surprising really for four o'clock on a Wednesday afternoon. I was always amazed by how many people there were who never really did anything but could just sit around all day getting pissed.

Our group shuffled down to the end of the bar. It said something about the place that not one person looked up to see what the commotion was all about.

An old guy was sitting on his own on a stool at the end of the bar. He had a mug of something hot and brown in front of him. It looked like cocoa. We stood in front of him.

"This is him," said one of the goons.

I looked at the old guy. Was this Mr Big? He really didn't look the part, not like Finch who was large and imposing and really scary. He just looked like an old granddad. Soft. Wispy white hair pulled back across his old head, sagging wrinkled face, and clothes you wore because they were comfortable and didn't care who saw you in them.

"Welcome, welcome," he said affably, gesturing me towards the stool next to him. I sat down.

He sniffed and looked at Darby who was still being supported by the goons.

"Take him away and do something with him." The old man casually waved a couple of fingers and the goons immediately shuffled Darby off somewhere. The old man smiled at me. This was where I needed to get on the front foot I thought.

"I wanted to have a word with you, I said."

"That's funny," said the old man. "I thought I wanted to have a word with you."

"No. If I didn't want to come, I wouldn't have come. Your two flunkies tried last time. They're not very good at being persuasive. But now I've got something to talk to you about, I've got something to offer you that I think you might be interested in. But if you just want to start getting heavy about what's been going on, then I'm out of here. I've got things to do. I don't want my time wasted."

The old man chuckled.

"Is this the way you always do business?" he said gently.

"I've just had a couple of jokers pull guns on me," I said. "I'm angry. If you wanted to talk to me you could have sent me a note. I don't appreciate guns being waggled in front of my nose. If you don't want me to be angry, don't start threatening me. Simple as that."

The old man sighed.

"Those boys," he said. "They mean well, but they don't really know what they're doing. Always they think they're in the movies. They think they're... that guy, what's his name..."

"James Bond."

"Jimmy Cagney. They think they're Jimmy Cagney, 'you dirty rat.' You know what I mean? They're good boys, but they're not very bright. You know that for yourself. Last week I send them out and I say bring back this man who has appeared out of nowhere and is suddenly charging me double what I usually pay. And they come back and they say, but he did this and he did that, so we couldn't bring him. And now, here you are in front of me, and you tell me you're here because you want to see me. What a crazy world we live in. Crazy."

The old man had a very slight foreign twang to his voice when he spoke, I only started to notice it after he'd been talking for a couple of minutes, but it was so faint I couldn't work out where it was from.

"That's right," I said. I was still trying to be bullish, but the old man's weary pragmatism had taken away a lot of my early oomph. "I do want to talk to you. I want to talk about what I can offer you...."

The old man held up his hands to silence me.

"Come, come, we can talk of these things later. Let us have a drink first and get to know each other.

"Okay," I said. "Sounds reasonable. Who are you for a kick-off?"

That made the old man chuckle again.

"So impatient, so impatient. Let me tell you, my boy, it's only when you get to be as old as I am, that you realise how long you're around on this earth, and that there isn't really any need to rush anything."

He paused, looking contemplative.

"Unless of course you're not going to be around for very long, and then … well, then that's very sad."

He broke off and stared at his hands for a while, before seemingly pulling himself together again.

"My name is Tomassetti, Aldo Tomassetti. But shall I be very honest with you?"

"Sure," I said.

"Then I will. If I'm very honest, and I have decided I will be honest with you, more people call me Horlicks than they call me Aldo."

He giggled. I looked at him blankly.

"Horlicks. Because I drink Horlicks all the time. I drink nothing else."

He gestured at the mug in front of him. I frowned.

"Never heard of it," I said.

"Oh my. Never heard of Horlicks?"

I shook my head.

"Then we must get you some, you must try it. You will love it. It's the drink God gave to his people. Max, get a Horlicks for my friend here." This was to the barman who was in the middle of re-stocking his beer fridge.

A Horlicks was duly deposited in front of me. I blew across the froth on the top of the mug and took a sip. It was all right, it was the way I imagined Cocoa must taste, another hot drink I'd never tried. I took another sip. It was quite calming in a funny way, although at that moment I could have murdered something a bit stiffer.

The old man smiled at me and I smiled back. He kept nodding his head enthusiastically as he stared at me.

"Good, it's good, isn't it?"

"It is. Surprisingly good. But a brandy would set it off nicely."

"Ach, you boys, you and your drinking. Every sip of alcohol kills off one of your brain cells you know. That's the trouble with my nephews, they drink like fishes, and now look at them. You perhaps don't drink so much? You've still got a lot of your brain cells."

"I don't drink so much," I said. "The occasional brandy for relaxation, but I don't overdo it. But this is good, very good, perhaps I'll have a Horlicks before bed from now on instead of a brandy."

The old man laughed happily.

"So now we have a bond. We can share a love of our drinks. Already we can relate to each other. It is a good start. Now, what is your name?"

"Jones. But everybody calls me Jonesy."

"Well I shall call you Mr Jones. Which I suspect a lot of people do although you don't say that. I don't like to be familiar."

He waggled a hand at the barman again, who immediately stopped serving the people in front of him and raced over. That was interesting.

"Yes, sir."

"A brandy for my young friend here."

The barman looked enquiringly at me.

"Cognac," I said. "Large one."

The old man sighed.

"Well, if it relaxes you, perhaps I shall enjoy watching you drink it. It will make me happy. But don't forget your Horlicks."

I drained my mug, genuinely enjoying it. The old man leaned over and squeezed my hand. This was one of the weirdest experiences I had ever been involved in.

"Tell me about your family," Tomassetti began, "Because for me, family is the most important thing in the world. It is the only thing that really matters. Me? Everything I do is for my family. My business, my life, everything."

"I don't have much in the way of family," I said. "But I can understand how that might be important to someone."

"Then I am very sorry for you my friend. To have no family is a terrible thing. But tell me, if you have no family, have you not managed to make a family of your own?"

I shook my head.

"No, I'm pretty much on my own. I don't seem to have enough time to think about things like that."

The old man perked up at that.

"Then I shall find a family for you, someone from my family. A very pretty girl who you will fall in love with, and then you shall become a member of the Tomassetti family, and we shall be close, like brothers."

He put his hand on mine again and squeezed. I took a slug of brandy with my other hand.

"But tell me a little more about yourself."

I shrugged.

"Well, I'm thirty-eight, single. I've lived in London all my life, didn't go to University, I own a few businesses and I spend a lot of time … trading things I suppose you'd call it, moving things around. And that's it in a nutshell. Not much else to tell."

"And your family?"

"Father ran off when I was two, don't remember him. Mother brought me up. Died of what I suspect was a broken heart when I was seventeen. That's when I started working the street and started making a living."

"Ah, alone all this time. That is so sad."

"No, not alone," I said. "I have friends, girlfriends, I'm happy."

"No, alone. I see it behind your eyes. Single. I don't like that a man is single. But I have a niece I think you will like, and I think you will enjoy being in my family."

I laughed.

"I don't think I'm the marrying kind."

"We are all the marrying kind. We all say we aren't until we meet the right person, and then we are the marrying kind. That's the way of the world. But this moving things around that you mentioned. Give me an example of this, something that will tell me about you."

I thought for a moment and then told him about the wine. I didn't tell him about Finch and I glossed over where it had come from, but I did tell him I'd already sold it once, and I told him I was now in the process of selling it again for a lot more money, and I went into detail about how we'd done the swap. I didn't mention that it was all Spike's idea. He seemed impressed.

"Very resourceful. Very clever. I wish I had someone with me who had brains like that. I think I need you to meet my niece very soon. But this wine, perhaps. ..."

He was interrupted by someone coming in through the front door and marching straight up to him.

"Mr Tomassetti, I'm back. I've got news from the Tennis Player, he's. ..."

The old man held up a hand.

"Shhh," he said. "We have a visitor. Where are your manners?"

The newcomer looked round at me in surprise.

"Who the hell's this?"

"My boy, my boy, such language. We don't want to hear that, especially when we have a guest. Ah thank you."

This last was to the barman who brought over two fresh mugs of Horlicks.

The new guy looked at me suspiciously. He was big, everything about him seemed overlarge, a huge round swollen football for a head, hands like shovels, and sausages for fingers. His head was shaved but you could tell from the stubble that he was ginger. I instantly hated everything about him, and from the look he was giving me the feeling was mutual.

"Carrot," said the old man. "This is Mr Jones. Mr Jones this is Carrot. Carrot is an employee of mine, not one of my family, but sometimes I just don't have enough family to do all the things

I want to, so I have to look elsewhere. Carrot, Mr Jones is the mysterious person who has become involved in our enterprise with Mr Darby. He is here because he wants to talk business with us, but perhaps in the future he will marry young Tabitha, and perhaps we will shall buy some wine from him."

My ears perked up at that. That was interesting. But Carrot just looked downright confused. He looked from me to the old man and then back to me, staring daggers. Clearly none of it made any sense to him.

I sipped my Horlicks and stared calmly back at him.

"Well we should bloody well tell him to sling his hook, and not do it too pleasantly either," said Carrot. "He's been sticking his nose in where it's not wanted and he needs to be given the message that it's our turf and he's not welcome here. A message that means he won't be able to walk again in a hurry."

"Carrot, Carrot." The old man laid a restraining hand on the other man's arm. I thought Carrot was going to explode.

"As it happens, I'm feeling good things about Mr Jones. I think he's someone we could work with perhaps. Who knows, perhaps he could be very useful for us, perhaps do things that nobody else can do. I suspect he has talents that would be extremely valuable. Now take a seat and let us listen to what Mr Jones has to say."

Carrot grabbed a stool and plonked it down next to us. He didn't take his eyes off me the whole time.

"You know, Carrot," the old man went on. "We need someone to take the place of Winslow, perhaps Mr Jones might be the very person."

"What happened to Winslow," I asked.

"He turned out to be not as trustworthy as I had hoped," said the old man. "So he had to leave us."

"Yeah," said Carrot with enthusiasm. "And he didn't enjoy it very much I can tell you that. It was a long and painful parting."

The old man tutted.

"It was very disappointing," he said. Sadly. "He seemed to be exactly the sort of person we needed, but you can never really tell. You have to be so careful these days. He disappointed me so much."

Winslow was the MI5 man, had to be. And they'd killed him by the sound of it. Christ, I needed to be careful here.

"Which doesn't mean we need this nobody," interrupted Carrot again. "He needs to be told he's not wanted in our business, and told in no uncertain terms."

"Carrot, Carrot." The old man shook his head. "Please, please. There's too much anger here. First Mr Jones comes in full of hostility, so we give him a mug of Horlicks and eventually we get him to find peace, and then you come in wanting to fight everyone, and off we go again. This is too much for me, too much."

He got off his stool, stretched a bit, and shuffled off towards the back of the room. He turned and looked over his shoulder.

"Mr Jones, I'm tired. Forgive me, but I have had enough for today. Would you be so kind as to come back here again tomorrow? At, say, five o'clock."

"But Mr Tomassetti, how do you know we can trust him? He could. ..."

The old man waved a hand, instantly silencing the big man. It was amazing the power he could wield with those wrinkly hands.

"Tomorrow," the old man said.

We watched him go, then Carrot leant over to me.

"Listen, you tosser. You might have the boss fooled for the moment, but you aren't going to fool the rest of us. I don't know who you are, but as far as I'm concerned you're just a chancer who thinks he can make an easy buck. Well, there's no place for you here. If I had my way I'd take you out the back and stick a knife in your ribs right now. I'll be convincing the boss tonight, so if you know what's good for you, you'll get lost. Don't come

A LOT OF NERVE

back tomorrow and don't get involved in this business any more. In fact, disappear."

He stood up.

"This is good advice, take it."

"Have a Horlicks," I said. "It's very calming. Might help you relax."

I thought he was going to leap on me. His already red face went a deep shade of crimson and his hands started clenching and unclenching. He was making a huge effort not to kill me. And then he just turned on his heels and walked off.

I finished off my Horlicks, nodded to the barman, and left.

I felt I should have been feeling more stressed, but I was actually quite relaxed. I'll stop off for a jar of the good stuff on my way home I thought.

CHAPTER TWENTY
TERRY THE GLOVE

I think I can still feel my heart beating. Don't think I've ever been so scared in my life. But that feller's been good to me. Slipping me those fifty notes. Felt I had to watch for his back again. There's no doubt he's grateful for what I've been doing for him. Reckon he needs me. I can see us doing a lot of stuff together. Could work out being very lucrative for me, he's loaded, you can see that a mile off.

God, I was frightened though. Didn't know I had it in me really. Quite proud of myself, especially as they had shooters. Mean looking buggers. Reckon they would have used them too. Soon saw them off though. They could see I meant business. Scared – I could see it in their eyes. That feller must have been impressed. Think he was thinking about a partnership already, but that would have convinced him. Bit of muscle and some back up can never do any harm for anyone.

Wonder what's happened to that prick Walton. Funny him just disappearing like that. Still, hope he got what he deserves, something nasty. Wonder what's going to happen to the pub if he never turns up again. Still I'm sorted. Me and that other guy got a good future ahead of us.

CHAPTER TWENTY-ONE
SAUSAGE SURPRISE

The fact that it was dark when I got outside surprised me, I must have been in the club longer than I thought. It was starting to get chilly, so I turned the collar of my jacket up and stuck my hands in my pocket. I tried to process what had just happened, but I think the Horlicks really had made me sleepy as I wasn't coming to any conclusions.

The one thing I was sure of was that I was completely nonplussed by Tomassetti. On the surface of it he was just a kindly old gentleman, wouldn't hurt a fly sort of guy, but on the other side of the coin he sure did exert a surprising amount of authority on those around him, there was a lot of fear there. And it did appear that they'd done the MI5 man in, Winslow, and enjoyed it too according to that thug Carrot. But the old man was extremely difficult to read ... was it really all an act? Or maybe he was a raging psychopath behind that mug of Horlicks. Or even, I thought, he was oblivious to what was really going on with the bunch of hoodlums around him.

It was as I was strolling aimlessly around Soho, ignoring all the various requests to come and have a good time or see a show with real live girls that I came to a decision. I decided it was time to bring Hernandez properly on board. I decided that she could actually be of help to me, that I needed some proper professional back up and that she would probably have access to all sorts of information that might prove useful down the road. I decided all of that, but mostly I just really wanted to see her again.

I rang her on my plastic Tesco phone.

"Jones, where have you been? I've been calling you."

Damn, I'd completely forgotten about checking my other phone, I bet there were loads of missed calls on there.

"Sorry," I said. "I had to change phones, but you can get me on this number from now on."

"Well thanks for telling me. Is this you trying to be as mysterious as ever?"

"It's a long story for another time, but what did you want?"

"I wanted to see if you were ready to share anything yet. I've been doing a bit of digging on Paradine and it's got me absolutely nowhere. It's bugging me beyond belief that those faceless civil servants are happy to let an ugly crime like that go unpunished. Unless, of course, you're one of those faceless civil servants now."

I laughed.

"Hardly. But they have roped me in on this unfortunately. Listen, I will share some of it with you. I can't tell you everything because, well, I just can't. But I'll give you some of it."

"Okay."

"But in exchange, I'd like you to get me some information if you can."

"If I can. What do you need?"

"I've just met a gangster called Aldo Tomassetti. I'd like all the information you've got on him."

"Well you're going to need a van for that, we've got several filing cabinets dedicated just to him."

"You know him then?"

"Know him? He's the biggest crook in London, runs just about everything illegal that goes on in Soho. Nasty piece of work as well."

"So how come he's not locked up then?"

"Nobody's ever been able to get close enough to pin anything on him, it's always his minions who carry the can. The suspicion is that there's someone senior in the force who's on his payroll. But I can tell you all about him, give you his background, what he's involved in, that sort of thing."

"Great, that would be really helpful. What else would be useful would be a picture of him."

"Okay, no problem. Anything else?"

"Anything you've got on two of the people he's got working for him. One guy, surname of Winslow, I've not met him so I've no description, and another guy who everyone calls Carrot. Big, heavily built guy, shaven red head."

"Okay, I'll see what I can dig up."

"Meet up later?"

She sighed.

"Wish I could, but I've got a ton of paperwork here, and besides it will take a while to dig up any info I can find on those two. I could meet you tomorrow for breakfast though?"

I was disappointed, but I agreed. We made arrangements to meet in a little café I knew in Notting Hill the next morning. It was as I hung up that I suddenly recalled all of Lambert's warnings. I'd only been out of the gangster's presence for five minutes and I was on the phone to the police asking about him, and doing it on the street in full view of everybody walking past. Lambert was right, I wasn't very good at this. I dropped my phone on the floor and stamped on it very hard. I scooped up the several dozen bits and dropped them into a rubbish bin.

Now I had two reasons to visit Tescos on the way home.

"I'd like you to buy some Horlicks for the office."

"Horlicks? What on earth for?"

Mimi's face was a real picture. She couldn't have been more surprised if I'd asked her for a date.

"I've acquired a taste for it," I said.

"Well, if that's what you want, of course. I sometimes have a mug before I go to bed of an evening myself. Very relaxing. Would have thought a double brandy would have been more up your street though."

"You'd be surprised what I get up to just before bed." We both laughed.

I sat down at my desk and signed the stack of papers Mimi had ready and waiting for me, and then gave her the number of my new plastic phone.

"What is it with you and these phones?" she said.

"Security." I tapped the side of my nose. "And another thing while we're talking about security. I'm going to phone you every night at seven o'clock. If you haven't heard from me after an hour, then I need you to call this person."

I gave Mimi Hernandez's card. She immediately got serious and her face hardened. You could see she was burning up with questions but she knew better than to ask.

"She'll know what to do," I said.

My toasted bacon sandwich had just been plonked down in front of me when Hernandez arrived. I was already half way through my second mug of tea.

"You take me to the nicest places," she said as she sat down. She looked round pointedly at the ragbag collection of builders, market traders and down and outs who filled the café.

"You're late," I said.

"Have you ever tried driving here from Dulwich? It's taken me forever. Nightmare."

"Dulwich? Where's Dulwich? I've never heard of it."

"Don't get south of the river very much then I take it?

"I get nose bleeds. Is that where you live, Dulwich?

She nodded. She was the only woman in the room and every other customer in there was continually eyeing her. Something someone that striking would be used to I guess. It was a good thing she didn't look like a policeman or the place would have emptied in seconds.

"Nice out that way is it?"

"It's okay. Bit dull and a bit remote. But it's all I can afford on a policeman's salary. I'd have to go down a different career path if I wanted to live in a smart part of town in a swanky apartment."

"That can be overrated," I said, not meaning it. We smiled at each other.

The girl came over to take Hernandez' order.

"I'll take some fruit and some porridge and a herbal tea, please."

The girl looked at her like she'd crawled out from under a rock.

"Fruit's off, porridge is off and herbal tea's off. There's been a lot of demand for it this morning."

Hernandez looked round at all the other breakfasts being consumed. They were mostly of the double egg, bacon, sausage, beans and chips variety. She looked at me.

"I'll have what he's having," she said.

"Bit too up market for you, this smart part of town is it?" I said.

She snorted. She snorted again when she took a sip of her tea.

"Too many herbs in it perhaps?"

"All right, all right, get your jokes out of the way, then perhaps we can get down to business."

"Okay," I said. "You first."

She reached down for her bag and pulled out a grainy photograph of Tomassetti.

"Yeah, that's him," I said.

"Jeez, have you really got involved with him? He's dangerous."

"He doesn't seem like it, he just seems like a really nice old man, you know, a bit past it and a bit eccentric."

"Don't be fooled by that. He's a killer. Really. Someone to be avoided. If he's the one responsible for Paradine, then I'm not surprised your friend ended up looking like he did. Seriously, whatever it is you're up to, there's nothing worth getting involved with this butcher for."

I tried to be cool, but there was that image of the meat again.

"I don't have a lot of choice as it happens. How about the other two, any luck?"

She shook her head.

"We don't have a lot on file about his current gang. Like I say, there's some payola going on there somewhere otherwise we'd be all over them like a ton of bricks. I took it at face value that it was a governmental thing that I was warned off the Paradine case, but now I'm not so sure. Perhaps it was just money changing hands."

"No," I said. "That was genuine enough. MI5."

Her eyes widened slightly.

"Tell me more."

"Well, I shouldn't, they really did make me sign the Official Secrets Act. I shouldn't be breathing a word about this."

"Well why are you?"

"Well…" I paused and tried to look as serious as I could. "…this is difficult for me to put into words, but I'm on a dangerous mission for my Queen and country. I'm putting my life on the line for all the ordinary people, all the citizens of this great nation of ours who get up every day and go about their ordinary, dull, boring lives without knowing that there's somebody like me out there, fighting for their freedom. My chances of making it through this alive are slim, who knows, I'll probably be dead by this time tomorrow. I thought I should make the most of my last day on this planet by, you know, spending it with the person I most want to be with."

I reached out and put my hand on top of hers.

"What a load of crap! You bloody con-man!" she exploded, making everyone on the adjacent tables look around. Interestingly, she let my hand stay where it was for a second or two more than she needed to, before pushing it off.

"All joking aside," I said. "This is dangerous."

"All joking aside, I know it is. I've just been telling you for the last ten minutes not to have anything to do with this psychopath."

"Well, like I said, I don't have a lot of choice."

"Because of MI5?"

I nodded.

"And what exactly do they want you to do?"

"Well, in a nutshell, it seems that Tomassetti and his gang are stealing some secrets on behalf of somebody else. Something to do with some new radar system or something that one of our big companies is developing. They want me to infiltrate Tomassetti's gang and find out who they're selling the secrets to."

Hernandez looked at me with one of those 'yeah, right' expressions on her face.

"Yeah, right," she said.

I shrugged.

"Believe me or not, that's the truth."

"And why would you do that for them?"

"Well, it seems that they might have discovered one or two things about me that might be … well, a touch awkward if they were ever to be made public."

"What, you mean they discovered you're gay? And you don't feel ready to come out of the closet yet? Or perhaps they discovered you're having an affair with your Polish cleaning lady who's really a Soviet spy."

We both laughed. It eased some of the tension that had started to build up between us. Clearly Hernandez wasn't buying anything that I was telling her though.

"What a load of codswallop," she said. "The only thing that's believable is that they found enough dirt on you to blackmail you into doing something."

"Everything I've said is the truth. It doesn't make any difference if you believe me or not, but I'd prefer it if you were on my side. I could do with a bit of back up."

I outlined my plan of calling Mimi every evening and Mimi calling her if she didn't hear from me. I gave her Mimi's phone number. For the first time I think, Hernandez started to wonder that, just possibly, this might be real.

"And what am I supposed to do if she rings me?" she asked.

"If I haven't rung, it's because Tomassetti and his goons are slicing bits off me somewhere. I thought you might be able to think of something to do."

"Why can't your new friends help, the faceless ones in the grey suits?"

I shook my head.

"I'm on my own in this. No help from them."

"Look, this is ridiculous. Pretending for a moment that this is even remotely what's going on, why aren't they sending in one of their own people?"

"They tried that already. Unsuccessfully. Tomassetti's mob killed him. They seem to think I might be able to stand muster as the real thing where he couldn't."

Hernandez sat back in her chair looking pensive. She was chewing the side of her cheek as though she was really worried about me. It was endearing.

"Bollocks," she said suddenly. "Absolute bollocks. You're the biggest blagger I've ever met. But let's go with it, let's pretend that this fairy story is real and that, notionally, I might try and help you out. What happens next?"

"I'm meeting Tomassetti tonight at five o'clock."

"Where?"

"Drinking club in Soho, just off Wardour Street. Meard Street. I think it's called the Albemarle Club."

"Okay, what's the meeting about?"

"I'm offering him some more secrets. He seems to like me, I'm trying to get a job of some sort in his organisation. But we're still in the getting to know you stage. We're bonding over a mug of Horlicks."

"Horlicks?"

"I told you, he's just a sweet old man. We had a mug of Horlicks, had a chat, and then he went to bed early. That's why I'm going back today."

"Well, if he's anything, he's not a sweet old man. He's very, very dangerous. Don't be taken in by any of that."

"I know, I'm being as careful as I can. So, are you in?"

There was a pause, a long pause.

"Why do I sense I'm being set up here?" she said eventually. "But yes, I'm in. But here are my rules. I want to know where you are all the time. All the time, got it? You check in with me on a regular basis, let me know where you are and what's happening. If I'm in on this, I'm in, properly. Not on the periphery, left in the dark."

"Perhaps you'd better move in with me while this is going on then," I said lightly. "We can be properly close then. Like you want to."

"I'll think about that," she laughed.

"Deal?"

"Deal."

"This could be the start of a beautiful friendship," I said.

A big bruiser of a bloke walked past holding a fry up. He stopped at our table, looked down at Hernandez and offered her his plate.

"Ere, want some of my sausage," he said.

CHAPTER TWENTY-TWO
MIMI

I really don't know what's got into that boy. Horlicks? That's not normal. And all these phones, I just don't know what he's up to these days. So mysterious all of a sudden. And he doesn't tell me anything. Can't trust his auntie Mimi any more, I suppose. Me. Me who knows everything about him, seen everything, changed his nappies, comforted him when he was crying, put plasters on his cut knees. I was there for him when his dad left, there for him when his mum died, and I'm there for him now keeping all his businesses running and keeping him out of jail more than likely. There's nobody else would be able to do this for him. Nobody. He'd be in a right pickle if it wasn't for me.

That Escobar coming in was a right result though. Burlington Bertie, hundred to thirty, that will do very nicely. Should make about a hundred grand out of that. I'm sure Jonesy wouldn't mind that I used his briefcase full of money to put the bets on. Good use of his money that's for sure. It's not like he's in need of a few bob.

Now I need to work out everyone's cut in the syndicate. They're all such babies, not one of them can work out what all the odds mean. You'd think at least one of them would have sussed out that I'm paying them a fraction of what they're owed. Babies.

It's such a pain having to traipse round all the different betting shops though, so time consuming. But the only way they'll pay out is if each bet is small. Small beer. If they thought I was a high roller I'd be banned straight away. Bookies are all very nice when they're winning, but if you get a bit of good fortune you're out of there straight away. The crooks. I'll have to get Jonesy to show me how to do the betting on the computer, that would save my poor old plates. Don't like leaving a trail though, that would worry me a bit. Happier working in cash. Cash on the horse, cash for the winnings. No one the wiser. Way it should be.

I wonder what's up with the boy though.

Horlicks. Bless my soul.

CHAPTER TWENTY-THREE
AN EDUCATIONAL INTERLUDE

Everything was the same when I arrived back at the Albemarle. I went up the steps and knocked on the door and the same milky white face looked out at me through the panel. Neither of us said anything, but the door was swung open to let me enter.

I don't think any of the customers had moved since the day before. Tomassetti was sat on his usual place at the end of the bar, and Carrot and the two goons were at a table over to one side. As I walked up a thought struck me, I wondered what had happened to Darby.

"Mr Jones." The old man looked genuinely pleased to see me. He shook my hand and made me sit on the stool next to him. A nonchalant hand gesture attracted the attention of the barman who instantly came running over.

"A Horlicks for me and my guest, please Max." He looked enquiringly at me and I nodded. That seemed to please him even more. I was conscious of three pairs of eyes boring into me from the adjacent table.

"Did you want to hear about what I've got to offer?" I said.

"You're talking about something from the same source as the papers you've been selling us?"

"That's right."

The old man looked thoughtful, then let out a big sigh.

"Yes, perhaps we should talk about that. But not here I think. Come, we'll finish our drinks, and then we'll go somewhere a bit more conducive to a business discussion."

Oh, oh, I thought. Every nerve in my body twitched. The thought of going off somewhere with the four of them...I assumed the others would be coming as well...was not very appealing. I felt quite comfortable in this semi-public place, even though I doubted that there were many people in there who come rushing to my aid. I really didn't want to go anywhere else. I racked my brains, but couldn't come up with anything very compelling to persuade him not to move on.

"I'm happy here," I said. Limply.

The old man smiled.

"No, no. We'll go. This is the place where I relax, I do my business somewhere else. I try very hard to keep my two worlds separate."

We finished our drinks in silence. I didn't say anything because there was a voice in my head screaming 'nooooo', and I was trying to ignore it.

"Come then," said the old man eventually.

He got up, took my arm, and we walked slowly past the bar to the front door.

"Mr Tomassetti," I said. "What happened to Darby?"

"Mr Darby? He's fine. We talked to him and calmed him down and got him looking and thinking like a human being again. He's a very frightened man, so it was difficult, the whole thing is difficult for him doing this. But he's back home now, and hopefully back at work again. He's too valuable to us to ever let anything happen to him. He's our only way of getting the information we need."

He looked over at me. Very pointedly.

"So he needs to be kept safe, and he needs to be kept as happy as we can make him. I think one of things that will keep him happy and safe is if he never sees you again."

Another pointed look at me.

"But we will talk more about poor Mr Darby later. As we try to put all the pieces of this mysterious jigsaw together."

Uh, oh, I thought. This doesn't sound promising at all.

At that point, I was seriously considering doing a runner. The moment the door opened I thought. Just sprint off, hope there's lots of people around so they can't shoot me, and keep running.

I still had that thought in my mind as we got outside onto the pavement, but just as we did, Hernandez walked past. I was so astonished I almost said something, but just managed to control myself. I'm sure if somebody had been looking closely at me they would have seen something in my face.

She just walked by, didn't look at anybody, and kept going. She was giving me as strong a message as she could possibly give. I wasn't on my own. I felt so much better it was unbelievable.

"Now, there is a woman," said the old man, watching Hernandez walk away. "A woman to admire. What do you think, Mr Jones? Would she make good family for you?"

"I'm sure she would," I said, trying to cover up my surprise once again. "Shall I go after her now and ask her?"

The old man laughed.

"Perhaps not just now. But if you see her again, I believe you should. I think in this life you do not get many opportunities with a woman such as that."

I was just thinking how weird this all was when the Bentley swept up in front of us. I was right about everybody coming, Carrot drove, with the old man next to him and me sandwiched between the two goons in the back.

What would be nice I thought, would be that we were going to their place in Mayfair, and not some meat packing company in Deptford or somewhere. I don't know why I was so keen, it wasn't as though I knew what went on there, it was just that Mayfair felt close to home and safe. It had to be a better bet than somewhere I didn't know out in the sticks miles away from civilisation.

We drove out along Grosvenor Street, and it was as we were passing the old American Embassy that I started to feel a bit better. We had to be going to Mayfair, this would be a stupid route to get to anywhere else. And as we pulled up outside the house I'd seen the goon's go into before, I began to feel a whole lot more comfortable.

And I felt even better when we went inside. Carrot led the way up the steps to the ornate doorway, and we all followed him in. A maid appeared out of nowhere and took the old man's coat. I looked around. It was just a family home, I could hear people talking from somewhere else in the house. It was all very normal. I say normal, but it was far from that really. Everything looked exquisite and very, very expensive. It wasn't my taste, too traditional and old fashioned, but there was no doubt that it had all been done very well, and at a huge cost I didn't wonder.

The old man led me into a room off the hall. A small sitting room, with some leather sofas and armchairs and couple of enormous paintings of horses on the walls. Tomassetti saw me looking.

"My passion," he said. "I have a stable out near Newmarket. I will take you there one day. I have a horse called Knobbler's Bay, we think that she will do great things for us. She will be a champion. Do you follow the horses, Mr Jones?"

"I stick a pound or two on the National every year, but that's about it, I'm afraid. I never win."

"Then we must educate you. The sport of kings they call it, and I'm inclined to agree. There is no finer pastime in the world."

"I'd enjoy that," I said. "I've never been racing, it would be a new experience for me."

"Splendid." The old man was looking quite excited at the prospect of taking me racing. "Splendid. We shall arrange a trip up to my stables. I shall show you around and let you meet my horses, and then we shall go racing together. I have a box at all the courses. We shall have great fun."

I could almost touch the resentment coming from Carrot's side of the room, but I was feeling a lot more confident now. Surely the old man wasn't contemplating doing something nasty to me if he was making plans for us to go racing together. The only thing though, was that look he gave me when he told me Darby was the only way he could get the information. I figured I wasn't entirely out of the woods yet.

He gestured me towards one of the sofas and sat down opposite me. Carrot and the two goons stood along the wall by the door.

"So, sell to me."

I took a deep breath.

"Okay," I said. "I muscled in your operation, and I'm sorry. I saw an opening and I took it. It's what I do, I see opportunities. But now I understand what's going on, I think I can offer you more than you're getting. I don't pretend to understand the technicalities of it all, but I understand the mechanics of getting and moving on information. Again it's what I do."

"Go on."

"You're gathering information about a highly secret development, and then you're selling that information on. I don't know who your customer is, but presumably they're getting that information to develop it themselves and as soon as there's a breakthrough, your customer will know and will have it out there before you can say Jack Robinson."

"And?"

"Well, what you're providing them is just a tiny part of the development process. I'm sure your customer would appreciate, and pay for, as much information as we can get our hands on. There must be a lot more data being produced than just those few sheets a week. You've got Darby, but he hasn't got the balls or the brains to do any more than you're getting him to do at the moment. That's where I come in. I can get in there and get it all. Whether it's physically or using technology, I can get in. Your customer would bite your hands off to get the rest of the development picture."

"And why wouldn't we do this ourselves? Why would we need the services of somebody like you?"

I looked over at Carrot and the goons and then back at the old man.

"Really?"

He pulled a sort of rueful face and nodded.

"And you could do this?"

"Absolutely. It's what I do."

"And you know what the development is and where it is being developed?"

I nodded again.

"Yep."

The old man sat in silence for a while.

"I thought you were going to sell me something specific."

"No. I'm selling me."

The old man nodded again at that.

"You've got nothing to lose," I said. "If I can't do it, you carry on getting the information you're already getting. And if I get caught, I'm on my own. There's nothing going to tie me back to you."

"This is just bullshit. I told you he didn't have anything to offer us." This was Carrot, who had clearly been trying hard not to interrupt, but couldn't hold it in any longer. "He's just a chancer, he's got nothing. I don't know why you're even listening to him, I say let's get rid of him now."

The old man held up a hand and Carrot subsided.

"Calm down, calm down," he said. He stared at me and I held his gaze. It wasn't easy, but I managed to keep my composure.

"Well," he said eventually. "I am intrigued, certainly, but I wonder if perhaps you really know as much about what is going on as you claim."

Uh, oh. Here we go I thought. I held my breath.

"But first," he said. "Let us have a drink. Carrot, will you ask Isabella for two mugs of Horlicks. I presume you boys won't join us?"

The three of them shook their heads and Carrot left the room staring malevolently at me. We sat in silence for five minutes or so until he came back, followed by the maid carrying two steaming mugs on a silver tray. She sat them down on a small, very ornate table. I had a sudden thought. I hoped Tomassetti wasn't poisoning me with all these Horlicks.

He took a sip and made an appreciative noise.

"To begin with," he said. "I shall be very honest with you as I hope you will be with me going forward. The bad news for you is that, firstly, we know a lot more about you than you probably suspect, and, secondly, it appears that you have absolutely no idea about what is really going on."

He stared at me levelly, and I swallowed hard.

"Did you really think we would just let you come muscling your way in on our trade and start demanding more money, without us doing something about it? Of course not. We have, in fact, been finding out all about you."

Uh, oh, I thought again.

"But fortunately for you, you were very easy to find. Very easy. There are a surprising amount of people in London who know you and have done business with you in the past. It was very unexpected that we were able to find out so much about you in such a small amount of time. And to sum up, you're well known, we've discovered a lot of, what shall we say, enterprises that you have been involved in, and we can trace a number of those back a good many years. We were able to prepare quite a large file about you very quickly. So, as far as we can tell, you are exactly the man you appear to be. You've come up smelling of roses in that respect, you might say. And in addition to verifying that you are, in fact, a real person, I think it's safe to say that we were very impressed by what the dossier we had had prepared had to say about you. Very impressed."

I wanted to let out a big sigh of relief, but I kept it in.

"Except. There was one thing."

Uh, oh.

"We discovered that you provide some services for a certain Mr Archibald Finch."

Archibald? I didn't know he was an Archibald. Who the hell names a baby Archibald? Although I don't suppose Finch was ever a baby, he was born big and ugly. It was very hard to imagine him as a child.

"And he isn't somebody I have very fond feelings for. In fact, my feelings are completely the opposite of fondness. It isn't exactly war between us, but it's getting very close. You can imagine that I wouldn't want one of Mr Finch's hired help knowing anything about my business."

"I can assure you," I said. "Nothing would give me greater pleasure than never having to see Finch again for the rest of my life. I sold some stuff for somebody a few years ago, and it turned out to be Finch behind it. I had no idea until afterwards. And he's kept using me ever since; I don't have any choice about it. Recently though, he seems to have taken against me. That wine deal I told you about, that's Finch's stuff, and he's making me sell more and more of it, and asking for a better price each time. And it's absolute crap. Like I say, I really need to get him out of my hair, but I just don't know how to do it."

The old man smiled.

"Yes, well, we can turn our attentions to Mr Finch later. Perhaps we can arrange things in a way that would result in Mr Finch's absence which would do all of us a favour."

I grimaced inwardly. There was the image of the meat again.

"But enough of that," the old man continued. "The other side of our, what shall we call it … investigation … was to discover what role you play in the appropriation of the test data with our Mr Darby. And as you know very well, you have no role at all, all you've done is insert yourself, very cleverly, between Mr Darby and us. So. You're an honest crook, trying to make a quick profit. Nothing more, nothing less."

I realised I hadn't breathed for the last minute or so, and I exhaled as quietly as I could.

"But to continue. If we work on the basis that you can do what you say you can do, and that your motivation here is to make some money, then let's explore some of the details of your proposal. Firstly, do you know what sort of development we are talking about here?"

"It's a new sort of new radar system. I can't give you any more detail than that at the moment, but that's what it is." I tried to sound as confident as I could, mentally keeping my fingers crossed that good old Google hadn't let me down.

The old man raised his eyebrows.

"Well, my dear Mr Jones, I'm afraid to tell you I don't think it is radar."

"It isn't?" I was surprised.

"No, it almost certainly isn't.

"What is it then?"

"To the best of our knowledge it's a battery."

"A battery?" I parroted. I was beginning to feel out of my depth. Knowledge is strength, and clearly I didn't have any at all.

"Yes, a battery. Not just any old battery, of course. A very special battery, one that will last forever. Can you imagine? Forever. Or perhaps not quite forever, but one that will last a very long time without the need for charging. Think how that will change the world. And can you imagine the power and the riches that will bring to the owners of such a thing?"

I could imagine. Easily. No wonder Paradine had died because of this. Thinking about it, and after listening to what the old man had to say, I'd lived a bit of a charmed life so far.

"I say, to the best of our knowledge, because this whole business is shrouded in mystery to be honest. It was Carrot, in fact, who managed to discover a little bit of what this is all about, that the information we are selling relates to this remarkable battery. He is perhaps not quite as stupid as you are thinking him to be, hmm?"

The old man had noticed my surprised look. I looked over at Carrot who was looking very smug.

"And who is it you think our Mr Darby works for?"

Ah, I was on firmer ground here.

"A company called Integrated Electronics. They do a lot of secret stuff there, lots of things for the military."

"And you know this how?"

"He told me," I lied. "We had a long conversation about everything."

The old man raised his eyebrows and stared hard at me, just as Carrot started sounding off again.

"See, this is absolute crap. Stop all this nonsense now. Let me take him outside and deal with him. This is crazy."

The old man held up his hand, still staring hard at me. I was starting to get worried.

"Well, Mr Jones, this has, in fact, been a very useful conversation. As I said, we have done some very extensive research on you, it is something we are very good at, and our conclusions were that you were somebody with a lot of promise, somebody who might be of interest. And meeting you confirmed that opinion, that you might be someone we could do business with."

He paused.

"But?" I ventured.

"But, as Carrot so eloquently put it, using different words to the ones I might use, you know nothing."

"I don't?"

"No. Our Mr Darby does not in fact work for whoever that Electronics company was you mentioned. He, in fact, works for the Ministry of Defence. A fact that we know very well, because, under our customer's instruction, we recruited him. We arranged the circumstances that would ensure he stays tied to us, and we run him. As it happens, it might be this company of yours developing this product, but I would be very surprised if Mr Darby knew this, or that he would have the nerve to pretend to you that he actually worked there."

It was my time to stare. I could feel the panic starting to well up inside me. That bloody Lambert had stitched me up good and proper here.

"But don't feel too badly, Mr Jones, things haven't changed very much. We know who you are and what you do. We had already assumed, as Carrot said, that you were a chancer and didn't have anything tangible to offer, and now we have confirmed that. You were taking a gamble, and while that may have failed, it doesn't stop us doing something together. Why, as you said earlier, it's you you're offering us."

I could feel Carrot glowering at me across the room. While I was feeling a tad more comfortable, he certainly wasn't.

"So, while you might not think this has gone well, we are still on good terms. There have been no surprises from my side."

The old man smiled at me. Reassuringly I thought.

"So, do you have any questions?"

I tried to pull myself together. I could still recover the situation here.

"So who is your customer? I asked, trying to sound as nonchalant as I could.

"Ah," said the old man. "I think perhaps that is something we should keep secret for the time being. It's not something you need to know right now, certainly."

"How did you get involved?"

"We were approached anonymously. We were told that somebody had heard rumours about this famous battery and they wanted to find out more. But they didn't want to get too close themselves, they needed some distance, and that's where we came in. We would do the dirty work for them. We would acquire the information, and if anything unfortunate happened to us, that would be the end of it. Their name could never be linked to ours. And we were happy to do that, because, obviously we were going to be very well rewarded for the sort of risks we were going to be taking."

The old man paused and took a sip of his Horlicks. I followed suit. It still surprised me every time how good it tasted.

"They instructed us on everything we had to do, all we had to do was do it. They told us what the information was, where we could obtain it, and then they gave us the means to obtain it. Darby. All we had to do was to come up with something that would make sure Mr Darby would always do what we wanted him to do. And that was very easy, of course. Mr Darby met a woman. A woman who took his breath away, a woman who made him feel alive for the first time in his poor, sad life. And, unfortunately for him, that woman had very expensive tastes, and he found that he was spending more and more on her every time he saw her. Money that he did not have. So when we turn up and offer him some very large sums of cash for not doing very much, then, of course, he is very grateful. We did of course mention that if he didn't cooperate we would have to tell his wife about his new friend, but to be honest he was more interested in being able to have money to lavish on his new love. And he does love her very much indeed."

"And she's your woman?"

"Of course."

"Poor old Darby."

"Indeed, poor old Darby. But he has some happiness now. It won't last forever, but he should enjoy it while he can."

We sat in silence for a while, the old man staring at me while I pondered everything he'd told me. The more I thought about it the more I realised how little I had to offer. I was feeling very vulnerable right now.

"So Mr Jones. After all that, do you still think you've got something to offer?"

It was as though he'd read my mind. He really was very good.

"Yes," I said. "As I told you, I'm selling me. You've found out who I am and what I do, so you know I'm kosher. You know you've got no worries on that score. But what I can do is bring something a little extra into your organisation. I'm willing to wager I've got a skill set that nobody else has got."

There was silence again. The old man had his head tilted slightly over to one side and he had a faraway look in his eyes. He was either deep in contemplation at what I'd said, or he was about to drop into a Horlicks-induced slumber.

"Bullshit! That's just bullshit." Carrot woke everybody up. "I'm not going to listen to any more of this. Let me get rid of him now. I've had enough."

Just as the old man held up his hand to silence Carrot, I had a sudden panic about the time. I dragged my phone out of my pocket to look. It was seven-thirty.

"I'm sorry, Mr Tomassetti," I said. "I was supposed to make a very important phone call. Do you mind if I make it now?"

He nodded and I pressed Mimi's number.

"Jonesy! You naughty boy. Thank goodness. I was just starting to worry that I would have to make that phone call. I'm not cut out for this cloak and dagger lark, you know. Are you all right?"

Her words came out in a jabber. It was actually quite difficult to understand what she was saying she was talking so quickly.

"I'm fine. Everything's fine. All under control."

"Well, that's good, but it isn't here. That Finch has been on the phone all day. He says you aren't answering your phone, and he wants his money for the wine. Now. He says he's coming round tomorrow and he'll take payment in kind if the cash isn't there for him. Jonesy, this is scaring me rotten."

Damn. I still wasn't checking my messages properly. I was going to have to start getting hold of this phone thing properly.

"Okay, okay," I said. "I'll ring him now and get things sorted out. If I need to tell you anything I'll call you straight back, but if you don't hear from me, it means everything's fine and just carry on as usual. But don't worry, it's just that I've got so much going on that I'm struggling to fit it all in."

"Well, you make sure you look after yourself. I worry about you, you know."

"I know. Anyway, let me make that call. I'll call you tomorrow if not before."

I hung up.

"That sounded like a precautionary call," said the old man. "A call somebody might make at a set time to tell someone he was all right. If he was worried about what might happen to him."

I didn't answer.

"Very wise, very wise," he continued. "It's a sign of someone who thinks things through, covers every eventuality. But it also sounded as though you have a problem of some kind."

I nodded.

"It's that wine I told you about. Finch wants paying now. He's starting to get heavy, says he's coming round tomorrow to get payment one way or the other."

"Hmm," the old man looked thoughtful. "We really need to think about Mr Finch and what to do about him. But tell me, what is the position with the wine, do you have a sale yet?"

"I don't know. I need to speak to the guy who's dealing with it for me. I haven't had a chance to talk to him for a while. Hopefully the deal's been done and I can get Finch out of my hair."

The old man smiled.

"Yes, lets hope so. But in the mean time I have a proposal for you. You wish to be of service to me, yes?"

I nodded.

"And you believe that with your talents you can provide my organisation with something we don't have at the moment?"

I nodded again.

"Then this is my proposal. Firstly, you go away and you talk to your wine person and you talk to Mr Finch and hopefully you sort things out. If you cannot sort things out then you telephone me first thing in the morning and perhaps I will help you sort them out."

He pulled a card out of his pocket and slid it across to me.

"And then secondly, you will come to dinner tomorrow night, here with my family at seven-thirty. And then after dinner we will sit down and talk, and I will give you a task. Something that you can do for me that will demonstrate your abilities. It won't be easy, but if you succeed then I see no reason why we shouldn't begin to start working together on other matters."

I heard a muffled snort of derision from Carrot's side of the room.

"Mr Tomassetti," I said. "That sounds fine. I would be delighted to do something for you. But I must tell you now, if this is something of a violent nature, if you need harm doing to somebody, then I'm not your man. There are plenty of people who can do that sort of thing for you and do it well, better than I ever could. What I can bring you something completely different. So if that's the sort of task you've got in mind for me, then you'll have to count me out."

"Excellent, excellent. Of course, of course. And you're right to say that, because, let's be honest about it, in my line of work there is a lot of persuasion that has to be done. And that persuasion, by it's very nature does have to be physical a lot of the time. It's the only thing that people can understand sometimes. But persuasion can take many forms, and that's where you might come in my friend."

He stood up and offered me his hand. I shook it.

"Anyway. You must go and deal with your problems. I will take a mug of Horlicks and think about Mr Finch, and then we will meet back here at seven-thirty tomorrow. As you are dressed now will be fine. That is a very elegant suit, if I may say so."

He clicked his fingers at Carrot.

"Please drive Mr Jones home."

"That's okay," I said. "I could do with a walk. And it'll give me chance to make some phone calls."

"Very well. Then Carrot, please show Mr Jones out."

We shook hands again. At the front door Carrot leaned in very close and whispered in my ear.

"That's a shame," he said. "I was looking forward to some alone time together. Thought perhaps I could tell you your fortune. But don't worry, there'll be another time I can drive you somewhere. In fact you can count on it. A long drive, one you won't come back from."

I sniffed loudly.

"Carrot," I said. "You smell."

I turned and went out through the door, savouring the look on Carrot's face. It's going to be him or me one day, I thought.

CHAPTER TWENTY-FOUR
HERNANDEZ

Why do I feel I'm being taken for a ride here? None of this makes any sense. And why am I the only person who seems concerned about Paradine? There are times when I just don't know why I bother.

It's not as though I haven't got anything better to do with my time. God knows I've got enough on my plate as it is. I don't know why I don't just keep my head down and get on with what I'm being paid to do. I'm doing three peoples' work as it is without doing some more on the side. And it's a good job I am doing it, because no one else here is. Mug, that's what I am.

And Jones isn't really telling me what's going on. He's too shrewd to do that. Tells me just enough to keep me interested and no more. And I'm not sure I believe much of it anyway. Although seeing him with Tomassetti was a bit of a surprise to tell the truth. Don't think I'd really believed him until then. And Jones didn't look like he was completely in control of the situation either. He's always so sure of himself normally. Confident, cocky, too much of it normally. All part of the charm I suppose. I liked seeing him like that. Shows he has got a vulnerable side to him perhaps.

But I'm doing this for me, not for him. If he gets caught in the crossfire, tough. I'm just out for what I can get.

God I hope he doesn't stay in that house all night, it's freezing just standing here waiting for him to come out.

CHAPTER TWENTY-FIVE
GOT IT?

"Spike, give me some good news."

"Ah."

Shit.

"No, not ah. I want to hear something positive about the wine. I want to hear it's been sold, I want to hear you've got a big pile of readies waiting to be pressed into my sweaty palms, I want to hear you've got a big queue of people banging on your door wanting to buy some more. Or at the very least I want to hear that there's a buyer all lined up and raring to go."

Naturally the first thing I'd done on leaving the Albemarle was to phone Spike. Getting Finch sorted out was now my only priority. I was stomping up South Audley Street desperately trying not to lose my temper with Spike and doing all I could to not start shouting at him.

"It's complicated."

"It's not complicated," I said, as calmly as I could. Somebody walked into me and I barged them aside. I could hear some muttered complaints behind me as I walked on. "We have some wine that you're going to sell to one of the many buyers that you had lined up. Simple as that. I need a quick sale, so if you have to give a bit of a discount that's fine. But it doesn't need to be any more complicated than that. I've got a rather nasty gangster on my back who's taking a very personal interest in this, and that's the complicated bit."

There was a silence on the other end of the phone.

"Spike?"

"Look, Jonesy, it is more complicated than that. I'm sorry. I meant to tell you earlier, but I didn't know how to. I suppose it's time I opened up about what's going on."

My heart sank. I knew everything had been going too smoothly. I felt something twinge in the pit of my stomach.

"Gawd, Spike, what are you doing to me? I just don't need this at the moment, I've got enough on my plate. Just tell me what's going on."

The silence went on for so long I thought he'd hung up, but then he started to speak.

"Well, you know I told you I'd lost some money on the gee gees?"

"Yes."

"Well it was cards. And the blokes I lost the money too started to kick up rough. Mean buggers too. They would definitely do all the things they threatened to do to me."

"How much are you into them for?"

"Twenty-five grand."

"Oh Spike. Poker?"

"Yeah. They had me done up like a right kipper. I had a jack straight flush. The other bastard had a queen flush. No way that was real, but nothing I could do. Like I say, nasty buggers."

"So I still don't see how stitching me up comes into this."

"I was desperate to raise the money to pay them off. I just haven't got that kind of dosh hanging around at the moment. Then I came up with the idea of switching your wine, but I never had any idea how we could sell it in bulk. My thinking was I could sell some of it through the shop and raise the money I needed that way."

"And have you?"

"Yeah, I've been doing it as a special. Three hundred quid a bottle or two hundred and seventy if you buy a case. It's been walking out the door. The funny thing is I've only had three bottles bought back, so I'm really starting to think that the bulk of it's probably okay."

"How much have you sold?"

"About six cases so far."

"What's that, just over twenty grand, so you've still got a bit to go."

"I scraped the rest together. Had to take out a couple of loans. So the debt's paid. I'm in the clear now. Last time I get involved with that crowd I can tell you."

"Okay, so that's good. But what about selling the rest of it? Why is that a problem?"

I could hear Spike let out a big sigh.

"Jonesy, there never were any buyers. I don't know anybody who'd buy slightly shifty wine in bulk. Think about it? What would they do with it? People who buy good stuff in those quantities are buyers for the supermarkets and the off-licence chains, and they need provenance, they need a history to go with the wine. They need proof it's what it says it is. And they need to know it's not hot. I'm not saying there aren't people out there who wouldn't buy some of it, but I don't know anybody off the top of my head. It would be a question of putting the word out and seeing what we could come up with. I'm sure we could do it eventually, but it's not going to be a quick process."

"I thought we were mates. How could you do the dirty on me like this?"

"I know, I'm really sorry Jonesy. I feel really bad about it. But I was scared stiff. These guys are the real deal believe me."

"Who was it?"

"Feller called Shady Doc. Heard of him?"

"Oh Spike, of course I've heard of him. He's a right nutjob. How on earth did you let yourself get caught up with somebody like him?"

"It was a couple of blokes I'd met down the boozer one night. I'd had a couple of drinks and before I knew it I'd been persuaded to get involved in a game. And of course they let me win a few hands at the beginning, let me get a bit full of myself. I feel so stupid now."

"Yeah, well. You could have told me the truth, you know."

"Yeah, I'm really sorry Jonesy. You don't know how bad I feel about it. But there is a positive side to this."

"I'd like to hear it."

"Well, we've got all this wine, which turns out to be not as bad as we thought. So I just keep selling it and we keep making a lot of money out of it. We get a nice little income on a regular basis. It ain't going to make our fortune overnight, but we can do very nicely out of it. And at the same time we can both keep our feelers out to see if we can offload any of it at any time. I bet you and I can come up with some buyers eventually."

I pondered all of that. Actually it wasn't all that bad a prospect really.

"Except I've got to pay off this maniac tomorrow or he's going to start cutting bits off me."

"Yeah, sorry about that. But you'll get all the profits from my sales until that's paid off. Honestly, this stuff's selling like hot cakes. It'll just be a short term hit for you, you'll see."

I grimaced. I didn't like the thought of hits, short term or otherwise.

"All right Spike, let's go with that. But I'll be round later. I want to sort out the details of all this, I want to dot the i's and cross the t's. I don't want any more surprises."

"Yeah, ok."

"By the way, do you know why he's called Shady Doc?"

"No"

"Ah. Best I don't tell you then."

"A hundred and fifty grand."

"But I only managed to get that last time because it was that idiot Walton. That's not a realistic price"

"Be careful I don't add a bit more on for all the aggravation you've been causing me."

To be fair, Finch was absolutely steaming when I phoned him, so the aggravation he was feeling was real enough. I listened to him rail off at me for about five minutes before he started to run out of steam. I'm sure I've been called worse in my time, but I can't remember when.

I'd told Finch that we'd had a buyer who'd pulled out at the last minute, but we had a couple of other prospective investors lined up. I told him I was very confident of it all going through, but it might take a little while longer and I might have to drop the price a bit. Finch wasn't having any of that. He said I was to be on his doorstep with his money at nine o'clock sharp the next morning. I told him I'd have to find the money from somewhere first, and he very generously gave me until ten o'clock. He went on at length about what would happen if I wasn't there with the money, and then he dropped the bombshell about how much he wanted.

"Listen, Mr Finch, I don't understand what's going on here. We've done a fair bit of business over the years, and I've always done a good job for you. And I've worked bloody miracles with this wine of yours. I just don't understand how you can just pitch up and demand I pay you a lot of money out of the blue, when all I'm doing is working my socks off for you."

Finch's voice was icy.

"What exactly are you accusing me of here?"

Uh, oh. Careful.

"I'm not accusing you of anything, Mr Finch. I'm just saying I don't understand why you're demanding money from me. It's not like I really owe it to you or anything."

I had this huge feeling I was overstepping the mark. It was a good job we were on the phone and not face-to-face I thought.

"Listen, you nonce," he said. Menacingly. "I'll spell it out for you. And this is the last time you ever question me or talk back to me again, got it? In your miserable, little scummy world, I am God. Got it? God. And you are just a dirty little maggot squirming around in the mud who deserves to be stepped on and squashed. Now, tell me in what Universe does that tiny little maggot turn round and question what God is doing?"

"Um, not this one?" I ventured.

"Certainly not this one. So If I tell you that you're going to come round tomorrow morning and give me the cash you owe me, then you say, 'Yes, Mr Finch' and you do it. You do it without thinking about it, you just do it. Got it?"

"I'm not a wealthy man, Mr Finch. I don't have that sort of cash just lying around."

"Then I shall enjoy extracting my pound of flesh from you in other ways. In fact I'll probably enjoy it a lot more than just getting the money off you. So if you care about me and my pleasure at all, you'll turn up tomorrow without the cash so as not to disappoint me."

He laughed. A really, unpleasant nasty laugh. My blood ran cold.

"And if can raise the cash tomorrow? Is that the end of it?"

"The end of it? No I don't suppose it will be the end of it. Perhaps just for the time being it might be. But not forever."

The phone went dead.

God, what a nightmare.

***

I was dying for a drink so I headed for the nearest pub. It was quite a small place, but it had been done up in a way that would hopefully fool tourists into thinking it was historic. I expected to see a 'Shakespeare Drank Here" sign up somewhere.

I grabbed a pint and a whisky chaser and sat down at a table in the corner. Christ, this was a mess. I was never going to get Finch off my back. Unless I used Tomassetti for help, and then I'd have him on my back forever instead. Why didn't I stay on at school and become an accountant I thought.

"Who's the other drink for? Expecting someone?"

I looked up in surprise. It was Hernandez. I think she must have seen how pleased I was to see her because she started smiling. Happily, I thought.

"Yeah, I thought you might turn up, so I bought you a pint of bitter."

She laughed. Again happily.

"Well, neither of us have got time for a drink. Don't ask questions, just follow me out. Now."

What was going on? Things were going from bad to worse.

Hernandez opened the door and stuck her head out, looking up and down for a few seconds. Satisfied with what she was seeing, or not seeing, she grabbed me by the arm and shuffled me out. We walked quickly up the street, keeping close in to the shadows of the shop fronts.

"Is there another pub close by?"

"Bound to be," I said. "This is a drinker's paradise around here. But what's going on?"

"Let's get somewhere first and then I'll explain."

We didn't have to wait long. After passing four or five side streets we could see a pub in the distance. It was very similar to the one we'd just come out of, fake as anything, but mercifully quiet. I bought my beer and scotch all over again and a brandy for Hernandez. She took off her coat and shook out her hair. She caught my eye as I stared at her, smiling again. Embarrassed, I took a long gulp of my beer. It was pretty tasteless, but the whisky did something to bring me back to normality. I was conscious of the barman watching us over his newspaper. I don't suppose we were his usual sort of customer.

"You were being watched," she said, before I could ask.

"Yeah?" Damn. I was so naïve at all this. I kept forgetting that I needed to be careful. After all that stuff that Tomassetti had told me they'd been doing for the last few weeks, I still wasn't watching my back properly.

"When you came out of that house. You got straight on the phone, but somebody came out right behind you. He was so close I suspect he could hear everything you said, so I hope you didn't give any state secrets away. He watched you go in the pub, spoke to somebody on the phone and then left."

"What did he look like?"

"Big bruiser of a guy. Shaven head, ginger."

I nodded.

"Carrot. That may or may not be official. Things are getting very personal between us."

"Well, my money's on him if it comes down to it."

"Hah! Thanks very much."

"You're welcome."

We sat in silence for a bit, looking at each other.

"Thanks," I said eventually.

"For what?"

"For, you know, having my back. I appreciate it."

She shrugged.

"I'm not doing it for you, I'm doing it for me."

"Yeah, you keep saying that. Tomassetti saw you when you walked past, you know. He said that I should ask you to marry me."

"You're kidding."

"No. He said if I ever saw you again I should ask you to marry me. Although the way he put it was to ask you to make a family with me."

"And are you?"

"Am I what?"

"Going to ask me?"

"I don't know, do you think I should?"

"I think that's your decision, not mine?"

"What would you say if I did?"

"I think you'd have to ask me to find that out."

That had all been said in a fairly light-hearted tone, it could all easily just be taken as our usual banter. But she was looking at me very intensely, and I had this peculiar prickly sensation in my stomach again."

I had no idea what to say next. I didn't know what I wanted to say, but I was saved by the bell as my phone rang. I duly noted the look of exasperation in Hernandez' face.

It was Mimi.

"I just wanted to check everything's okay, dear," she said. "I'm wetting myself over the prospect of Finch and his gang of thugs turning up tomorrow."

"No, it's fine, Mimi," I said. "It's all sorted. I'm going over there first thing tomorrow to pay him off. So there's nothing to worry about any more. All back to normal tomorrow."

"Phew, that's a relief. And you? You're all right, dear?"

"Yeah, I'm fine. I'm just having a drink to unwind. It's been kind of a stressful day."

"Well if you need anyone to talk to, you know where to find me."

"Thanks, I appreciate the offer."

I hung up. Unfortunately the call had killed the mood between me and Hernandez completely. She was staring at me with another of those 'oh, yeah?' looks on her face.

"Mimi?" she said.

"My assistant. She's the one who'll call you if she doesn't hear from me."

"Right. I suppose she runs your dry cleaners as well."

I smiled. A little bit of jealousy is always good to hear.

"She runs all of it, as a matter of fact."

"And what was that offer you so politely declined?"

"Just business," I said. "Nothing for you to worry about there."

"I wasn't worried, I was just curious. Not that it's any business of mine what you get up to anyway."

That was so cold it was freezing. It was an amazing what a phone call from another woman, even it was someone old enough to be her grandmother, could do to a relationship. I decided not to let on that Mimi was the wrong side of sixty.

But with the moment well and truly shattered we dropped into our business-like roles. Hernandez started to tell me how she'd spent all evening standing in the cold waiting for me to come out of places. As she talked I started to think of all the TV partnerships I'd seen over the years, and wondered which one we were most like. Sapphire and Steel? Mulder and Scully? Dempsey and Makepeace? Cagney and Lacey? Jimmy Cagney more like. I smiled.

"Something funny?"

"I was just imagining us as a crime-fighting duo. Hernandez and Jones. It's got quite a ring to it don't you think?"

"Well, you can stop imagining right now. There is no duo. There's Hernandez and there's Jones. Separate. Got it?"

A lot of people had been asking me if I'd 'got it?' today. I was getting tired of it.

"Sure. But who are trying to convince? You or me?"

She pulled a face and carried on telling me what she'd been doing. Then it was my turn. I gave her a flavour of what had been said. Everything I told her was true, and there was enough to have justified the time I was with the old man, but it wasn't all of it by any stretch of the imagination.

"So what's in these papers that all the fuss is about?"

I took out my smartphone that I hadn't switched on for days and showed Hernandez the pictures. A quick look at the screen showed me I had fifty-seven messages.

"Wow," she said as she scanned through them. "So you've no idea what any of this is about?"

"Well, not really. It's possible that it's to do with the development of some sort of long lasting battery. Or possibly a new type of radar, but I'm not sure. Any ideas?"

"Not my strongpoint, science."

She carried on studying the pictures intently.

"But I can tell you where they're from."

"You're joking. How?"

"Didn't you think to research the references at the bottom of the pages?"

"Just gobbledygook aren't they? Just like all the rest of it."

"Dstl?"

She looked at me. I looked back. Blankly.

"How about the Defence Science and Technology Laboratory?"

"And what's that when it's at home?"

"Well, I suppose you might know it better as Porton Down, you know, where they do all the nuclear stuff, chemical warfare, that sort of thing. It's run by the Ministry of Defence."

Ahh. I hadn't told her that I knew about the MoD. I tried to act surprised.

"You're joking."

"Nope."

"So how do you know all this?"

"Case I worked on once. Somebody was poisoned with something strange and we got involved. The Dstl bit stuck in my head. So you didn't know?"

I shook my head.

"So what did the spy boys tell you?"

"Nothing like that I can tell you."

Hernandez grunted.

"Well at least I think I believe you that MI5 are involved now. Mind you, I think it's definitely a bad thing that you're involved in the stealing of state secrets. I wouldn't want to be in your shoes if this all goes pear shaped."

"No." I didn't want to be in my shoes either. And what the hell did chemical warfare have to with batteries?

I contemplated my drink for a while and when I glanced up she was giving me that look again.

"And you're seriously going to do a job for Tomassetti?"

"Looks like it. It's the only way I'm going to get accepted on the inside."

"Something criminal?"

"I guess so. That's what he does. He sure as hell isn't going to ask me to take his library books back."

There was another famous Hernandez look.

"Well I'm not backing you up on anything like that."

"No, I understand. I'm not asking you to."

"Do you have any idea what it might be?"

I shook my head.

"None, but I told him very clearly I wouldn't do anything violent. I don't think it will be, he's got enough brain-dead imbeciles to do that for him already."

"Well, that's something I suppose. Let me know when you find out, there *might* be something I can do to help."

"Okay."

"By the way, what were you saying to your dry cleaner about paying somebody off?"

I grimaced.

"Somebody trying to put the squeeze on me. God knows why, decided he doesn't like me, I suppose. I've got no choice but to pay him off and then try and lay low for a while."

"Who is it? Anybody I might know."

"Gangster called Finch. Big time villain down Canning Town way."

"Finch! God almighty! Finch is into you for money! You're lucky you're in one piece still. Jesus! How did you get involved with him?"

"It's a long story," I sighed. "And not a happy one. But come back to my place for a nightcap and I'll tell you all about it."

That made Hernandez laugh again.

"Nice try," she said, getting up. "But I'm going home, I'm knackered. Got an early start tomorrow. But let me know what's happening, yeah? You need to watch yourself if you're involved with both Finch and Tomassetti. Give me a call tomorrow?"

Was that genuine concern in her voice?

"Sure."

The barman came over to collect her glass after she'd gone. I was staring reflectively into my pint.

"That's the trouble with birds like that," he said as I looked up. "Tread all over you. Lead you up the garden path with all sorts of promises and then leave you on your own with your beer. I know, I've been there."

He was probably in his late fifties, bald, apart from a few wispy bits of hair combed over from one ear to the other, and a big, red-veined hooter that was testament to the fact he clearly liked a drink. He was wearing a dirty old patched cardigan covered in stains, and he walked with a really heavy, lop-sided limp.

"You should tell me about it sometime," I said.

"Ooh, don't get me started. The tales I could tell you."

He started to limp back to the bar, but paused to call over his shoulder.

"Women, eh?"

He raised his eyes to the ceiling.

CHAPTER TWENTY-SIX
FINCH

I hope that little toe-rag can't raise the money. That would be so nice. He can join that imbecile Walton. I think I would enjoy being inventive with our Mr Jones. He certainly wouldn't, that's for sure. I'll have to get my thinking cap on, and get Smiley John involved. He can be very imaginative with these things.

But supposing he does manage to raise the cash. I don't want him walking out of here thinking he's in the clear. No, that's definitely not the message I want sent out. So, what to do? One plan for if he does turn up with the money and another for if he doesn't. I want him to either feel a lot of pain or to feel really stupid. Yeah, either of those will do nicely. Need to give this some thought tonight.

I think I need to take over his business too. Time I extended my portfolio a bit. Bet he's got some interesting things going on that I could get my teeth into.

Once I've taken my teeth out of him, of course.

CHAPTER TWENTY-SEVEN
IT'S A FAMILY AFFAIR

At eight o'clock the next morning, I found myself staring at a row of left-luggage lockers at St Pancras station. When I'd first started storing some money here, about three years ago it must have been, I'd felt very melodramatic. This was the first time I'd ever had to use it and I was now feeling very grateful to myself.

My locker contained four non-descript holdalls, each with fifty thousand pounds inside. Reaching inside, I moved the money out of two of the bags into a third, took that bag out and locked up. I looked around me for five minutes, decided everything was cool, and then headed down to Canning Town for the big meeting. This was going to be the end of it. Pay him the cash and then get the hell out of it. And enjoy the prospect of the nice profit I was going to get out of selling his wine.

"Mr Jones, I'm waiting with baited breath. Is it money or pleasure in store for me this morning?"

I was getting all too familiar with the inside of the Rat and Ferret. The empty tables, the dark ambience, the two heavies looking slightly bored, it was the scariest place I had ever been in. I idly wondered what was out the back, whether he had a desk there covered in papers, or possibly a computer. He wasn't somebody who struck you as being terribly interested in admin really.

I heaved my bag onto my lap and took out the bundles of fifty-pound notes. They were sealed into packets stamped and authorised by the Bank of England. I stood up and placed them on Finch's table.

To say he looked disappointed was an understatement. He stared at them for a few long minutes before letting out a big sigh.

"Is this all of it?"

I nodded.

"Where did you get it from?"

"I borrowed it. Had to go to a Shylock. He's charging me twenty per cent, the crook."

"Oh dear, I hope I haven't left you in any financial difficulty."

I wanted to say something snappy back, but I bit my tongue.

"I'll be able to pay some of it off quite quickly," I said. "I've got a buyer for the wine lined up, but I'm not going to get a hundred and fifty grand for it. I'll be lucky if I clear fifty."

"Ah."

Oh, good grief, there was that bloody 'ah' again.

"Yes. I've changed my mind about what I'm going to do with the wine."

"You have?" I could see the pleasure behind his eyes. This wasn't going to bode well for me I could tell.

"Yes. I'm going to buy the wine back from you."

"You are?"

"Yes."

"Oh. Well, ok then."

I wasn't sure what to make of this. I would be saying goodbye to a bit of a profit for me and Spike, but, to be honest, to get him off my back and come out of it even, would do for me at the moment. If he was doing this just to give me a warning, I'd take it like a good boy and be off.

"Yes, and I'm prepared to make you a very generous offer."

"You are?" I was very conscious I was starting to sound like a parrot, but he was taking me by surprise every time he spoke.

"We both agree that it's rubbish don't we? We both agree that it's going to be very hard to sell. I actually find it very difficult to believe that you really have got a buyer lined up. I think that if you had you would have finalised the sale by now. And at such large quantities, it really is going to be hard to shift."

I swallowed hard. Perhaps now was the time to tell him it was actually good stuff. No, admitting that I'd been cheating him would be to sign my death warrant. I felt my stomach twinge again. What was doing that?

"So," Finch continued. "I'm going to make you the very generous offer of one thousand pounds for the lot."

My mouth dropped open. I started to protest, but Finch held up a warning hand and I instantly subsided. I knew where complaining was going to get me.

"Good," he said. "A nice bit of business. Get the wine over to me early next week and we'll say no more about all the aggravation you've caused me."

"Umm," I said. "There is one thing. I'm about six cases short now. I've been giving people samples, trying to get them interested."

"Ah. Well, not a problem. I'll just pro-rata the payment. One hundred cases less six... that's about... no, I'll tell you what, I'll just give you five hundred quid and we'll call it even. Okay?"

He reached over for one of the plastic packets and tossed it to me.

"Now piss off."

I stood up clutching my little packet of fifty-pound notes. I wanted to say something so desperately it was hurting. But there wasn't anything I could say. Not without somebody else's army behind me.

Finch called out to me just I was about to go through the door.

"Oh," he said. "I'm thinking I might take over your business by the way. I'll be in touch."

I could see the hint of a smile on one of the heavy's faces as I pushed past him. He was thoroughly enjoying himself.

He was another one who was going to get his one day.

A couple of brandies at home and a long hot bath made me feel a bit more human, but it didn't do anything for the seething resentment that I was feeling inside me. I was desperate to do something, anything, now, but I knew there was nothing I could do. But I would, I promised myself. Once this other business was out of the way, then I would put my mind to it.

I rang Spike and told him what had happened. I could sense his disappointment even over the phone.

"Have you sold any more?" I asked.

"Nah, just those six cases."

"Okay. Listen, I need to get the wine over to Finch by Tuesday. Reckon you could organise a van for me?"

"Sure, not a problem. Going to break my heart seeing all that good stuff going to waste though."

"Yeah, I know. Still, we're still alive, that's the main thing. I'll call you on Monday."

I wasn't sure who would have had the worst of it, I thought as I hung up. Me with Finch or him with Shady Doc. Neither of us would have looked good afterwards that was for sure.

So at seven-thirty sharp that night I was getting out of a cab outside Tomassetti's sumptuous Mayfair townhouse. I'd put on my best whistle, polished my shoes, and was, as they say, up for anything. I'd phoned Mimi at seven to say everything was ok, and Hernandez to tell her where I was going to be spending my evening. I wasn't sure if she was going to be standing guard over me again, but it wouldn't make me unhappy if she was.

The maid let me in. I thought her name might be Isabella. She showed me into a room off the hall, bigger than the one I'd been in before but just as ornately and expensively, decorated. Isabella looked at the ground the whole time, not catching my eyes once.

The room was full, probably about twenty people in there. There had been a lot of noise coming through the door before I walked in, but as soon as I did it went deathly quiet. I could feel the full force of forty-odd eyes boring into me. It was all I could do not to turn round and immediately walk out again.

"Mr Jones. Welcome. Welcome."

Tomassetti put down his mug of Horlicks and came over to greet me. I thought he was going to hug me at first, but we just shook hands in the end while he patted me reassuringly on the shoulder. He really did look genuinely pleased to see me. I was finding it more and more difficult to treat the whole thing as an act. If it was, he was bloody good at it. I was actually enjoying being in his company, and I'd found myself looking forward to this evening when I was getting ready to go out.

"Come, Mr Jones. I want you to meet my family. They are all here to meet you, I have told them all about you. Everybody, this is Mr Jones. This is the young man who is going to make us all a great deal of money, so we can all retire happily."

I looked over at him in surprise.

"No, no," he laughed. "It's just my little joke. Indulge me, I am very happy today, very contented. As I hope you are after your business with Mr Finch. But we will talk more of that later."

I nodded.

The old man took me round the room and slowly introduced me to everybody there. I felt like royalty as everybody bowed and scraped in front of me. I would have loved to know who he told them I was.

First there was his wife, Marta. She looked a lot younger than him, old, but still good-looking in a stern matriarchal way. There was no arguing with her, I thought. She said she was pleased to meet me, but her eyes said different.

Uncle Adlai was a different kettle of fish. He did seem pleased to meet me. He was ancient, although still reasonably sprightly. He slapped me on the back and said he had been waiting to see what I looked like. As we walked on to the next introduction, Tomassetti whispered to me that it was important that I impressed him later.

I struggled with all the names after that. There were a few more uncles and half a dozen aunts, and a whole stack of cousins who all blended into each other by the time I'd been introduced to them all. None of them seemed as pleased to see me as Uncle Adlai.

But then finally, there was just one person left to meet. Tabitha. Tomassetti introduced her as his niece. She was small, probably in her early twenties, had short black hair cut almost boyishly, and looked extremely pissed off. The atmosphere in the room changed as we shook hands and I instantly realised why I had been brought there tonight. Well, I could play charming if it got me what I wanted I thought.

Isabella came round with a silver tray bearing some drinks. They were of some sort of brown liquid in very small glasses. There didn't seem to be any choice so I took one. Sweet sherry. It certainly wasn't my drink of choice, and it didn't have the effect that a stiff double brandy would have, but at least it was alcohol. I had a feeling I would need more than a mug of Horlicks if I was going to have to perform tonight.

We stood around and chatted for a while. People came and went. It was all inane stuff, although, to be honest, it was mostly

Tomassetti telling me wonderful things about Tabitha. After about half an hour, Isabella put her head round the door and quietly announced that dinner was ready. We all shuffled off to the dining room. It was as we walked that I realised Carrot and the goons weren't there. Significant?

The dining room was enormous. If the table had been longer we could have squeezed another fifty or so guests in, as it was, there was plenty of elbow room for those of us who were there. I was in the middle of the table. Tabitha was on my left, a bloated pudding of an aunt was on my right, and Uncle Adlai sat opposite me. There wasn't much in the way of conversation that the whole table joined in, it was all fairly muted. In fact, quite a few people hardly said anything all night, these were mostly the younger cousins who all looked bored stiff and didn't care who knew it. So my evening revolved around talking to Tabitha who, unfortunately, didn't have a great deal to say, the Aunt, who turned out to be Tabitha's mother, and Adlai, who made it very clear from the word go that it was his family, his business, and that he was the one calling the shots.

So, over a meal that consisted of about twenty different courses, and several glasses of quite spectacular wine, both red and white, the four of us talked. Not all together. One at a time, with me.

The mother asked all the questions you would expect a mother to ask of a prospective son-in-law. What did I do? Was I well off? Had I had many girlfriends? Why hadn't I married before? Did I believe in God? I did my best. I think I answered everything pretty much to her satisfaction, and I lied about a lot of things. I could tell it hadn't worked though. I still wasn't good enough for her little girl.

Uncle Adlai asked some very telling questions. He started off by wanting to know what I did and I gave him a flavour of some of the things I got up to. I couldn't see any point in lying about any of that because it seemed like they'd pretty much found out everything about me. He then went on to pose me a whole load of different scenarios and asked for my views. If somebody did this and somebody else did that, what would I do? If this happened or that happened, how would I deal with it? It was all hypothetical of course, but I suspected that these had all been real occurrences at one time or another. Most of the situations involved dealing with people who weren't doing what you wanted them to. I wasn't sure how to play it at first, but there was no point in trying to second-guess a gangster, I didn't have the same outlook on life as them. I suspect my answers were a lot more humanitarian than Uncle Adlai's would have been.

And I asked Tabitha some questions. Every answer was monosyllabic. She might have been shy, or even stupid I suppose, but I got the impression that she just really didn't like me. I couldn't get anything out of her. She didn't ask me anything in return.

Then, after dessert and coffee had been served and consumed, Tomassetti banged on his mug with a spoon to get everyone's attention.

"Thank you everybody," he said. "Thank you all for coming to my home tonight. It was wonderful to see you all. And thank you to Mr Jones for being our guest tonight. I hope he can see as much as I what a wonderful family I am blessed to have."

"A wonderful family," I said. I raised my wine glass to the room and drained what was left of the wine inside it. There were some muted mumblings in reply from assorted spots around the table.

"And now, perhaps it's time for the ladies to withdraw. If the men would like to adjourn to the games room for their drinks, I would like to have a few words alone with Mr Jones and Uncle Adlai. We will join you later."

After everyone had left, Uncle Adlai and I moved up to sit either side of Tomassetti. One of the waiters came back in and asked us what we wanted to drink. Another Horlicks for Tomassetti, a glass of milk for Uncle Adlai and a brandy for me. We clinked glasses and mugs together when they were served.

"I can see what you were saying," said Adlai to Tomassetti. "He is a very clever young man. You're right, I don't think we do have anyone like him. He's smart but he's also very soft. I don't know that he'd be hard enough for the things we have to do. But there's a long way to go before we can even begin to think about the sorts of things you have in mind."

I assumed he was talking about me, but it was as though I wasn't there.

"Of course, of course," Tomassetti said. "But you can see why I was intrigued. He's certainly more suited than anyone else. Hopefully there won't need to be any panic about making any decisions, that will be a long time away yet."

"And of course he has to be family," said Adlai.

"Yes, yes." Tomassetti turned to me. "So what did you think of our little Tabitha. A wonderful girl is she not? Those big brown eyes, she would make a man a wonderful wife you know."

"A man would think himself very lucky to be in a position where she might consider him for a husband," I said carefully. "However I don't think her mother thought very much of me. I suspect she would like something better for her beautiful daughter."

The two men smiled. I was saying the right things, but inside I was starting to panic. What was this? What was being planned for me?

"But now, down to business," said Tomassetti. "Firstly tell me how you got on with our Mr Finch."

I told him what happened, and I played it straight. He got the whole story.

"So, the wine you will be returning to Mr Finch could actually be quite decent, but he believes he is getting back the vinegar that he gave to you."

I nodded.

"So then I will buy it off him. Through somebody else of course. What do you suppose he would want for it?"

"Probably about fifty thousand for the lot. Somewhere in that sort of region."

"And what could I sell it for?"

"If the wine is okay and hasn't been spoiled, it's worth about four hundred thousand retail. If you could find a buyer you could maybe get three hundred for it. But finding someone to buy that much wine without it having a proper history won't be easy."

I noticed Adlai half raise an eyebrow and, almost imperceptibly, nod.

"Then I shall buy Mr Finch's wine," said Tomassetti. "And then, later, I shall decide what to do about him selling me such bad wine. It will give me some considerable leverage. You and I will talk about the details of that later. Can I ask where you were able to get one hundred and fifty thousand pounds in cash from at such short notice?"

"I had a contingency fund," I said. "It's not as big now as it once was."

"Very wise, Mr Jones. You seem to always have a contingency. There isn't anyone you would like to telephone now?"

I smiled.

"No I'm fine."

"Good. Now to the second part of our business. I talked about you doing something for us, something that would prove the abilities that you say you have. Something difficult, something that not many people would be able to do well."

I swallowed.

"Yes of course, I'll be pleased to."

"Have you heard of a gentleman called Strutter?" Raymond Strutter?

I shook my head.

"He's sometimes known as the Ragman."

Ah, that rang a bell. Another nasty piece of work. I didn't like the sound of this already.

"I see you have heard of him," Tomassetti continued. "He would like to think of himself as, how shall I describe it, a rival? A competitor? Of course he isn't, he's small change compared to us. But he's starting to be a nuisance, an irritant. And what I want to do is give him a warning, something subtle that will scare him and make him think, 'hmm, perhaps I should step off Aldo Tomassetti's toes, I think he is too dangerous for me'. And this is what I want you to do for me."

"That's exactly the sort of thing I said I wouldn't do for you," I said.

"Hear me out, please. Perhaps in the normal circumstances, there might be something physical taking place, perhaps someone might get hurt somewhere. But this time I want it to be different. I want to scare him, make him realise how vulnerable he and his family really are. So it needs to be something quite imaginative, quite clever, but something where nobody actually gets hurt. I don't particularly want to start a war at this time."

I looked at him blankly.

"So, next Saturday, the Ragman's only daughter is getting married. He has a very large house in North London. The ceremony and the reception will be held there. There will be a lot of people attending and the security will be formidable, as you would expect he has many enemies. What I want is for you to do something at the wedding that will make him realise that I can get at him any time I want to. Him and his family. So I want you to make something happen, and then I want him to find this."

He reached down and produced a small jar of Horlicks.

"He will know exactly who is threatening him when he finds this."

I swallowed hard.

"What did you have in mind?"

"Ah, that's for you to decide, my friend. This is your challenge, your opportunity to show us the talents that you keep telling us about. It won't be easy, it will be like perhaps getting into Fort Knox. And it will be very dangerous. So, what do you say?"

I didn't know what to say. This was so stupid I could hardly take it seriously. But what the hell.

"Okay," I said. "This is a bit outside what I'm normally used to, but I'll give it my best shot."

The two old men gave each other a look.

"Excellent," said Tomassetti. "I'll get Carrot to help you, he can be your assistant. He has all the details of the Ragman. All that's left for me to say is, good luck."

Carrot. Oh no.

"I don't need Carrot," I said. "I prefer working on my own. You might have noticed that we don't exactly get along too well."

"Yes, indeed I have noticed. Nevertheless, Carrot is my man, and if you want to become my man too, you're going to have to learn to work together. I have told Carrot this too. But I want Carrot to be with you while you do this. If you don't want to use him, then that's up to you, but I need him to report back to me what it is you did and how you did it. Somebody independent, yes?"

"But not Carrot. He's not independent. He's never going to say anything good about me. There must be someone else you can send who can tag along."

For the very first time, I sensed a very slight hardening of the old man's mood.

"Carrot will accompany you."

And that was it, he didn't say another word. He stood up and solemnly shook my hand. Then he and Uncle Adlai walked slowly out of the room, leaving me staring at a small jar of Horlicks.

CHAPTER TWENTY-EIGHT
UNCLE ADLAI

Too soft, much too soft. That's the trouble with all of them, the whole lot, too soft. It wasn't like that in my day. We ruled with a rod of iron. If someone stepped out of line, they knew it. We didn't give people warnings. If they did something wrong they got hammered.

And look at all the information you can get on somebody these days. Who can read it all? In my day you saw how someone handled trouble, how he stood up to it, then you knew if he was a man or not.

So they produce a file on that Jones. A file! They give me a dossier on him. Twenty pages thick. The only thing it doesn't say about him is the size of his dick. This is the man we want, says Aldo. He can take over our business when we can no longer do it. He will take us forward. Forward to what, I ask.

So he's clever and he does deals, so what? We can all do that. Can he make the decisions, the hard decisions? The ones that hurt? 'We need someone ruthless, someone single-minded, someone who doesn't mind treading on everyone else to get what he wants. Because if we don't have someone like that, then there are plenty of people out there who are like that and who are going to come along and tread all over us and take everything that we have away. Everything that I've worked for.

It's no good having someone who likes all the fancy clothes and fancy drinks and fancy women, someone who says, I'm not going to hurt anyone, that's not what I do. That's not what I do? Good god, that should be all what we do. You hurt someone first, then you find out if it's fair or not. People have to be scared, it's the only way to get respect.

Look at this damn file. I don't know where to start. I don't even understand what the headings mean.

Well, let's see how he handles the Ragman. Probably send him a letter asking him nicely to get out of our business. On pink stationary. That would go down well. And apologising for the inconvenience.

I'd just hit him over the head with a hammer. Then I'd apologise.

CHAPTER TWENTY-NINE
A BIT OF PHYSICAL

It turned out to be a busy week.

Carrot phoned me on Monday morning. He gave me the Ragman's address, told me the wedding ceremony was at two-thirty on Saturday, and was there anything he could do to help. Then he laughed. Very unpleasantly.

"Remember," he said, just as I was about to hang up. "Mr Tomassetti wants us to work closely together on this one."

I put Carrot's number into my contacts with a heavy heart. I really didn't want to be this close to him. We'll end up being Facebook friends next, I thought.

Mimi was out dealing with a problem with one of the businesses when I got into the office. I made myself a mug of really strong tea and sat there cradling it, thinking about what I was going to do next Saturday. The trouble was, this was outside my expertise, I didn't have any points of reference.

Eventually a few thoughts started coming together in my head. I googled Raymond Strutter and came up with his phone number. It was amazing how much personal information you could find on the Internet these days, including crooks' phone numbers.

A female voice answered when I rang.

"Hello," I said. "This is Robinson from the catering company. Could I speak to whoever I need to speak to about a query with the guest list for Saturday, please."

"That would be Mrs Strutter, but I'm afraid she's out at the moment. She won't be back until late this evening."

"Ah, that's a shame. We've got a bit of problem this end. Who am I talking to?"

"This is Mrs Briggs. I run the household for Mrs Strutter."

"I don't suppose you have a copy of the guest list by any chance?"

"Well, I know where one is, but I'm not sure about letting you have it. I don't remember seeing you here with the other members of your company when they visited. Why isn't Miss Cole calling us?"

"I've just been drafted in from another branch to help out. They've had a lot of sickness here, including Miss Cole. I've been trying to piece things together while they're all recovering. The problem is I've got two guest lists here, and I don't know which is the up-to-date one. I've got things like table settings and place names to put together."

Please, please let there be table settings and place names and not a walk-up buffet. Please.

There was a silence on the other end of the line. Then ...

"Well, this is all highly irregular, but I suppose I can send you a copy. Where do you want it sent to?"

"Don't suppose you've got a fax machine by any chance?"

"As a matter of fact we do."

"Brilliant. You're a life saver."

I gave her our number and she promised to send it over that morning. I was still amazed by how many people still had fax machines. I'd thought about throwing ours out loads of times, but it was interesting how many times it came in handy.

The fax came through about twenty minutes later.

I'd had a vague idea that perhaps I could add my name to the list and then somehow substitute it for the real one, hope no one would notice. It wasn't much of a plan, but it was all I had. I scanned the list. About fifty people or so. I read down the names.

And ... bingo, I hit the jackpot.

One name came leaping out of the page at me. I couldn't be this lucky, I thought. Somebody up there really was smiling down on me.

Jane, the girl I'd met at the old girl's party. Smythe-Bannister. It was such an unusual name there couldn't be two of them.

I googled her, found the number and rang her straight away.

"Jane," I said, when she answered. "How are you?"

"I'm all right. I thought I might have heard from you by now."

Frosty. Not a good start.

"I'm really sorry, Jane, I had to go away the day after I saw you. I've been all over the place. Africa and South America mostly. I've tried ringing you loads of times, but it's nigh on impossible getting a signal in those sort of places."

"I thought you ran a dry cleaners?"

"I do. But it's a lot more complicated than you might think. Involves a lot of travelling."

I could hear her brain clunking round as she processed this.

"Listen," I said. "I'm coming back into the country Saturday morning and then flying off again on Sunday. I'd love to see you, I've been thinking about you all the time. We'd could go out for a nice meal somewhere, have a few cocktails, get to know each other a bit better. What do you think?"

"We-ell, that would be nice." I could feel her mellowing. "The trouble is, I've got a wedding to go to on Saturday, old school friend. We're very close, I couldn't let her down. When are you next back?"

"Not for another couple of months, I'm afraid. This is a real flying visit. I really wanted to see you."

"Well, you could always come to wedding with me, I suppose. I'm her Lady-in-Waiting, and she asked me not to bring a date so I could spend more time with her. But I'm sure she would understand if I explained the situation."

Thank you, thank you.

"Okay then," I said. "You've twisted my arm. So who's getting married?

"Just an old friend from boarding school."

"What does her dad do?"

"No idea. Business, I suppose."

"Oh, well, sounds interesting. I'll look forward to it."

We made arrangements for Saturday. She was going to have to get there early to help the bride do all the things brides have to do before they get married, so I was going to have to make my own way there. She promised to ring Amelia straight away to make sure everything would be ok.

"By the way," she said, just as I was about to ring off. "Where are you?"

"Luxembourg."

"Ooh, how exotic. I love those fancy sounding islands."

My next call was to Tweezer, the guy I sold the first lot of Finch's dodgy wine to. Tweezer was a good man, we'd done a lot of stuff together over the years, and he was as solid as anything. One of the really good things about him was he knew everybody and he could get hold of just about anything you could ever want.

"Jonesy, my man. Don't tell me you've got some more dodgy plonk that you want to get rid of?"

I laughed.

"No. But I could probably lay my hands on some if you really wanted me to."

"No I don't, thank you very much. I'm still using the last lot to put on my chips. But what can I do you for?"

"I've got a question. Hypothetical. Okay?"

"Okay."

"Supposing someone wanted to make a bit of noise some-where. A bit of an explosion, say. Because they wanted to let someone know that they could. Wanted it to be a bit of a warning. How would you go about doing something like that? Wouldn't have to be anything big, just make a lot of noise and cause a little bit of damage. Nothing that's going to hurt anyone, but would make them think twice about it. You know what I'm saying?"

"Hmmm. Hypothetical eh? Well, hypothetically I know a guy who does that sort of thing. Hypothetically of course. Want me to put him in touch with you?"

"Yes please." I gave Tweezer my new number. "Thanks, mate, good talking to you again."

"No problem."

After I hung up I remembered I was going to ask Tweezer how he'd got his nickname. I thought that every time I spoke to him, but I always forgot.

Good as his word, I had a call from Tweezer's contact a couple of hours later.

"My name's Joe Kettlestone, Tweezer asked me to call. He thought I might be able to help you in a little project you've got in mind."

I explained what I wanted. A lot of noise, lot of smoke, a little bit of damage, perhaps a bit of a fire, but nothing lethal.

"I think we can manage that," he said, "Why don't you come round to my workshop tomorrow morning and I'll sort some-thing out for you."

He gave me an address in Battersea and we arranged to meet at ten o'clock. I told him I'd have someone with me.

Then I rang Carrot, told him what I was doing, and said he could come with me tomorrow if he wanted. He said he'd meet me there. I told him I'd wangled an invite to the wedding, but there was no way I'd be able to sneak him in as well.

He laughed that horrible weasily laugh again.

"Don't you worry about me," he said. "I'm going to be there all right. Somebody's got to keep a beady little eye on what you're up to. Oh yes, I'm going to be there all right, watching every little move you make."

The rest of the day I spent going through the pile of paperwork that Mimi had ready for me, feeling thoroughly depressed every time I thought about Carrot. I really had to do something about him.

I'd arranged to meet Hernandez for a drink later to have a catch up. I'd originally thought about meeting in my local, but I was finally waking up to how stupid I was being with someone probably watching me, so I suggested a boozer in Pimlico I'd used a few times about ten years ago. It was handy for Hernandez' office in Victoria if nothing else.

Of course, when I got there it wasn't a pub any more, it was an expensive block of apartments. Hernandez was standing outside with her arms folded and an exasperated look on her face.

"So is this the little place tucked away where you take all your girlfriends then? Don't think you're getting me in there, buster."

I looked sheepish.

"It was the Kings Head last time I was here."

I caught a hint of a smile. Not really upset then. We could see another pub up the Vauxhall Bridge Road towards Victoria, and we set off. I asked her how her day had been and she had a bit of a moan about her bosses and her workload. Same as everybody in the world does.

In the pub, I told her about Strutter and what I was going to do.

"No, absolutely not."

"What do you mean, no?"

"I'm not letting you do it. Absolutely not. The thought of you going round throwing bombs at people makes my blood run cold. I forbid it."

"You forbid it?"

"Yes. Besides you might get hurt."

Ah, now we come to it.

"You're worried about me. That's very sweet."

"No, I'm not worried about you. I'm worried about the safety of the general public and what sort of trouble there's going to be if someone starts letting bombs off in the middle of London."

"It's in Chipping Barnet."

"You know what I mean. There could be all sorts of problems, you know that. And I'm not going to come and bail you out of jail if you get caught."

We bickered backwards and forwards about Strutter for another half an hour or so, but didn't resolve anything. Eventually we settled down to just chatting about stuff. She told me quite a lot about herself and I told her a little bit about me and made some things up. It was really nice and I could see her visibly relax in front of me. We had a few drinks and about ten o'clock she said she had to go.

We stood outside the door of the pub. It was starting to get cold of an evening and she pulled her coat tight around her. We were standing very close, almost touching. She was looking at me hard, unblinking. I put my arms around her and she stayed very still, not moving. I bent in towards her and kissed her very gently. She didn't respond but she didn't pull away.

"I don't think I'm ready for this, Jones," she said, her voice sounding very hoarse.

"Ready for what?"

"You know what, don't be bloody stupid."

She punched me on the arm, but then moved in and held me very tight, her face buried in the crook of my neck.

"Ouch," I said. "Look, why don't we go back to my place and talk about it? No pressure, just a chat. You can't run away from this for ever."

She pulled her head up and looked into my eyes. Those few moments seemed to go on forever. Then she grazed my lips with hers and pulled away out of my arms.

"No, you're right," she said. "I can't run away for ever. But not yet. I'm not ready yet. Okay?"

I nodded. She kissed me again, squeezed my arms, and then turned and walked off. I watched her until she'd disappeared out of sight. She didn't look back.

Carrot was outside waiting for me when I got to the guy's workshop in Battersea the next morning. It was really out of the way down a maze of back streets by Battersea Power Station near Nine Elms. Even the cab driver had trouble finding it. I was no help, I got nose bleeds whenever I crossed the river.

"You take me to the nicest places," Carrot said as I paid off the cabby. I gave him a look.

Joe Kettlestone turned out to be everyone's idea of what an absent-minded professor should like that. Dishevelled, a mass of unkempt grey hair, a pair of glasses pushed on to the top of his head, and an annoying habit of talking to himself all the time so you didn't know if he was saying anything to you or not. The only thing missing was the white lab coat.

He took us through to a workshop filled with hundreds of tools, and dozens and dozens of other unidentifiable vaguely mechanical looking bits of kit. There were quite a few work-benches around, but every inch of surface was covered with something or other that looked like it was in the process of being built.

I explained to him again exactly what I wanted, more for Carrot's benefit than his.

"Then I think this will do the trick nicely," Kettlestone said. He produced out of nowhere a pack of Marlboro cigarettes and a lime green disposable lighter, one of the type you can pick up for a pound just about anywhere.

"Do you smoke?"

I shook my head.

"Well, no matter."

He flipped open the lid of the cigarette pack and Carrot and I looked inside. It was a jumble of wires, a lump of something black and what looked like a tiny circuit board.

For the next twenty minutes, Kettlestone told us what it was, what it was made of, how it worked and what it did. I gave up listening about two minutes in. Even Carrot looked over to me at one stage and raised his eyes to the ceiling. It was all highly technical stuff, and it was all completely over my head. But it was exactly what I wanted. Igniting the lighter would set off the explosion, which would cause damage to about a three feet radius. If there was something flammable in the vicinity then it would almost certainly catch fire, Kettlestone said. He also said it would be a good idea to cut up some actual cigarettes and put the tops in the packet to hide the real contents.

"How much?" I asked.

"Do you think you'll be bringing any more business my way?"

"Could be," I said. "If this goes well, could be very likely." I could see Carrot scowling out of the corner of my eye.

"Ton, then."

I pulled two fifty-pound notes out my wallet and gave them to him. We shook hands.

"Nice to do business with you," he said.

"You're a brave man," said Carrot when we got outside.

"How's that then?"

"Throwing a bomb at the Ragman at his only daughter's wedding, you've got a real death wish. You must really want to work for Tomassetti badly. Why is that I wonder?"

"Well, it's none of your business, you ginger pig," I said.

He swung at me then, which I knew he would, and I easily stepped inside his clumsy haymaker. Then I hit him, very hard with my clenched knuckles, in the centre of his stomach, just below his ribs. He doubled up against the wall, struggling for breath. I leant over him.

"Listen, you prick. You think you're so tough, but I've been taught how to do this by people who are really tough. They'd eat you up and spit you out. So if you don't want any more of that then you stay out of my way. You say you're going to be at Strutter's on Saturday, fine. But stay out of my way. Got it?"

I gave Carrot, who was purple in the face by now, a little shove and he fell sideways onto the pavement. I walked off. I felt very smug as I searched for a cab, in fact, I hadn't felt as pleased with myself for ages. It's amazing how satisfying it can be filling a few of those caveman urges occasionally.

That smug feeling disappeared very quickly when I got out of the taxi at Spike's place. A black car swept up, Lambert opened the rear passenger door, pulled me inside and the car sped off again.

"Want to buy some wine?" he laughed.

"Listen, you bastard," I bristled, turning towards him. "What's going on here? Not one thing you've told me so far has turned out to be true. What's your game? You've been stitching me up good and proper."

Lambert leaned away from me, actually looking a bit concerned, which was very gratifying. The big bruiser who was driving, turned round and gave me a menacing look. He looked ready to climb over his seat and tear my head off.

"Okay, Giles," Lambert said, holding up his hand. "There'll be no trouble here, we're all friends, all on the same side. Aren't we Mr Jones?"

"Well I'm not sure after all the nonsense you've been giving me," I growled. "I could almost believe you've been setting me up on purpose here. For starters, Darby doesn't work for Integrated Electronics, he works for the bloody Ministry of Defence, the stuff he's stealing isn't from IE either, it's from bloody Porton Down, and it's a battery, not bloody radar. So if we're on the same side, tell me where all those bloody nursery rhymes you told me came from."

Lambert looked genuinely puzzled.

"Radar?" he said.

I remembered I'd googled the radar, it was speculation, not anything he'd told me.

"Well," I said. "That's not important. What's important is you've told me this pile of bollocks. It's almost as though you wanted me caught."

"Well, obviously you haven't been," Lambert said levelly, trying to recover himself I thought. He wasn't quite so smiley as he usually was. "But I'm curious to know how you found all that out and how you're still alive."

"I think Tomassetti likes me," I said. "He told me all that himself. I looked like a proper prat though telling him all the stuff I could do for him and everything I said to him was rubbish. That could have gone very badly for me. No thanks to you, you bastard."

"So have you found out who they're selling the secrets to?"

"No, not yet, bloody hell, give me a chance. Although I did find out one other thing."

I paused.

"Your man, your agent, Winslow, he's dead, I'm afraid. They were on to him."

"Winslow?"

I nodded.

"Sorry."

My anger subsided when I told him that. He might be a bastard but it couldn't be easy hearing that sort of news. He was certainly a lot quieter after that.

"Winslow? And he's definitely dead?"

I nodded again.

"But what about all that bullshit you've given me?" I said. "What's going on?"

He shrugged.

"I don't know what to say. Everything I told you is what I'd been told. If it's not true then I don't know what's going on myself. Are you sure Tomassetti's telling you the truth? That he's not leading you on?"

Actually, that hadn't occurred to me, and I pondered that.

"I don't know," I said. "It all seemed genuine enough."

"Well, let me investigate. Let me go back to the office and see what I can find out."

He dropped me off outside Spike's lockup.

As I watched the car drive off I felt my stomach twitch. Who was lying to me, Lambert or Tomassetti? What a nightmare.

Spike and I took the wine back to Finch's warehouse. Apart from anything else, all this being moved around and shaken up couldn't be doing the stuff any good. Hope it all goes rancid, I thought.

Spike looked a bit wistful once we'd got it all loaded and the doors locked.

"Shame, init," he said. "That was a good little wheeze I came up with there, wasn't it?"

"Yeah," I said. "A great little wheeze. Right up to the part where you stitched up your best mate."

"Oh. Yeah. Sorry."

He tried to look crestfallen, but not very successfully.

"Come on," I said. "Let's get this over with."

I clapped him on the back and we got in the van.

It took ages to get over to Finch's place from Chelsea. It wasn't very far in real terms, but it meant crawling through the centre of London. I don't reckon we ever made it over five miles an hour. Spike spent most of it telling me about all his problems. I spent most of it trying to stay awake.

CHAPTER THIRTY
JOE KETTLESTONE

Cor, what a Herbert. Some people are strange. He wants a bomb, but he doesn't want to hurt no one. What's the bleeding point, I ask you. If you want to scare someone off and you want to use a bomb, of course you've got to hurt them. There's no sense in a bomb otherwise, what's the point. If he thinks his bomb isn't going to hurt anyone then he's an idiot. It's going to hurt a lot of people.

Now, if it was me, I could be very imaginative. You could do just a simple explosion with lots of shrapnel, of course, and it would be very effective. But suppose you really wanted to scare someone, do something a bit different? Now, what about a chemical bomb, or a biological bomb? Once it went off, you could let them know how the symptoms would develop over the next couple of days, let them know exactly how it would go. First would come the respiratory difficulties, trouble breathing, then the sweats and the fever, and then the rashes and the sores. And then of course you could tell them exactly how long it was going to take them to die. And how painful it was going to be. Exquisite. Of course, a nice little wrinkle would be to offer them an antidote, if there was one. But only if they did exactly what you wanted them to. Brilliant. Much better than just chucking a stupid cigarette bomb at them. That's not going to scare them, just make them angry.

Or what about a jelly bomb? Oh yeah. Incendiary, one that sticks to human skin. Throw that into crowded room and then watch the fun. Watch them running around screaming their heads off. That's the way to scare people.

CHAPTER THIRTY-ONE
TIME FOR NUPTIALS

Wednesday was shopping day. I had to trawl round quite a few places and see quite a few people before I found exactly what I was after, something very suitable for Amelia's wedding. When I got home I put a lovely little package together, wrapped beautifully in wedding paper with some elaborate ribbon on the top. I took it round to the office.

"Can you deliver this for me," I asked Mimi when I got there. She looked puzzled. I gave her Jane's name and address.

"Will you say I wanted to get something nice for Amelia, and because I was out of the country I got you to do it for me. And because I'll be rushing to the wedding straight from the airport, I thought it best that you took it round now so she could take it with her. What's important is that she doesn't know I'm in the country. I'll explain it all later once it's over and done with."

The confusion on Mimi's face was a real picture. It kept me amused thinking about it for the rest of the day.

Isabella answered the door to Tomassetti's house when I got there. She showed me in to the little room where I'd been the first time I came round, and Tomassetti joined me about five minutes later.

"Two mugs of Horlicks, please Isabella," said the old man.

He shook my hand and sat down.

"Thank you for Saturday," I said. "I enjoyed it very much. It was nice to meet your family."

"What did you think of young Tabitha?"

"She was very nice," I said.

He laughed.

"A very good reply," he said. "I appreciate you saying that. And she is very nice, but I suspect being very nice isn't going to bring you back to her every night. Did she have very much to say to you?"

I shook my head.

"Not really. I don't know if she was shy or nervous, but she didn't. I tried."

He sighed.

"I know, I saw. You did nobly, my friend. But I suspect you are going to need something more to make you settle down than a big pair of brown eyes. Someone like that young woman who passed us in the street the other day."

I was instantly on the alert. What was this? Did he know about me and Hernandez? Did he suspect something? Did he know she was a policeman? My mind was racing.

"Why, do you know her Mr Tomassetti?"

"Know her? No. Why should I know her? She was just a beautiful woman who passed us in the street. Why would you ask that?"

Aagh. Now I was really on the back foot. Don't get defensive. I thought quickly, and bang, it was like a little light bulb switched on above my head.

"I've seen her before."

"You have?" Tomassetti was looking puzzled.

"Yes. I've seen her with Carrot. That's why I thought you might know her as well."

The old man looked up, startled.

"Where was this?"

"Well, when I left here the other week, I spotted Carrot following me. I went into a pub and watched him through the window. He hung about for a while, and then left. So I followed him. He ended up going to another pub, and he met her in there. I recognised her as the woman you'd pointed out. I assumed you did know her and I didn't think any more of it. I thought you must have been teasing me the other day because you knew who she was."

The old man pursed his lips and stared at me. A bit nonplussed, I think.

"Well. Well, I really don't know what to say. I don't, in fact, know her. And I would be surprised if Carrot does either. While I could see someone like her being attracted to you, Mr Jones, I'm not so sure I can understand her seeing very much in someone like Carrot. For all his good points, he's not exactly a ladies' man."

I bit my tongue. I was desperate to say some more, to lead the old man in the right direction, but I knew I'd said enough. The seed of doubt was there.

"Very strange. And puzzling. But enough of Carrot for the moment. You are working with him on the Strutter wedding? Everything is going smoothly? I don't want to know any of the details yet, just to know things are proceeding."

"It's going very well, Mr Tomassetti. I think you're going to be very pleased with the outcome."

"Good, good, that's exactly what I want to hear. I shall wait with bated breath to find out what happens. Now, on to other things. You will be pleased to hear I have purchased Mr Finch's wine."

"You have? How did you do that?"

"An associate bought it for me, done in a way so that it can never be traced back to me."

"How much did it cost you?"

"Forty thousand pounds."

"That's not bad. In theory you could make ten times that out of it."

"Ah, but I didn't buy the wine to make a profit out of it. I bought it because I want to teach Mr Finch a lesson."

"And what will that lesson be?"

"I haven't decided yet. I thought that next week, once we have got Saturday out of the way, you and I can sit down and discuss how we might proceed with causing Mr Finch a great deal of inconvenience and aggravation."

Okay, this was giving me even more incentive to succeed on Saturday. I might be being forced to do this by MI5, but Finch was personal, and I was going to get a lot of pleasure out of seeing him get his comeuppance.

Saturday came round before I knew it. But at two-thirty sharp I was standing in line outside the Ragman's palatial mansion in Chipping Barnet waiting to get through security. This consisted of three blokes and a girl, all wearing sunglasses, patting each of the guests down and going through their pockets. It was all fairly perfunctory, I guess they knew most of the guests by sight already. Until it got to me.

As my name was being ticked off on a big list, one of the sunglasses whispered in the ear of one of the others. I took notice of him for the first time. To my absolute horror it was Carrot.

He stood there with a huge grin stretching from ear to ear, while his compadre asked me would I mind emptying my pockets. I walked over to the table he was indicating and did as I was told. Bloody Carrot had really blind-sided me here. Was I being set up? Was the old man involved? I was going to have to be very careful.

I emptied everything out onto the table. Wallet, keys, change, just the usual stuff. Oh, and a packet of Marlboro and a lime green disposable lighter.

It was as I put those down that Carrot leaned over and whispered in the other guy's ear again. The guy picked up the packet of cigarettes and, holding it very gingerly and as far away from him as possible, opened it. Time seemed to stand still. Cautiously he flipped open the top. Finding a full packet of cigarettes staring up at him the guy looked questioningly over at Carrot. Carrot made a sort of flipping gesture with his hand.

Some of the other guests waiting in line had picked up on the tension that was starting to build up, and they began to watch what was going on with rapt attention. It was very quiet.

The man carefully held up the packet and tipped it upside down. Twenty cigarettes fell out. Everybody leaned over and peered into the box. Which was empty. There was a sort of anticlimactic sigh from the crowd.

The security guy made a snorting noise and looked exasperatedly at Carrot who came over and whispered in his ear again.

"Sorry sir, would you mind if I pat you down," he said. "We have to be very careful, you understand. I nodded and held my arms out. The guy gave me a very thorough and prolonged going-over, he'd done this sort of thing before. He found nothing.

"Thank you, sir, sorry for the inconvenience."

As I passed through, I noticed Carrot's face had turned purple. I thought his head was going to explode.

I found Jane surrounded by a bunch of bridesmaids. She seemed pleased to see me. I think she would have liked us to spend more time together, but she had to go off and help the bride do bridely things. The ceremony was to be held outside in Strutter's safari park of a garden. Fortunately the weather was good, so we weren't going to get wet.

I grabbed a seat at the back, which was fortunate, because it was all I could do not to nod off. It was the longest wedding service I could ever remember attending. Strutter was sat in the front row with a tiny, mousy woman who I guessed was his wife. He looked as mousy as she did. Short, greasy haired, thick black-rimmed glasses, he looked like he should have been working in an accounts department somewhere. Extraordinary. I had no idea why he was called the Ragman. Hopefully, I would never find out. He probably had the worst reputation of any of the London gangsters, the stories about him were legion. The most violent, the most psychopathic, the most evil of all of them. If half the tales told about him were true then he really was somebody to be feared, respected and be very scared of. Presumably that was why Tomassetti had chosen this to be my task.

The ceremony wound it's weary way on, with the bride and groom reading out vows that surely would have made the Guinness Book of Records, both for length and for naffness. All the way through, Jane looked at me and giggled from the front, and Carrot stared at me hostilely from the side, where he stood with the rest of his security team.

But eventually, thankfully, it was all over, and we filed noisily over to a marquee where champagne was waiting to be served. Jane told me she had to sit at the top table, mine was about as far away from the top table as it was possible to be. I think it was for all the black-sheep cousins and disreputable members of the family. Everybody was single and they all looked decidedly odd. I decided I wasn't going to be able to sit through very much of this.

Strutter got up to make his welcoming speech.

Carrot was over to one side of the marquee still staring daggers at me. Carefully holding his gaze, I took the lime green disposable lighter out of my pocket and held it up so that Carrot could see it. The look on his face was a real treat. I could see him tense up.

I thumbed the ignition and the marquee suddenly shuddered to the noise of a deafening explosion. A mushroom cloud of smoke rose lazily above the centre table where all the wedding presents had been piled up, and hundreds of thousands of small pieces of silver confetti shot up in the air. People screamed and jumped to their feet, sending chairs and glasses flying, but the hubbub of panic was replaced, as equally suddenly as the explosion, by 'oohs' and 'ahs' as fifty pairs of eyes watched the tiny pieces of confetti float back down again, shimmering in the light. It was a truly beautiful sight.

The guests burst into thunderous and instantaneous applause. The ovation went on for minutes, and then everybody sat down again, noisily discussing what had just happened. The place was buzzing. Everybody seemed to think it was the best wedding ever.

The only person who didn't was Strutter himself, who, ashen faced, was staring at the centre table where once had stood a beautifully gift-wrapped present, but was now just a small mound of charred remains and ashes. In the middle of that mound of ashes, slightly singed but mostly untouched, stood a small jar of Horlicks.

By this time, I was standing next to Carrot whispering in his ear.

"If you think you're going to blow the whistle on me for this," I said. "Then you're going down with me. You're as vulnerable as I am here. So I think it's in both our interests that you keep stum about this. In fact, considering that you're security, and we've just had a rather serious security breach, I would probably make myself scarce before my psychopathic nutjob of a boss wakes up to that fact."

I could see from Carrot's face that that thought hadn't struck him yet. He looked at me wide-eyed, and then, without a word, slipped quietly out of the marquee. The last I saw of him he was running for the trees like all the hounds of hell were after him.

"I still don't really understand what happened."

"Me neither," I said.

Jane and I were lying in bed after what can only be described as an energetic session. We were both sweaty and exhausted.

"Poor Mr Strutter looked like he'd seen a ghost."

Strutter had, in fact, continued staring at the jar of Horlicks, white-faced for a good five minutes or so while Mrs Strutter tried manfully to get the party back on track. Not that any of the guests had a problem, they were all still a twitter at the excitement of having half a ton of confetti unexpectedly rain down on their heads.

Strutter made it to the best man's speech, before getting suddenly to his feet and leaving. He looked like a man sleepwalking. A couple of minders appeared out of nowhere and hurried after him. The rest of the evening went without a hitch.

"People were saying it was a real bomb, but it couldn't have been, it was just a confetti bomb. I thought it was beautiful. Everybody loved it."

"I heard somebody say they thought it was a bomb as well," I said.

"How silly. But they're saying that one of the security people disappeared straight afterwards, so they're saying he's the one responsible."

"Which one, do you know?"

"The big, ugly bald one, do you know who I mean?"

I nodded.

"Amelia says Mr Strutter is very cross with that security man. I wouldn't like to be in his shoes when he finds him."

I lay back with my hands behind my head and smiled. You know, it hadn't been a half bad day in the end.

Sunday turned out to be a day of feedback, first Tomassetti and then Hernandez.

The old man was first. I got a text saying could I meet him at the Albemarle at lunchtime. It was difficult getting away from

Jane who came over all clingy, and in the end I had to just push her away and slam the door behind me. I'd had a great time with her, a fabulous night, but the whole needy thing put me right off. Shame.

It was fortunate that the whole story about me flying straight off was still holding, so that took the pressure off. When she asked me where I was going, I said Zanzibar. I assumed she would think that was in the middle of Europe. I told her it was unlikely they had phones out there, let alone signals, but I would do my best to ring her.

I could hear her crying behind the door as I walked away.

"I've had an emissary."

"Oh?"

"Yes, from Mr Strutter. He wants to discuss terms."

Tomassetti and I were sitting at his usual end of the bar sipping on our mugs of Horlicks. I was feeling a bit self-conscious that I'd pitched up unshaven and wearing yesterday's suit, but I thought I was bearing up pretty well considering. Certainly, the old man didn't notice, he just looked very pleased to see me.

"Is that a good thing?" I said.

"Oh yes, very good, very good indeed. I take it as a sign that yesterday went very well."

"I'm not sure I quite understand."

"Well, emissary. All of the various, what shall we call them, factions, in our business here in London have unofficial methods of communication. An associate here might have contact with another associate there, that sort of thing. So, late last night I had a message from one of my associates who had been contacted by one of his associates with the message that Strutter wants to discuss terms."

"What sort of terms?"

"I suppose you could compare it to what happens at the end of a war, the First World War for example. The two sides get together to discuss the terms of victory, what the loser will do for the winner."

"So Strutter's surrendering?"

"No, not exactly. Again, the First World War is a good example here. Germany did not actually surrender, but when the two sides agreed to stop fighting there was clearly a winner, England. And they were given some compensation by Germany in exchange for not fighting any more. That is the situation we are in at the moment, I am England and the Ragman is Germany. We have an understanding in our business of what it means exactly when people say certain things. And this is exactly what Mr Strutter means when he says he wants to discuss terms. We will negotiate, and I will tell him exactly what sort of business he can conduct from now on and where he can conduct it, which I can tell you, will be much reduced from what it is now and very far away from me. And in exchange he will give me some form of recompense. And then that understanding will become the status quo for a little while, and then he will become a little more ambitious and then we will go through the whole process all over again. It is the nature of our business and the nature of the people who perpetuate our business unfortunately. Such a waste of time."

He looked thoughtful for a moment, before perking up again.

"So, I assume your mission went well for there to have been such a swift and positive response. I hope you didn't have to kill his daughter to achieve such a result."

For the next thirty minutes I told the old man exactly what had happened. I left nothing out, he had it all, chapter and verse. He had a slightly surprised look on his face by the time I finished.

"So it was just a firework?"

I nodded.

"Yes, but a very good one. It took some tracking down to get someone to make me something that was powerful, would make a lot of noise and smoke, would create a dramatic effect, but wasn't in the slightest way dangerous. Fortunately I know people who can help me out with this sort of thing."

"It obviously had a dramatic effect on Mr Strutter."

"It was the jar of Horlicks that did that. That was a brilliant touch. He just stood there staring at it for ages. I think he could see his life flashing before him. It's amazing how scary a bedtime drink can be. He was very, very frightened."

"Indeed, indeed. But to pull off this trick, you had to leave poor old Carrot carrying the can?"

"Not at all. Showing him the cigarette bomb was a bit of an insurance policy for me. I didn't think I could trust him and I was absolutely right. He tried to expose me. If I had had the bomb on me, I would be dead meat now, hanging in Strutter's freezer somewhere. And, by the way, what was that all about, Carrot being on Strutter's security team? If I didn't know better, I'd say you'd gone out of your way to make things as difficult as possible for me, it's almost as though we were working on different sides, that you wanted me dead."

I started to get a big angry. I hadn't really thought about the implications of Carrot being there before, I had been enjoying the thought of him being hunted down too much. The old man smiled and patted me on the arm.

"Of course I made things as difficult as possible, of course I did. I wanted to give you a proper test, to put you through as challenging an examination as there could possibly be. What was the point of it otherwise? What would it tell me if you achieved something easy? So what? So of course it was difficult. But you made it look easy, didn't you. I must tell you that I think Uncle Adlai will be very impressed at the result of this, although he will also be very disappointed that nobody got hurt."

"But how was Carrot there anyway? I don't understand?"

"In our business, knowledge is power. So I have a few of my boys doing jobs for my competition. Bits and pieces here and there.

They keep me informed of what is going on. It's a very complicated business you know, what we do. So, originally I was going to get Carrot to do something that would give Mr Strutter the message, but then you came along saying you could do this and you could do that, so I thought I would kill two birds with one stone as it were and give you the opportunity. So instead of having Carrot going in like a battering ram, we had your much more elegant solution, which, because it was elegant, and so well put together, would, I am sure, have been much more frightening for our Mr Strutter. Straightforward violence I believe he can deal with, something with some brains and forethought behind it, I think would be much more terrifying. Something he knows he can't compete with."

The old man fell silent for a moment, clearly miles away, before carrying on.

"The only downside for us, of course, is that you made Carrot the scapegoat for the operation, and now Mr Strutter is devoting a great deal of time and energy looking for him. That was unfortunate."

"No, I didn't do that. Don't forget, I had no idea Carrot was on the security team. He'd told me he was going to be there, I'd assumed he got a proper invitation, same as I had. He didn't have to do a runner either, that put the finger on him straight away. Really stupid."

"Yes, I suppose you're right, you couldn't have known."

"So have you heard from Carrot?"

"I had a message from some associates down in Hastings. He turned up there last night, looking very much worse for wear. They will look after him for the time being and keep him safe. When I talk to Mr Strutter next week I shall imply that the operation was nothing to do with his security people, and perhaps that will take the pressure off Carrot a little bit."

"So you haven't spoken to Carrot yet?"

"No, not yet."

"I don't suppose his story will be the same as mine."

"No, I don't suppose it will be. It will be interesting to compare the two."

The old man yawned and stretched a bit.

"Will you excuse me Mr Jones, I had a very late night last night, and I admit I'm beginning to feel a bit sleepy. I think I will go home for my afternoon nap now. But if it's convenient for you, I would like to get together next week and talk about a few things. Mr Finch for one, perhaps you can come up with another of your elegant solutions for him. And then you and I need to talk about the future, our future, and what we might do together."

I said I would be happy to. He got up, patted me on the shoulder, and shuffled off. The goons appeared out of nowhere and followed him out.

I was a bit stunned how well all this was going. I could actually see some light at the end of the tunnel. Now I was close to being accepted surely it wouldn't take too long to find out everything that MI5 needed. The only problem for me was that I needed to work something out so that Tomassetti and his hoodlums weren't going to come looking for me for the rest of my life. I needed another elegant solution I laughed to myself. And that's where Carrot was going to come in very useful again.

Hernandez and I met up for dinner in a little bistro in Chelsea later that evening.

"I was outside when I heard the explosion."

"You were?"

"I thought you really had let off a bomb. It was bloody loud."

"Yeah, it was wasn't it? Scared everybody witless. Completely harmless of course. Tomassetti called it an elegant solution, and I'm inclined to agree with him."

"You're too smug for your own good you are. You want to be careful, you know what the say about pride coming before a fall."

"No, what do they say?"

Hernandez gave me one of her looks.

"So it was in the present that you got your girlfriend to take along?"

"Yep."

"Couldn't they work out which one it was? Didn't your girl-friend twig that she was the mule?"

"Nope. Strutter's heavies took all the presents out and disposed of the lot of them in case there was a real bomb in there as well. They couldn't take any chances. One or two people moaned a bit, but everyone was having too good a time to complain too much."

"So it all worked out just the way you wanted it?"

"Pretty much."

"And now you're Tomassetti's man?"

"Well, I guess so. I'm not sure exactly what's happening on that front, but it looks like I've passed the audition. As it happens I think he's got big plans for me doing something significant in his organisation."

We sat in silence for a while, Hernandez wasn't eating, just playing with her food.

"I didn't realise you were outside," I said.

She nodded.

"I thought you were asking for trouble with all these plans for blowing Strutter up, so I thought I should be there in case it all went wrong. I couldn't decide what to do when I heard the explosion, but eventually I sneaked in so I could see what was happening. I could see that you were all right."

"How long were you there?"

"Until you left."

"So you saw. ..." I tailed off.

"Yes, I saw you leave with your girlfriend."

"There's nothing in that. I told you about her beforehand. She was the only way I was going to get in. There's nothing between us. I used her, that's all."

"Yes, you used her all right. Same as you use everybody."

"That's not fair."

"Isn't it?"

I didn't know what to say. She was right of course, but it wasn't very nice to be confronted with it. I put my hand on hers but she snatched it away. I started to say something, but she got in first."

"Look Jonesy, I can't deny there isn't anything between us. Of course there is. I'm tighter than a wound-up spring every time I see you. I'd like nothing better than for you to be something other than what you are, an accountant or something, and then we could get together and have a nice normal relationship and be together. But I'm a police inspector and you're a bloody crook for god's sake. Where's the hope in that for us? How on earth can there ever be an us?

I shrugged.

"And you are using me, just like you're using that girl, and everyone else you ever meet. I know that. You aren't telling me half of what's going on. You're using me for what you can get out of me, and then you'll dump me and move on, just like you do with everybody."

"That's not true...."

"It bloody well is true."

Hernandez was getting angry now, and loud. A few of the other diners were looking our way, presumably hoping for some entertainment to brighten up their own boring meals.

"Look, I'm not saying you haven't got feelings for me, but you're still using me, I'm not stupid."

"Then why are you here?"

"I don't know," she said. "I just don't know. Part of it's because I'm using you as well, I suppose. I want Tomassetti because I don't like to see graft in the police force. And I want Paradine's murderers. Badly. I'm the only mug who seems to care about that poor bloke's death."

She stared at me for a while, grim-mouthed.

"I could change," I said. "I could stop doing what I'm doing. MI5 are going to be paying me a lot of money when this over. I can retire. Then it'll just be you and me."

"Change. That's a good one. The day that you change will be when hell freezes over."

"That's a bit dramatic, isn't it?"

"That's how I feel about it, it is dramatic. I'm frustrated because I want there to be an us. But you're a bastard, and that's all there is to it."

"This is because you saw me with that girl yesterday, isn't it?"

Hernandez sort of groaned and stood up. She picked her wine glass up, emptied the contents into my face, and stormed out.

I looked round. Every single person in the restaurant was staring at me. They were all having a thoroughly enjoyable time.

"Drinks are on me then," I said.

CHAPTER THIRTY-TWO
JANE

I wonder if Amelia's dad would let me use their house for when Jones and I get married. It was perfect.

One of those confetti bombs would be nice too.

CHAPTER THIRTY-THREE
SAFE AS HOUSES

The next couple of weeks just sailed by. I spent most of them with the old man, with an occasional visit to the office to see Mimi shoehorned in whenever I could.

I clearly had passed the audition because Tomassetti was showing me his business. We slogged our way round half of London while he briefed me on all his various operations and introduced me to all his top men. It was very surreal. It was as though we were visiting royalty and everyone was on their best behaviour, trying very hard to impress and not say the wrong thing. Except when the old man wasn't actually standing next to me. Then all I got was unrestrained hostility.

I tried on a few occasions to talk to him about what was going on, what he wanted from me, but he wasn't having any of it.

"Indulge me, my friend," he said after one such attempt. "Allow me the pleasure of showing you around my little empire, and then, once you have seen everything, then we can sit down over a mug of Horlicks and talk about what we might do going forward. And who knows what the future might hold."

"Supposing I don't want anything to do with this?"

"Then that might be the outcome of our talks. But don't forget this all started because you came to me and said you wanted to do business with me. So you were the instigator here. Has that changed?"

"No, not at all. I still want to. It's just that this seems to have escalated a bit."

The old man laughed.

"Yes, it has hasn't it? Who would have thought that when you decided to try and extort a few thousand pounds from a miserable little man sitting in a pub that, just a few weeks later, the two of us would be sat here discussing the future of my organisation? Amazing, isn't it?"

Amazing wasn't the word for it, it was so much more than that. I didn't feel like my feet were touching the ground as he took me on my whirlwind tour.

The main thrust of the old man's business was drugs. He had a huge network that either imported the stuff or manufactured it, and then sold it on to the dealers on the streets. It was enormous and must have been worth millions to him. It seemed to be cocaine mostly, but as far as I could tell there was also heroin, crystal meth and ecstasy. And anything else that came his way in truth. The operation was efficient, well organised and streamlined. In fact, the only difference between his and a successful legitimate company was that that his end product was illegal and killed people.

In addition, there was prostitution, gambling and extortion, each of those being pretty big businesses in their own right. Then there were nightclubs, pubs, betting shops, casinos, property companies, tanning salons, nail parlours, the list was endless. Some of those were legit, it helped with the enormous amount of money laundering that went on, but most of it was extremely crooked and fronted for a lot of the other stuff. It was a kingdom, there was no other word for it. The sheer scale of it all took my breath away.

He ran his businesses from his townhouse. Except that it wasn't just his townhouse, he owned three other houses next door, all full of people working extremely hard for him.

I think I was standing there with my mouth open when the old man first showed me, because he started laughing.

"What, you thought I could run all this without help? You are surprised, I think. But, impressive is it not?"

I nodded.

"Very impressive. I'm amazed, I had no idea. You've got quite a set up here."

He smiled happily, obviously very proud of the empire that he had created. Or perhaps Uncle Adlai had created, I thought.

"This is why I go to the Albemarle for my Horlicks. To get away. If I am here, even in my own house, then I am always available. People can always come to me. Which is fine of course, it's what I am here for. But sometimes it's nice to pretend that I'm just an ordinary old man who sometimes goes out to meet his friends for a drink and a chat about old times."

An ordinary old man I thought. Hah!

We adjourned back to the first little room. I could hear the sound of children playing somewhere in the distance.

"I just don't understand how you get away with it all," I said. "There's so much of everything, and so much of it is transparently illegal, why aren't you all in prison?"

Tomassetti made the universal money sign by rubbing his forefinger and thumb together.

"How do you think?" he said. "I spend a fortune keeping people on my side. A small fortune. Occasionally things go amiss of course and we find ourselves on the wrong side of the law, and we have to close down a small piece of business, or one of my people has to go to prison for a short time, but generally speaking it all goes very smoothly. I have enough people in important places to make sure nothing evil befalls us. It's easy enough to do as long as you have enough money. Our biggest problem is not usually the authorities, it's the threat of somebody else coming along and trying to take over what we do. A new kid on the block, you might say. That is my constant worry. I spend a great deal of my time working out what everyone else is up to and then making sure that I'm always one step ahead of them. You know, I've thought for a long time, I should be the person running the spies in this country... what's his name? M? I think I would be very good at that."

We both laughed. He would certainly be a lot more personable than the harridan I'd met at MI5 I thought.

One day when we were driving somewhere in the back of the Bentley, the old man told me he'd had his meeting with the Ragman. I was surprised because he hadn't mentioned it beforehand. Obviously I wasn't being let in on everything that was happening.

It all went as anticipated apparently. Strutter played it all very supine and agreed to Tomassetti's terms without argument. One of the old man's demands was that there was to be no comeback against any of his men, so in theory Carrot was off the hook.

"Have you spoken to Carrot yet," I asked.

"Oh yes. He's back in London now, but we've decided it would probably be best for everyone concerned if he laid low for a while."

"What did he say about the wedding? Was his story the same as mine?"

The old man laughed.

"More or less, more or less. Although the part he played in his story was a lot more heroic than it was in the one you told. And he does blame you for what happened to him."

"Me? How does he blame me exactly?"

"Well, he couldn't say precisely, he just kept saying it was your fault. I think I have a pretty clear picture about what happened that day now. So once again I offer you my congratulations. A job well done. If only you could have head-butted somebody on the way out, then I think we might have received Uncle Adlai's blessings as well. He still has reservations that you aren't hard enough for this type of work."

"I have reservations too," I said. "I agree with Uncle Adlai that I'm not hard enough. I have no talent or desire to get into anything that requires violence."

"No. For a long time I had wondered, hoped in fact, that a partnership might have been the ideal solution for some of the things I am thinking about for the future. Someone comfortable with the physical side of our work, with a propensity for it even, allied with someone more suited to the cerebral side of things. I had high hopes for you and Carrot becoming that partnership."

I snorted.

"He's an idiot," I said. "That one's a non-starter straight away."

"And yet I thought at one time putting the two of you together might work. Carrot isn't an idiot, he actually has done good things for me. He's reliable, hard working, trustworthy and resourceful, a good man to have on your side. I confess I like Carrot very much. He hasn't been with me very long, but he's impressed me a great deal. To use another wartime analogy he's someone I would like beside me in the trenches. But from the moment you appeared he took against you. I don't know what it was, I know it wasn't your fault, it was him right from the start. From then on, all the time, he's telling me not to trust you, that you're not who you say you are, that I should get rid of you."

"But you don't believe him?"

"No, I told you, we have acquired a great deal of information about you. Enough to be satisfied that you are who you say you are. But, I fear, his antagonism towards you, for whatever reason, means you and Carrot can never work together. It's you or him, I'm afraid."

"Well, that's for sure. So what will you do about that?"

"Oh, I don't know yet. There's a long way to go before we need to make any big decisions, so there's no rush. But I have decided not to give him any more jobs to do for the time being, I have left him to his own devices. It will be good for him to have a little break perhaps. I think, in the short term, it will be a good thing for you two to stay out of each other's way for a little while."

"You'll get no argument from me there."

"And I am slightly troubled about you seeing him with that rather attractive young lady. I am always smelling rats and I don't like the smell of that. I'm sure Carrot will have a perfectly acceptable explanation when I eventually ask him, but I have decided not to ask him just yet."

"No?"

"No. I shouldn't tell you this really, but I am having him followed. Just in case. We'll leave things like that for a few weeks and then we shall see what we shall see."

We both subsided into silence as we thought about the implications of that.

The car eventually pulled up outside a seedy-looking shop right in the middle of a grimy little side street full of tiny two-up, two down terraced houses. I hadn't really kept up with where we were going, but it looked like we were somewhere in the maze of streets north of Kings Cross station.

The old man quickly got out of the car, which drove off immediately, almost without completely stopping.

"Come my friend, I have one more surprise to show you."

We stood in front of the shop. It looked like something out of the forties. Black, peeling paint, dirty, grubby windows you couldn't see through, it didn't look very inviting. The sign above the shop said, "**Mandelbaum's**", although it was so obscured by dirt it was almost indecipherable. A yellowing, curling cardboard sign with a picture of a sewing machine on it was hanging in one of the windows and was the first clue as to what actually went on inside. 'Custom Tailoring and Alterations," it said. "**By Professional Clothiers.**" As I pondered what a Clothier was, I read the sign in the other window. It was as washed-out and distressed as the first one, although I suspect it might have been quite colourful once. "**Mens, Youths and Boys Suits. Made to Measure. 7/6.**" Ah, well that was a bit of a giveaway as to how old the place was. Pretty good price for a suit though, I thought. I wasn't exactly sure what seven and six was in current money, but it had to be less than fifty pence.

We pushed our way inside. The door didn't really swing very easily and I had to give it a bit of welly to get it to open properly. The inside of the shop was the same as the outside, ancient, dirty and neglected. The only real difference was that there was more dust. There was a counter and nothing else. A door behind the counter slowly opened, and a very old man shuffled out. He was about as Jewish as you could possibly imagine.

"Chaim!" Tomassetti said with a beaming smile. "How are you my friend?"

He pulled up a flap in the counter and the two men embraced.

"Chaim, I want you to meet a new colleague of mine, Mr Jones. Mr Jones, this is Chaim. He looks after this place for me."

We shook hands. His skin was wrinkled and dry. He had to be ninety if he was a day. I looked at Tomassetti.

"He makes your suits?"

Tomassetti laughed.

"Perhaps one day they used to make suits. But that isn't the purpose of this place now. Come, I'll show you."

We went through into the back room. Chaim didn't follow us. He hadn't said a word so far. Very spooky.

There were some rickety old stairs at the back and we went down them into the basement. I was thinking it might have been the coal cellar at some time. The stairs weren't easy to navigate, and Tomassetti took some time to make his way down. The basement was decrepit, peeling paint, musty smelling and with signs of damp everywhere. There was another door at the end, and we pushed through that into another room, identical to the first except that this room contained six battered old filing cabinets.

I looked at the old man enquiringly.

"Welcome to Pandora's Box," he said, and swept his arm round at the cabinets. He laughed at the obviously non-plussed look on my face.

"Here are all my records. The real records, the records that no one must ever see. Obviously it is extraordinarily dangerous to keep written records of these things, but sometimes it is necessary. For example, there are the details of all the bribes I have given to policemen over the years to keep them on my side. Who, where, when, it's all here. It's a very important insurance policy for me. Perhaps one day I'll need all this information for bargaining chips."

"Isn't that a bit risky having all that stuff here? Surely the police could get in anytime?"

The old man smiled.

"That's what Chaim is here for, who never leaves this building. He carries a pager with him at all times. That pager is there solely for the purpose of informing him that it is time to destroy this building. He knows exactly what to do, the whole place is primed, and would be ablaze within minutes of him being informed."

"Wow." I didn't know what to say.

"You are very privileged being allowed to see this. Only my most trusted people are allowed in here."

I nodded. I felt privileged.

"I confess I'm starting to feel a little tired now," continued the old man. "I suggest we go home and take one more drink together and then I'll leave you to your evening. Do you have plans?"

I shook my head, I hadn't done anything social for weeks.

We went back upstairs, said goodbye to Chaim and left. Just as we got outside, the Bentley slid quietly up to meet us. How did the old man keep doing that? As we drove off I made a careful mental note of exactly where we were.

It was when we were back home sipping the inevitable Horlicks, that I finally got the chance to ask the question that was burning away inside me.

"I'm still curious about one thing," I said.

The old man looked at me enquiringly.

"Who you're selling those test sheets to."

The old man smiled.

"I'll be honest with you," he said. "I confess I don't know. As I told you, we were approached anonymously and told how to blackmail and recruit Darby, and then teach him how to steal those papers. We've never known who our customer was. The first time we performed a handover of the information, which I did myself, some of my people followed me. We decided it would be good to have some knowledge of who we were dealing with. The idea was that my people would follow the person I was handing over to back to wherever he had come from."

The old man paused, looking pensive.

"What happened?"

"We estimate they had at least twelve operatives hidden around our meeting place. They picked up all four of my people almost immediately. My boys were returned eventually, looking slightly worse for wear, with the message that this was our last chance to behave. I have made no other attempts."

"So you've no idea who it is?"

"None whatsoever."

"And you've made no more attempts to find out?"

"No. Occasionally I think about it, but they pay me what amounts to a small fortune for not doing very much work, so I count my blessings instead and leave things as they are, undisturbed. This is why I didn't want you to start meddling in my affairs. This is perhaps a bigger bit of business than you at first thought."

I nodded. You could say that again.

"But perhaps you would like to do the next handover for me. I stopped doing them myself a while back. The boys do them, or Carrot does occasionally. We give them the papers and they give us a large amount of cash in return."

"Yes, I'd be pleased to."

"Good, the next meeting is the day after tomorrow. You never know, perhaps with your skills you can talk them into paying us some more money."

He laughed. My god though, I was thinking, the perfect opportunity to finally figure this business out once and for all. As I was savouring that thought and registering everything he'd told me, I realised the old man was still speaking.

"...doing things. The sad thing about my business at the moment is that there is not one person in the entire organisation that I would trust with making the really big decisions. Not one. Not because they're not good people or that they're not trustworthy, but because they're not strong enough, not capable enough, not dynamic enough to deal with something of this magnitude. I have lots of people who do a very good job for me that I would trust with my life, but they couldn't operate at this level. If only there was somebody in the family who showed just a modicum of talent. Then I would devote all my efforts into grooming them, preparing them, tutoring them... but there isn't anybody, it's very sad for me, but there it is."

He looked over at me.

"Now, if you and Tabitha. ..."

He tailed off.

"No, I don't think so unfortunately. But still. Anyway, that is a conundrum that I have yet to resolve. But now let's talk about you. Obviously you have had to give Mr Finch a rather large sum of money. Is this going to put you in financial difficulty?"

"No, I'm fine, thank you. It's not ideal, but I'll survive."

"Good, I am pleased that you say that. But let's see if there isn't something we can do to get you evened up on that score. What about all this wine of Mr Finch's that I've got cluttering up my warehouse? Have you come up with a way that we can both get our money back and do something about the infuriating Mr Finch?"

I had been giving that a lot of thought. A rough plan was starting to come together in my head.

"Well," I said. "It just so happens that I have had a bit of an idea."

Tomassetti looked interested.

"Good, I'm pleased to hear that, so tell me what you have in mind."

"Its just a thought at the moment, I'm not sure exactly how we put it all together in practice, but I think it might have some legs."

"Go on."

"It's to do with a big charity event that Finch hosts at the Guildhall every year, you've probably heard of it. My idea's a bit complicated, but together I think we could wangle it so that Finch ends up serving the crap wine at his big do. Could be an absolute disaster for him."

I went through the scheme in detail.

Tomassetti broke into a big smile when I'd finished.

"I think it's brilliant. I love it. Public humiliation. Perfect."

"The only problem is finding someone who can do it," I said. "Obviously it can't be you or me."

"Well," said the old man, contemplating. "I believe I have just the man who can do it for us, this is entirely up his street. If anybody can do it he can."

"He sounds impressive, who is he?"

"An associate of mine. Gobbler."

"His name is Gobbler?'

"Yes."

"How did he get a name like that?"

"I've never asked him. And I haven't because I suspect I won't like the answer. I don't like crudity, as you will have noticed."

The old man did one of his amazing invisible summoning's, and a fresh-faced youth wearing a suit two sizes too big for him came haring into the room.

"Ah, Cristiano. This is Mr Jones. Mr Jones, this is Cristiano, a nephew of mine. He is learning the business."

I nodded to the boy and he blushed.

"Cristiano, would you be so kind as to get hold of Mr Gobbler and ask him to come here straight away. Thank you."

The boy scuttled off. The old man and I settled down to another mug of Horlicks each, and talked about his horses. Now he'd shown me everything he wanted to, he said, it was time for a trip out to see his stables and perhaps have an afternoon's racing. He was really passionate about the subject talking effortlessly and in some detail about all his different horses.

And within thirty minutes Gobbler arrived. I don't know where he'd come from, but I got the impression that if he'd been in Timbuktu he would still have got there within the hour. The two men greeted each other warmly, hugs and cheek to cheek kisses.

Gobbler wasn't exactly what I'd expected. He was short, if he was over five feet that would be pushing it, pudgy, thick black hair cut short and a five o'clock shadow that looked like it was permanent. He didn't look English, but I couldn't pinpoint where he was actually from. It was when he spoke that he really lit up. Confident, assertive, self-assured, this really was somebody you'd buy a second-hand car from.

Tomassetti began by telling me all about Gobbler, all the business that they'd done together, and how persuasive Gobbler was and how there wasn't anything he couldn't do or anybody he didn't know. And then he outlined the plan to Gobbler. Gobbler sat there and listened, and when the old man had finished, he didn't ask any questions, he just nodded his head a few times like he was computing it all in his mind.

"It will be a pleasure," he said.

And that was it. Tomassetti told us to liaise. Gobbler and I exchanged phone numbers and off he went.

I was quite stunned by the speed of it all. The only thing I was certain of was I was going to have to get a ticket to Finch's big bash.

By this time I was on about my sixteenth plastic Tesco phone, and I was being really, really careful about where I went and who I was seen with. I'd got into the habit of assuming that there was always someone watching me, and I acted accordingly. Occasionally I thought I was being a touch paranoid, but then I reminded myself that Tomassetti probably still had someone following me, MI5 quite likely did as well, and there was a good chance that Hernandez was lurking around somewhere. And, god forbid, for all I knew Jane had a private detective out there somewhere trying to hunt me down.

I now rang Mimi twice a day to check-in, at midday as well as seven, and Hernandez knew to send in the cavalry if Mimi ever phoned her.

Hernandez and I had had a big get-together and formulated a plan of action. We'd met in a pub about a twenty-minute walk away from where I lived, that had taken me an hour and a half to get to. There was no way that anybody was still trailing me when I did eventually get there, exhausted.

It was Tomassetti telling me that he was having Carrot followed that gave me the germ of a plan, and in the pub I spelled it out to Hernandez. She had a big part to play, but she was also going to be rewarded big time, so that was fair enough I figured. I was counting on discovering who was behind the whole business when I did the handover for the old man, then I was going to get the hell out, get the money from MI5, and then see if I could get Hernandez to change her mind about us. And I wanted to do all of that very quickly.

"I have a plan," I said.

"Do tell," she said sarcastically.

I told her I'd planted a seed of doubt in the old man's mind about Carrot, and I told her that he was now having Carrot followed.

"So Carrot's going to be my scapegoat," I said.

"How's that then?"

"Well, once I've got all the information I need for MI5 and I've handed it all over, I assume they'll come steaming in to do whatever they do in these circumstances, and all hell will be let loose in Tomassetti's mob. They'll be looking for whoever let the cat out of the bag, and obviously I'm going to be a prime suspect, only having been around for five minutes. And that's where you come in."

"I do?"

"Yes. I want you to manufacture a meeting with Carrot, perhaps you can arrest him for questioning or something. It needs to be really obvious that you're a policeman, so either take him back to a police station first, or have a uniformed bobby with you at the beginning, but then I want the two of you to go to a pub or a café somewhere. And don't make it too difficult, this is all for the benefit of the person following Carrot, I don't want him to miss anything."

"And then what?"

"And then, when you leave wherever you are, I want you to give him this. In the doorway of the café or the pub, and in a really obvious way, so that no one can miss it."

I handed her a large brown envelope.

"Is this what I think it is?"

I nodded.

"Fifty thousand pounds."

"Oh god, you idiot, this is awful, I hope nobody's watching us now. I could be strung up for this. And anyway, what am I supposed to say to this Carrot while we're in the café or the pub or wherever we're supposed to be?"

"It doesn't matter. You can talk about the weather, or football, or knitting or anything you like. You can say you fancy him if you want. It's not real, it's just so he can be seen taking money from you. You're a resourceful sort of woman, I'm sure you can think of something."

She blew out a long breath.

"Well, I suppose I can do something like that, but what do I get in exchange?"

"Me?"

"What's that, second prize?" she said, giving me one of her looks. "No seriously, what do I get out of it?"

"Tomassetti has a safe house in Kings Cross. He keeps all his really secret stuff there."

I paused for emphasis.

"Such as details on all the coppers he's bribing."

Hernandez' eyes lit up."

"Once I'm out and safe, I'll tell you where the house is. You're going to have to be very careful though, by the sound of it he's got half the Met on his payroll. You're going to have some very powerful enemies if you try to roll this lot up."

"And this house really has all that information there?"

"Yep."

She sat back looking impressed.

"Well, if all that comes off, I guess I might start thinking a bit more fondly of you again."

I started to say something, but she immediately got up to go.

"But for the moment it's just business, nothing more."

She turned round and flounced off.

"Keep in touch," she shouted over her shoulder.

CHAPTER THIRTY-FOUR
GOBBLER

So Mr Tomassetti comes up with a job for me. He's got some other geezer with him, some smarmy bastard from up west. So they're trying to do a number on that gorilla Finch, and they want to use some dodgy wine that's doing the rounds.

The first thing I do is go over and clock the wine that's being stored in one of Mr Tomassetti's warehouses. It looks pretty impressive. . . . Chateau Margaux . . . looks very fancy. I open up a couple of bottles at random. I don't know much about wine, I'm a gin and tonic man myself, but it seems pretty tasty. It can't stay at the old man's of course, got to keep his name out of it, so I carts it round to my drum. There's a ton of it, so it wasn't easy, I had to get a couple of muckers to help.

Anyway, once that's all done, I go and have a bevy in a pub where I know some of Finch's boys hang out. We all know each other pretty well, everybody in London knows I'm a straight guy, somebody everybody likes dealing with. Hah. If only.

So I get talking to some other faces I know in the pub, and tell them the story I've heard about Finch's wine. The rumour going round is that there was a little switcheroo at some stage, and that the wine Finch got rid of was actually the real deal. I tell it like it's a very funny story that Finch has got stiffed.

A bit later on, I'm on the other side of the pub with some other blokes, and I see the geezers talking to Finch's boys. Very animated too, they had to be telling them about the wine, hoping there was a few bob in it for them.

So, bait taken hopefully. Next port of call was to Jimmy Bean, who was the guy Tomassetti used as the front to buy Finch's wine in the first place. I give Jimmy instructions, that if Finch comes calling, to say he's passed the wine on to Fish Face Barney. He's to say Fish Face Barney always was the buyer, Jimmy Bean was just the middle man, receiving a small commission.

Now, Fish Face Barney is what you might call a small to medium gangster. If Jimmy Bean had still had the wine Finch wouldn't have thought twice about just taking it all back, but Fish Face Barney was a different kettle of … well … fish. Finch could lean on him a bit, but he would have to be a bit careful that he didn't start a war.

So, we get the wine round to Fish Face Barney's, and sure enough, Finch turns up demanding to try a few bottles. Fish Face Barney says, what's all this about? This wine's crap, we both know that, that's why it only cost me forty grand. Let's see, says Finch and they open up a few bottles. It all tastes beautiful. Fish Face Barney acts all surprised. I want it back says Finch. Not a chance, says Fish Face Barney, I looked this stuff up and there's four hundred grand's worth here. So Finch gets heavy, and Fish Face Barney stands up to him a bit and then concedes a bit when Finch starts threatening him, and in the end, they settle on a hundred and fifty grand. You can see Finch isn't entirely happy with the outcome, but equally you can see he doesn't want to take on Fish Face Barney at the moment. Anyway, Finch tells Fish Face Barney that he needs the wine tomorrow as he's going to serve it at a big charity event he's throwing. So far, so good.

First thing in the morning, I'm in the van with two other blokes driving down to some warehouse in Sussex that the smarmy geezer told us about. Lo and behold there's a load of wine, looking exactly the same as the stuff we've got. I get hold of the salesman and take him to one side where I can talk to him quietly. Look, I say, I've heard that this wine's a bit dodgy, proper pony, but I've got a little deal going on where this wine would come in handy. At the right price, of course. It'll be about three hundred grand, says the bloke, although he might be able to swing a bit of a discount. No, I say, I've heard it's proper rough, and I'll do him a favour by taking it off his hands, a hundred thousand knicker. The bloke starts to protest, but I tell him we can do it the easy way or the hard way, I can give him a ten grand bonus, cash in his pocket for being so accommodating, or my boys here can start slicing bits off him until he agrees. Naturally enough he goes for the cash option.

With the wine loaded up, we hot foot it round to Finch's place, drop it off and are on our way before anybody can say how's your father.

So everything's worked out tickety-boo, so far. Then came the difficult bit, getting in to the Guildhall where the big do is. But I have a bit of a brainwave, I pitch up a couple of hours before it's supposed to start, video camera in hand. I'm the official photographer, I say. We've already got one they say. Ah, but he's just for the photos, I say, keeping my fingers crossed. I'm here to do the video. But we've not been told about you, they say. Okay, I say, do you want to be the one to tell Mr Finch why there isn't a video, when he comes looking for it? Hmm, they say, you'd better go in then.

I find a nice little balcony in the corner, with a great view of everything, and I set the camera up.

Everything goes swimmingly at first. I reckon there's about five hundred people there, and Finch is right at the head of the table, acting like he's the king or something. He gets up and gives a welcome speech, thanking everybody for coming, and thanking them for their generosity. He says there's a silent auction after the dinner, and he expects them all to dig deep for the charity. The pride of place in the auction is a particularly fine wine that he will be serving to the guests later, but they'll have the opportunity to buy some for themselves at what could be a very good price. He hopes that they will match his generosity in donating the wine in the first place.

The first course comes along, served with some white wine or other. And then, the main course. Beef it looks like, accompanied by Finch's Chateau Margaux. At first, there are just a few puzzled expressions as people try the wine, then someone at Finch's end of the table actually spits his wine out all over his food, and then so do several other people. This isn't even wine, shouts someone, it's bleach! It's pandemonium, there's wine being gobbed out everywhere, the food's ruined because it's covered in the dodgy plonk that's being spat out, people are shouting and complaining, and quite a few of the most important looking blokes are walking up to Finch's end of the table and asking him what the hell's he up to? Is he trying to poison them or just swindling them by serving up something that isn't even wine.

It's hilarious. Finch just sits there, he hasn't a clue what to do. And the party breaks up. Everybody demands their money back, which of course Finch has to agree to, he hasn't any choice. He sits there looking stunned as everybody leaves, grumbling away and giving him a piece of their mind. I talk to one of the manager chappies a bit later, and he reckoned Finch will have lost a fortune, taking into account the room hire and the food and the other drinks and stuff. Such a shame.

And the best bit of all? I've got it all on film. I think Mr Tomassetti will enjoy having a bit of a sit down and watching that later.

Old Finchy will never be able to show his face in London Town again.

What a lark.

CHAPTER THIRTY-FIVE
FILE UNDER DANGEROUS

So, I pitched up at the old man's house about nine'ish on the day of the handover. It was due to happen at three, and I was overflowing with nervous energy and excitement. It was all I could do to look calm and collected and normal.

"I could do with a hand," said Tomassetti when I walked in.

"Happy to help," I said.

"We're thinking of expanding."

"Yeah?"

"Yes. Uncle Adlai and I have been discussing taking over someone else's business. They're a small operation, but a couple of things they're involved in are quite interesting, could be good additions to our portfolio as it were."

"So where do I come in?"

"Well, taking them over isn't going to be a problem, as I say, they're too small to be able to stand up to us. But usually in these circumstances, there are one or two people who might be worth bringing on board. That's never difficult. Most of these people are happy to work for whoever's the strongest, and as long as they're being paid it's not an issue changing bosses. The difficulty for us is deciding who to keep and who to get rid of. So, what we do is, we have files on all our competition. Everybody. As detailed as we can make them. So, for example, I have files as thick as your arm on people like Finch and Strutter, and files, smaller ones, on all their senior people. Know your enemy, as they say. And we go in for profiling. I have people who do that for me. Experts. It can be very useful. You should see the file they produced on you. Old Uncle Adlai had a fit when I gave it to him. He doesn't believe in such things, he would judge you purely by how many people you've killed."

I raised my eyebrows.

"But I think it is very useful," he went on. "It is surprisingly accurate an awful lot of the time. I wouldn't want to rely solely on that kind of information of course, at the end of the day I trust my instincts over everything else, but it is a useful tool to have in your armoury. Anyway, I thought you might help me go through the profiles of the characters we're going to be dealing with and help me decide who, if any, might be worth keeping on."

"I'd love to," I said. "I've never done anything like that before. I think I'd find it very interesting."

"Excellent," said the old man. "I suspect it's something you might be very good at. All right, let's go. We've got plenty of time before you do the handover."

And off we went, back to the secret house in Kings Cross. Everything was the same when we got there. The Bentley dropped us off and disappeared in a cloud of dust, the old man and Chaim embraced as though they hadn't seen each other for years, and we worked our way down to the basement. The funny thing about the street, I thought, as we inched our way down the stairs, was that on both my visits, there hadn't been a soul to be seen anywhere. I wondered if he owned every property there. I wouldn't put it past him.

"There are six people I want to have a look at," he said, when we'd got inside. "You take that filing cabinet and I'll take this one. You'll find Artie the Glass, E for B and Mincer in yours. It's all in alphabetical order."

"Blimey," I said. "Are these real people? Where do they get these names from?'

The old man laughed.

"Take out the whole file, and we'll go back to the house to look at them."

They were easy enough to find. Everything was very ordered, very neat, and immaculately filed. A lot of the files were of people, but there were also files with business names, what I took to be the names of operations and all sorts of other stuff that I had no idea what they were.

I took out Artie the Glass and E for B, but just as I reached for Mincer I realised his file was neatly sandwiched in between one labelled Metropolitan Police and one labelled Ministry of Defence. Jesus. I couldn't believe it, I almost stopped breathing I was so surprised. What an opportunity. This might be the answer to all my prayers.

"Everything all right?" called the old man.

"Just coming," I was sure the old man would notice what I was doing, but he seemed oblivious.

I held my breath and pulled the name tags off the Police and MoD files, put the files underneath the two I was already holding, and put Mincer's under those. I turned round just as the old man did, holding his three files under his arm. I was convinced he would be able to hear my heart beating.

I was conscious I was staring at him and he looked at me a bit quizzically.

"Here," I said quickly. "Let me carry those for you."

He handed the files over and I tucked them under the five I already had. It was quite a big pile by now. The old man closed everything up and we went back upstairs and outside. The Bentley appeared out of nowhere.

We sat in the back together and I placed the files on the floor between my feet. We arrived back at the house and I let the old man get out momentarily before me. As he did, I slipped the two extra files under the seat in front of me and put my phone on the floor.

The next few hours were spent going through the files together. It was fascinating stuff, profiling was something I'd never come across before. Some of the conclusions they came to from very little information was astonishing, but like the old man said, it was useful as a tool, nothing more. Especially as these guys were just a bunch of thugs and hoodlums, it wasn't like we were recruiting them for their brains.

After a while the old man announced that it was time for a break and did I want a Horlicks? I reached for my phone, couldn't find it, and ostentatiously patted down all my pockets.

"Can't find my phone," I said. "Can I check the car?"

"I'll get Carlos to look for it." Carlos had been our driver for the last few weeks.

"I'll do it," I said. "I wouldn't mind getting a breath of fresh air at the same time, clear my head. I'm not used to all this paperwork, I get somebody else to do it for me usually."

The old man laughed. Ten seconds later Carlos appeared. How did he keep doing that?

"Give Mr Jones the car keys please, Carlos. He might have left something in the back."

Carlos gave me the keys and I went outside. Again, my heart was beating like a hammer drill. I really wasn't cut out for this line of work.

I opened the car and got in the back. Quickly picking up the phone, I dialled Hernandez. God be praised she answered the phone straight away.

"Listen," I said. "This is urgent, I haven't got time to talk. Get round to Tomassetti's house straight away. You know the Bentley he uses, under the car behind the back wheel are two files. Get them and get the hell away. Copy everything in the files, and then when you have the meeting with Carrot, give him the original files along with the money. Got it?"

"Jones?"

"No. No, no time to talk or I'll get blown. Can you do that?"

"I guess so, but..."

I hung up. I slipped the files behind the back wheel of the car and rushed back into the house. I put the car keys down on the little ornate table.

"Find it?"

"Yeah, it was just on the seat. Thanks."

"And the fresh air?"

"Bracing. I'll take a coat next time. I don't get enough fresh air, I think. I should go for a nice stiff walk every day probably, I'm sure it would do me the power of good."

"Very wise, my friend, very wise. A healthy mind in a healthy body, as they say."

We went back to work. We concluded that none of them were really suitable. Artie the Glass might work at a very low level, but with a name like that I really had my doubts about him.

"What about the boss," I asked. "No file on him."

"Sadly he won't survive the take-over. Very unfortunate."

I had no answer to that.

A couple of hours later I found myself sitting outside a café-bar in Covent Garden. I couldn't help it, but it was impossible not to imagine myself a real spy as I waited for my contact to turn up. I felt like I was in the middle of a Le Carre novel or something; I tried to look enigmatic and mysterious.

There was an espresso and a brandy chaser in front of me, and a large Marks & Spencer carrier bag at my feet. Rather obviously. That was my identification. I looked round at the other tables, all of which were full. It had turned out to be quite a nice day and the tourists were out in force. The place was heaving;

what were the chances of at least one other person having an M&S bag with them I thought?

My bag contained Darby's latest sheets. The bag I would end up taking away would, in theory, contain a large amount of money. As I sat there sipping my drinks and looking round, I identified at least four characters who I reckoned could be my contact's minders. It wasn't anything obvious, they all looked normal, were dressed very conservatively, weren't doing anything unusual, but there was just a sniff of something about them. It was just an instinct, but I would have bet my bottom dollar they were who I thought they were. This was a great place for a meet though, huge open space with thousands of people milling about. Tomassetti had told me that they moved the meeting place round every few weeks or so, but it was always somewhere very public like this.

A tall, thin man walked into the square and instantly I knew this was my guy. He looked ordinary enough, but there was just something about him that made him stand out, something imperceptible. It was when he came a bit nearer and I could see the M&S bag swinging at his side that I knew I was right. My instincts were still good, I thought. I was pretty sure I was right about his guards as well.

The guy looked around for a bit and then came over and plonked himself down at my table. Well I say plonked, but it was more like he folded himself into his chair, he was all arms and legs like a preying mantis. He was in his forties, balding, very conservatively dressed and with an almost featureless face. He would be very difficult to describe to someone else. He put his bag on the floor next to mine.

"Morning," he said. "You're new."

"Is that the code phrase?" I asked. "You say 'You're new', and I reply by saying 'the clouds are in the east tonight' or something."

He laughed.

"Bit corny all that sort of stuff," he said. "We're not in the movies you know."

"And that's not corny?" I looked down at the two M&S bags sat side by side.

The guy laughed again.

"Point taken. But I'll be honest with you, sometimes we do things for show, just to keep you people entertained. None of it really matters how we do it."

He ordered a cappuccino from a passing waiter and refolded his legs under himself.

His drink came and he raised his cup to me in salutation.

"Good to do business with you," he said. "Are you going to be the regular meet from now on?"

"Perhaps," I said. "I'll see how it goes. I need to find out a few things first before I decide if I'm in or not. Who are you people for a start?"

"No, I don't think so," he laughed. "If you ever find out who we are then that's the end of this bit of business. Better for everybody that way. You're being paid to be our fall guys if anything ever goes wrong. Would be no point if you could put the finger on us, would there? Anyway, no skin off my nose if it's you or somebody else doing the handover."

He drained his coffee noisily and got up to go.

"Wait," I said. "What about the stuff we're giving you, the battery development, can you tell me anything about that?"

He gave me a sort of sideways look and sat down again.

"Battery development? What are you on about? This isn't about battery development."

"No? Well what is it then?"

He snorted.

"Well, I suppose there's no harm in telling you, to be honest we'd assumed that you people would've worked it out by now.

You have all the details, wouldn't take anybody with half a brain too long to work out what it's all about."

"Well we haven't."

"Obviously not. Well, it's to do with a new sort of nerve agent that's being developed. Chemical weapons and all that, you know?"

I felt my mouth sag open.

"You know what a nerve agent is right?"

I nodded. I was dumbfounded, I'd only asked him the question to take his attention away from a little kerfuffle that was taking place on the other side of the square where two of my guys had started an altercation with one of the minders. Pleasingly it was one of the people I thought I'd spotted.

"They told me it was an everlasting battery," I said.

"Then either they're leading you up the garden path, or you guys really aren't as bright as we thought you were. Anyway it's a good job your government hasn't managed to develop this stuff yet, otherwise they'd be in big trouble. You'd better hope that they don't manage it. See you."

With that he picked up my M&S bag and was off, leaving me stunned and not a little confused. Every time I discovered something more about this business it got a little bit heavier and a lot more perplexing.

"Piece of cake."

I was in the Spotted Horse savouring a pint of proper beer with two old mates of mine, Spook and Beaky.

"You were right," Beaky was saying. "There were twelve of them watching what was going on, very professional by the look of them, knew what they were doing I would say."

"But there was no problem?" I asked.

"Nah," said Spook. "Easy. We took out the one furthest away from the others. Waited till there were a lot of people close to him, then Beaky knocked into an old lady who fell on top of him, I tripped over them as well and lifted his wallet while I was on the way down."

"We were in and out in a couple of seconds," went on Beaky. "He was left on the floor under the old girl with his mates none the wiser while we hopped it. Here. You might be surprised at this"

He tossed a small black wallet onto the table. I held my breath and opened it. In the see through section of the wallet was a pass. It said it was issued by the United States Department of State and was a Diplomatic Identification Card. It went on to say that someone called Nat Spikesly was a member of the United States Embassy, London. A picture of Nat Spikesly was embedded in the card. He looked thoroughly dislikeable.

"Wow." I looked up at Beaky.

"Yep," he nodded. "CIA."

I was supposed to take the money in the M&S bag to the old man the next morning. I was desperate to take everything I knew straight round to MI5, but I didn't want to bring the spotlight down on me too early. It was important to carry on as normal before everything hit the fan. Once I'd delivered the money we were supposed to be going out to look at one of the old man's stables. He was going to show me his horses. With any luck I could duck out of that and sneak over to Millbank later in the afternoon.

I was just locking my front door before going to look for a cab, when I realised somebody was standing very close to me. I looked round, it was the two goons.

"Hey boys," I said. "You didn't need to come and get me, I can catch a cab easily enough."

Then something hit me very hard on the back of the head and the last thing I remember thinking as I slid into uncon-sciousness, was how would I find a cab now.

I woke up tied to a hard backed chair in a small dark room. My head was killing me. My mouth was bone dry and there was a good chance I was going to be sick any moment. There were no clues as to where I was. Tomassetti was sitting in a chair in front of me and the goons were standing behind him looking like they were thoroughly enjoying themselves. The old man was staring sadly at me.

"What's going on?" I said. "What is this?"

The old man slowly got to his feet. He stood looking down at me and then he hit me in the face, very hard, with the back of his hand. I felt my nose crack and blood gush down over my mouth and chin. The old man went back to his chair.

I spat out a mouthful of blood and tried again.

"What? What is it?"

One of the goons made a move towards me, but the old man put up a hand to stop him. He was still staring at me with those sad old eyes. He took a handkerchief out of his pocket and wiped the blood off his fist. He sighed.

"Mr Jones, I can't begin to tell you how disappointed I am. Not because you've let me down, that's human nature unfortunately; that's always going to happen. But because I had allowed myself to like you, allowed myself to think that we could do something very special together. You've left me feeling very stupid and very embarrassed. I'm disappointed in myself. And now I've got everybody telling me that they told me so, that they all knew you were no good. You've put me in a very difficult situation, something that I'm going to have to work very hard at to turn round because now everybody thinks I'm a stupid old man."

I started to shake my head, but the pain made me stop immediately.

"What have I done?" I said. "I don't understand." All I could think of was to keep protesting my innocence. Some plan. I was certain there would be rows of frozen meat carcasses hanging behind me if only I could turn round and look.

The old man sighed again.

"Oh Mr Jones. Don't do this. Don't spend the little time you have left in this world being such a person. Live the rest of your short life like a man. Take responsibility for your actions. Stand up and be accountable for what you have done."

"But I don't know what I'm supposed to have done. Tell me, for god's sake, I haven't a clue."

"Oh Mr Jones, that makes me so sad I can hardly bear to talk to you any more. But let's get this over with. I was going to say this hurts me more than you, but I don't suppose that's actually true. But it pains me a great deal even so that it has come to this."

I tried to say something, but my mouth was so full of dried blood where I'd tried to breath that I couldn't talk properly. I mumbled something, but even I didn't know what it was I said.

"I went back to Chaim's house last night, Mr Jones. There were one or two things I needed, and as luck would have it, I needed something from the filing cabinet last touched by you. And of course, I quickly realised that there were two files missing, two very important files."

I felt my whole body go limp. There was no way back from this. He reached over and pulled my head up by the chin so that we were looking at each other.

"Tell me why you took them. I need to know if you're working for somebody else or if you just saw an opportunity to make some money because of your greed. I need to know, and I can assure that I will find out, because I have ways of being very persuasive. Listen to me, Mr Jones, this isn't going to be very nice for me, but it's going to be appalling for you. Tell me what I want to know, tell me everything, and it will be a lot easier for both of us."

He flicked a couple of fingers and one of the goons threw a bucket of water over me. I had no idea water could hurt so much, but it cleared my mouth a bit.

"It wasn't me," I managed to say quietly. "I don't know anything about it. You have to believe me."

I tried to shake my head for emphasis, but I couldn't move it. It was all I could do to keep it from slumping down onto my chest again.

"Oh, Mr Jones. This is so foolish. I will find out, you know, you will tell me everything. It won't take me very long, but it will be a miserable death for you. You deserve better. Come, let's make a deal, you tell me what I want to know and I'll promise you a quick death and a decent burial. Perhaps I will invite your friends so they can pay their last respects. Otherwise, you'll just be slung into the alley with all the other rubbish, in several bin bags. So, how does that sound?"

"There's nothing I can tell you," I croaked. "You've got the wrong man."

"Oh dear. So unfortunate. Well, Mr Jones, I'm afraid to say...."

But I never found out what he was afraid to say. At that moment the door opened, and somebody I couldn't see came in. There were some whispered words between the pair of them, and then they all went out, the goons included.

It was very quiet and very still. Alone with my thoughts I started wondering if anybody would miss me when I was gone. I had a lot of friends, a lot of people I got on with pretty well, had a good time with. But would they really miss me? They wouldn't even know I wasn't around any more in all honesty.

Would Hernandez miss me? I hoped so. Perhaps there would be quiet moments when she would remember and wonder. I remembered the time I'd kissed her outside the pub. I could almost taste it.

I was still savouring that kiss when Tomassetti walked back in. Here we go I thought. I closed my eyes and steeled myself.

"It appears there has been a misunderstanding."

What? What? What?

"What?"

"It appears I have made a mistake in jumping to the conclusion that I did about you. We have in fact found the real culprit. This is going to sound very hollow, but I hope you can accept my sincerest apologies for what has happened."

None of this filtered through to me properly, I was in shock. Was this some sort of horrible new game they were playing on me?

They untied me, and the two goons helped me out of the room. My legs didn't work very well, so I was half carried, half dragged. I realised I must have been in the basement of Tomassetti's house. They took me to his little room and sat me on a sofa.

"We have a doctor here for you," said the old man. Tenderly. He was standing over me looking concerned.

A man came over and started wiping the blood off my face. He then examined me, concentrating on the back of my head and my nose.

"You've got a very big lump here," he said, fingering the swelling. "It must have been quite a nasty bang. There's only a small abrasion, so you don't need stitches. It's going to hurt quite a bit and you will almost certainly have a concussion that you will need to monitor carefully, but there shouldn't be anything to worry about long term. Your nose is definitely broken. I'll put something on it to protect it, but you'll need to go to hospital and have it x-rayed as soon as possible. You're going to be shockingly bruised tomorrow, your eyes are looking pretty bad already. But other than that you're as fit as a fiddle."

A syringe appeared in front of my face.

"This might sting a bit," he said. "But it will help." I felt something sharp in my arm, and then nothing more.

I awoke slowly, my eyelids didn't seem to work properly. Everything looked very woolly. I had no idea where I was or what had happened.

"Ah Mr Jones. Welcome back."

It was the old man. I blinked hard a couple of times and he slowly came into focus.

"How are you feeling?"

"I don't know," I said slowly, mentally examining all the aches and pains in my body. "Well … surprisingly good, actually."

"Aha, he is a bit of whiz is our Doctor Manjelligan. You've been asleep for about an hour, enough time for the concoction he gave you to work its way through your body. It's a very clever mix of all sorts of good things, his own recipe, you might say. And not something you would want to take too often either. But in the circumstances I think your body deserves something nice happening to it."

We stared at each other for a little while. The old man did look genuinely upset. I didn't want to say anything because I didn't want to land myself in trouble again. I still wasn't entirely convinced that this wasn't some trick to catch me off guard and fool me into saying something I'd regret.

"I'm afraid we weren't very kind to you," said the old man eventually. "But the doctor has given you a good going over, and he tells me there is nothing too serious. I know it's difficult for you to think this at the moment, but we can all be very thankful things didn't get any worse than they did. We were very fortunate with the timing."

"What's going on?" I managed to croak.

"Well, when I discovered the files were missing, you seemed to be the obvious culprit, I think you can understand the reasons why I came to that conclusion. You were the newest person into our organisation and you were the last person to have access to my files. The evidence pointed to you. Hence why I acted the way I did. But fortunately, in the nick of time you might say, we were able to discover who the real perpetrator was."

"And who was it?"

"Carrot."

"Carrot? You're joking."

"I only wish I was my friend. It has upset me that it is him, as much as it upset me when I thought it was you."

"But how do you know? What happened?"

The old man let out a big unhappy sigh before continuing.

"I was having Carrot followed. You seeing him with that woman had put a little bit of doubt in my mind, and as you have come to realise, I am a very, very careful man. So he has been watched. And lo and behold, he gets picked up by a police car, and inside the car are a uniformed policeman and ... that very same woman you saw him with. When we investigate, we discover that she is a Detective Inspector in the Metropolitan Police."

"Wow."

"Yes, indeed. My first thought was how can such a woman be doing such a thing, but that's by the by. Anyway, the car drops them off at a public house, and this Inspector and Carrot go inside. My people observe them at a distance. They talk for a while, we don't know what about, but eventually they get up to go and the woman gives Carrot a large brown envelope, which we later discover contains fifty thousand pounds ... and my missing files."

"Christ, I can't believe it." I managed to put a lot of surprise in my voice, but the thing I was having trouble believing was that Hernandez had acted so quickly. How did she know? "When was this?"

"Earlier today. Just in time to save your life as it happens."

I swallowed hard. I didn't like to be reminded how close to being a death experience it had been. I forced myself to continue to act as though this was all a complete shock to me.

"How did he do it? How did he get the files?"

"Unfortunately, I do not know. He talked his way into the house somehow I suppose, paid someone perhaps. He might have had the files for some considerable time for all I know. But because of my boys' overzealousness it looks like I will never find out."

"Why, what do you mean?"

"Come, I'll show you. Can you walk?"

I got to my feet. I felt a bit woozy at first, but my head cleared and I found I could move okay. The old man took my elbow as a precaution anyway.

We went back down to the basement where I had been held, and walked down a dark miserable corridor until we stopped outside a nondescript metal door. Tomassetti turned the handle and pushed the door open.

Carrot was inside, tied to a chair exactly as I had been. His head was lolling on his chest. There was blood everywhere. He tried to stir at the noise of the door opening, but it didn't look he had much life left in him. Eventually he managed to raise his head a fraction. His face was covered in so much blood that all I could see of his features were two terrified eyes staring out at me. He opened his mouth as though to say something, but all that came out was an agonised sounding croak. His mouth looked like a vivid crimson gash. His head slumped back onto his chest.

"What happened to him," I whispered. I was appalled.

"He was making a lot of noise apparently," said the old man. "The boys got so fed up they took out a lot of their anger on him. Amongst other things they cut out his tongue."

I turned away, I couldn't look any more. The old man came and took my arm again and took me back to his room. I tried to get the image of Carrot's mutilated face out of my mind by focussing on the fact that he was a violent, murdering psychopath and deserving of everything he got.

"Are you all right?" asked the old man.

"I told you before, I'm not a violent man. I haven't come across anything like that before. It's left me a bit shaken to be honest."

"Yes, I can see that. Perhaps Uncle Adlai was correct when he said you wouldn't have the stomach for our line of work. Unfortunately the boys never liked Carrot, so at the first opportunity they got their own back on him. They have left him very close to death. That is a great pity, because it means I will probably never find out how he got the file. I'm going to have to make a lot of assumptions about who may or may not have helped him. Chaim for instance. I have known Chaim my whole life, but he has let me down, whether knowingly or unknowingly, and he will have to pay the ultimate penalty."

He sighed.

"And of course it also means I will also have to discipline the boys for being so impetuous and so stupid. But there you are, what will be, will be. I have decided to give Carrot a quick death. He is almost there now, there is nothing to be gained by prolonging things."

Oh Jesus, another carcass for the freezer.

"My next problem of course," the old man went on. "Is discovering what this Police Inspector will do with the information. I will have to call in a lot of favours and spend a great deal of money ensuring nothing comes of it, I fear."

The old man paused.

"And then there is you and I, Mr Jones. What of us?"

We looked at each other for a while. I was determined not to fill this silence. I wanted everything to come from him.

"To my eternal regret," he went on eventually. "I suspect that our friendship is over. When something like this happens, there will always be a doubt lurking at the back of both of our minds. Something that will always stop us trusting each other. And without that trust there can be nothing. What we had has been irreparably broken I fear. It is my fault I know, and for that I am truly sorry."

I pretended to think about what he'd said for a while.

"Yes," I said. "You're right. I think it's going to take me a long time to get over this."

The old man nodded, and then with a big sigh, got up out of his chair.

"It would be my hope that we part, if not exactly friends, then as something a little more than people who met once and did a little business together. I will always be here if you need some help of any kind. But I must leave now, I have to go and talk to some policemen. You are welcome to stay here as long as you like, but if you want to go now, Carlos will drive you."

"No, I'm fine," I said. "I'll walk, I could do with some fresh air."

The old man smiled. He came over and we shook hands.

"So, with sorrow and my deepest apologies for what has happened, I will say goodbye. Good luck, Mr Jones."

He turned to go.

"Oh, by the way," he said. "I'm giving you the wine. As an inadequate way of trying to make amends. Call me some time and let me know where you want it delivered."

I nodded again.

"It's the good stuff," he said.

CHAPTER THIRTY-SIX
THE PREYING MANTIS

I've told you, I've no idea what's going on. I didn't know anything had happened. We did the swap, same as always, I took the papers and he took the cash. If something went wrong it wasn't from my end.

Yeah, he was new, never seen him before. But I had no reason to suspect there was anything wrong; he had the papers in the bag, knew exactly what was supposed to happen. I would say he had a bit more about than some of the others though. The old man is all right of course, we know all about him, but the younger ones he sends along, I'd be surprised if they even know what day it is. And that shaven-headed thug who's been doing it lately, what a liability. He always looks like he's about to jump up and kill someone.

He did ask a lot of questions though. None of the others ever seemed the slightest bit interested, especially the thug. Not even the time of day from him. But this one was curious. Wanted to know who we were. Didn't tell him of course. But then he wanted to know what the papers were about. So I told him, I would have thought they'd have worked it out by now anyway. He seemed genuinely surprised when I told him. They really hadn't worked it out. But what do you expect from a bunch of gangsters.

I don't think that was the wrong thing to do, I disagree. I don't see that had anything to do with anything. It was that Spikesly's fault, letting himself be jumped like that. He only had one job and he failed. Miserably. There's only one person to blame here.

What would I do now? I'd put the heavies on Tomassetti and gang, find out what they know and what's going on. I'd track down the guy who I did the handover with, and I'd waste him. And whoever was with him that lifted Spikesly's wallet. Silence them once and for all.

And I'd probably silence the old man and his gang so that there's no danger of anybody lifting the lid on this. This is too important. We can get somebody else to get the information for us, or we can do it ourselves. Not a problem. They're all expendable.

But I won't be doing it? Why not? I didn't do anything wrong. I'm on tomorrow's flight back to Washington? But that's not fair. This is nothing to do with me.

What about my wife? What do you mean I'll never see her again?

No, please.

CHAPTER THIRTY-SEVEN
ALL WRAPPED UP

Outside the old man's house I gratefully breathed a big lung-ful of fresh air. It felt wonderful. In fact I felt surprisingly good considering what I'd just been through. It occurred to me that perhaps the doctor's injection was just a big dose of con-centrated Horlicks.

My phone rang.

"It's me." It was Hernandez. "I'm watching you from the other side of the street. Don't look round. Find yourself a cab and drive to a pub a long way from here. Take a circular route. I'll follow you in my car and see you there."

She hung up.

I did as I was told. There was a cab waiting at the end of the street and I jumped in it. It was the same driver I'd asked to fol-low the goons all those weeks ago. He recognised me.

"Hello," he said. "It's Dick Tracy. Stone the crows, you look a sight."

I put my hand up to my face. My nose was covered in plaster. I hadn't realised, the doc must have done it while I was out for the count.

"Want me to follow someone again?" he laughed.

"Well funnily enough, I want you to make sure I'm not being followed," I said.

I looked over my shoulder and winced at the effort it took. I could see Hernandez' car behind us.

"Do you see that Ford Focus behind you? Well, I want to keep that one with us, but I need to make sure nobody else tags along, so take as stupid a route as you like and take as long as you like."

The cabby let out a raucous laugh.

"Blimey, you're a right one you are, I've heard it all now. But whatever you say, guv, you're the boss. Where to then?"

My mind went a complete blank, with a million pubs in London I couldn't remember the names of any of them. Was this the concussion I wondered? And then one suddenly flashed into my mind.

"The Leg of Lamb. Farringdon."

"I know it," said the driver, and we set off.

I sat back. It was probably a stupid choice, but I felt like seeing it again, just for old times sake. Just as long as it wasn't Wednesday I thought suddenly, I didn't want to walk into Darby doing his handover.

I thought hard, but for the life of me I couldn't actually remember what day it was.

"Hello Terry."

Terry the Glove looked up from the newspaper he'd been reading with a start.

"What? Oh, hello. Cor, who's been knocking you about then? That looks a sore one."

The Lamb looked the same as ever, reassuringly so. Deathly quiet though, there was only one other customer in there, sitting morosely in the corner over his pint.

"Bit of a misunderstanding that's all," I said. "All sorted now. How have you been?"

He looked even more glum than he usually did.

"Not so hot really. Guess who turned up?"

I shrugged.

"Walton."

"Really?"

"Yeah, they fished him out of the Grand Union Canal at Paddington a couple of days ago."

"Oh no. Dead?"

"Might just as well be. He's gone doolally. Hair's turned completely white and all he does is mumble nonsense to himself. Nobody's been able to get a sensible word out of him. Reckon someone scared him so much he lost his mind."

"I'm sorry to hear that."

"Naah, he was a tosser. Trouble is, now they've found him, they're selling the pub. Somebody will buy it and turn it into some poncy gastro pub probably. Won't want me any more."

Terry looked so fed up and so pitiful, that I actually felt a little bit sorry for him.

"Don't worry Terry, I'll look out for you."

He brightened up a bit at that, and then looked over my shoulder.

"'Ere, who's this coming your way? This your bird then?"

I looked round. Hernandez was walking towards us. The state of my face made her give me a second look.

"Christ," she said, startled. "Hope the other guy looks as bad as you."

"Funny," I said. "Brandy?"

She nodded. Terry brought us the drinks and I took them over to Darby's table. It made me feel all sort of warm and nostalgic. I think that whatever that doctor had given me was still coursing up and down my body. I bet I was going to feel rough in the morning though.

"I can see I was right to have been worried about you," she said, looking closely at my face. "Are you okay? You look terrible."

"I'm fine. Their doctor pumped me full of something, so I'm feeling pretty good at the moment, nothing really hurts."

"It looks like it should hurt."

"Yeah."

I paused.

"You know, it was pretty much touch and go in there for a while."

"I thought it might have been. That's why I didn't waste any time."

"Yeah?"

"Yeah, it was your auntie Mimi phoning me that started everything off. You hadn't rung her, so I figured the best thing for me to do was to incriminate your mate as soon as possible."

Ah, of course, my security calls. When I first considered doing them I thought I was just being melodramatic. I would have laughed if somebody had told me they were going to save my life.

"So what did you do?"

"Well, ever since we last talked, I've had a team tailing your man. And we've been keeping an eye on the other two who have been watching him as well. Very amateurish if I may say so, they had no idea we were there as well. So as soon as I heard from Mimi, I jumped in a squad car, grabbed a PC and hared round to where my guys told me Carrot was. Walking down Oxford Street as it happens. So, making it as obvious as we could, we screech up beside him and bundle him into the car. And then, very slowly, we drive to a pub round the corner, and Carrot and I go in."

"So, it turns out you're very good at this then," I smiled.

"I'm a natural. We sit there for a while, he keeps asking me what's going on, and I just keep talking nonsense to him. His two trackers are in the corner watching us, but they wouldn't have been able to hear what we were saying. Then I get up to go. And as I do, I say to him, 'you might find these of interest' and I give him the file and money. And I make sure the whole pub can see it. I leave him sitting there opening up the envelope. I wait outside for a bit, hidden, and then they all come out, with the other two holding Carrot very tightly by the arms. A car pulls up a few minutes later and they all get in and speed off."

"Poor old Carrot."

"You say that, but you said he was the one who killed the MI5 man. And he was probably the one who tortured poor old Paradine to death."

"Yeah, it was. He really was a nasty piece of work. He didn't deserve any better."

And then a thought hit me.

"Well, actually, I say that it was him, but I don't really know for sure. I've no real evidence, to be honest."

"Oh well, hopefully I'll be able to sort out who did what when I start making a few arrests. But tell me what happened to you."

So I told her. Everything. From when I'd got up that morning until she'd rung me as I was leaving Tomassetti's. And it was tough telling it. It didn't help having to watch the growing concern on Hernandez' face as I described the sheer horror of what had gone on.

"My god," she said, when I'd finished. She shuddered. "There must have been just minutes in it. If something had come up to delay me, you'd be dead now. I don't even like to think about it. You know, I shouldn't let you out of my sight. You're not to be trusted on your own."

"That's a nice thought," I smiled.

"At least you're alive, that's the main thing," she said. "Anyway, what have you got for me?"

I told her everything. I told her about the secret house in Kings Cross, and I gave her the address, which she wrote down in a little notebook. I told her about Chaim, if he was still alive, and I told her about the filing cabinets. I told her about all the other people I'd met, I told her about the command centre in Mayfair, and I told her as much as I could remember about everything else the old man had shown me. And then I told her that the last thing he had said to me before I left, was that he was off to keep her quiet. He was intending to spend a lot of money making sure of it.

I could see the light of battle in her eyes.

"Are you sure you're up to taking on the rest of the police force on your own?" I said.

"Ready? It's what I've spent my whole life getting ready for. You won't believe this or understand it, but I believe passionately in what I do. The police force, and everybody in it, should represent everything that's good about our society, and they, more than anybody else should be above suspicion, should be whiter than white. I believe in honesty, and I believe in fairness and decency, for everybody, no matter who they are or what they do. It eats me up inside that there are people at the top of our profession making money out of letting animals like Tomassetti get away with the misery they inflict on innocent people. I wouldn't expect you to understand that for a moment."

I sat back, I was quite overwhelmed by how much passion she'd shown saying all that.

"No, I do understand," I said. "I think I feel the same way deep down, but somewhere along the way, my life turned in a certain direction, and I just seemed to have been stuck with it."

I wasn't sure that was exactly the way I felt, but it seemed a good thing to say. The really worrying thing was that I'd actually felt quite defensive when she described Tomassetti as an animal. I'd almost said something in his defence, but managed to bite my tongue.

Hernandez gave me one of her looks.

"Yeah, right," she said.

"Seriously though," I said. "You're going to have to be really careful, you're going to make an awful lot of enemies."

She laughed.

"Well, that's my problem, I'll figure it out somehow. Don't forget I'm a professional, and I'm bloody good at my job, and, despite what you may think, there are still a lot of good, honest coppers around who will be on my side, fortunately not everybody at the Met is bent. Anyway, did you get a chance to see what was in the files you stole?"

I shook my head.

"No, it was a bit of a rush job. It was very hairy getting them out at all, I can tell you."

"I can imagine. Well, the police file is amazing; names, dates, places, amounts, everything I could possibly have dreamed of. The only thing that can stop me putting them away for a long time is them closing ranks against me. So I need to move very quickly before they react. You've really come through for me with this."

I looked at her hopefully.

"The other file is very disappointing though, I'm afraid. Nothing much of use in there at all, all it does is implicate their contact at the MoD. I'm afraid you're back to square one with finding out what's going on for your spies."

She stopped when she saw the smug expression on my face.

"What?"

"All sorted. I know who it was."

"Who?"

"Well, I can hardly believe it, in fact I'm not sure I do believe it. Turns out it's the Americans, the CIA, stealing the details of some sort of nerve agent that we're supposed to be developing.

"What? You're joking, like chemical weapons?"

"Yep."

"But why would the Americans be stealing from us? We're on the same side."

"God knows. I don't understand any of it. All I know is I'm off to MI5. I'm going to tell them everything, get my money and get the hell out again."

"Well I suppose it ties in with the fact that the information was coming out of Porton Down. That's amazing though. How did you find out?"

I explained what had happened and she whistled softly.

"That's really something."

I nodded.

We sat in silence for a while and looked at each other across the table.

"Do you know," she said. "That purple bruising really brings out the blue in your eyes."

We smiled at each other.

"You saved my life," I said.

"I suppose I did. That must mean you'll be in my debt forever."

"That sounds a like a good thing."

"Maybe."

We subsided back into silence for a little while. She was still staring intently at me.

"So this is it," I said.

"I guess so."

"It's been an adventure."

"You can say that again."

I paused, I didn't know what to say or how to say it.

"You and me...."

Hernandez put a finger up to my lips to stop me.

"There isn't a you and me, I keep telling you that. At this moment, in this pub, in this now, there is no you and me. All there is, is a policeman and a crook getting together in a temporary collaboration to achieve their own ends. That's all. Although...." she stopped and smiled. "...I have to say, they do make a very good team."

We sat there for a while, just looking at each other, until eventually she took a big breath.

"I'd better get going," she said softly. "I've got a big operation to put in place before Tomassetti and his cronies get everything wrapped up. I don't want to, but if I don't go now. ...."

She tailed off, smiling.

"Somehow I don't think this this is going to be the last we're going to see of each other."

I laughed.

"Like a bad penny I am, I'll always turn up. Don't worry about that."

We stood up and embraced. We did kiss, but only briefly, my nose got in the way and it hurt.

"We'll come back to that when you're recovered," she said. "Are you sure you'll be all right if I leave you here?"

I nodded.

"Let me know how you get on with your spooks."

Terry came over as Hernandez made her way to the door.

"I'd give her one," he said, as we watched her walk away.

"You do know she's a police inspector, right?"

"What? Ere, you're not plod an all, are you?"

"No," I laughed. "But I am considering a change in career."

"Yeah? Not thinking of going straight, are you?"

"Maybe. Who knows."

"Don't talk bonkers, you'll never change."

He snorted derisively and walked back to the bar.

I did feel terrible when I woke up the next morning, there wasn't one bit of me that didn't hurt, but I needed to get everything out of the way, so I rang Lambert at the number he had given me. I told him I'd found out who was buying the secrets.

"You're joking?"

"No, I know. And I've got proof."

There was a long silence.

"You'd better come round to the office then."

I thought he might have sounded a bit more enthusiastic, but there you go. I cabbed it round to Millbank straight away. If I thought I'd get in a bit quicker as it was my second visit, I was sadly mistaken. Apparently I didn't look like my photograph any more, which wasn't altogether a surprise considering what had happened to my face. But I did get in eventually, and without having to sign the Official Secrets Act 1989 again, which was a bonus.

So, sometime later, I was sitting in Lambert's broom cupboard of an office, watching him watching me.

"So?" he said eventually.

I threw the wallet across the table to him.

Gingerly he picked it up and looked inside. He did his best to conceal it but I could see the surprise on his face.

"Where did you get this?"

"Out of the pocket of one of the people who were watching their agent do the handover with me."

Lambert let out a big breath.

"Tell me what happened."

I told him.

"So, let me get this straight," he said, in a slightly strained voice once I'd finished. "You and Tomassetti became best friends, he let you do the handover of the stolen information, and while you were doing that, you took one of their people's wallets?"

"With a little help from some friends, but yes, that about sums it up."

Lambert stared at Nat Spikesly's picture for a while.

"You know what this means?"

"Well I assume it means they're CIA and they're stealing secrets on behalf of their Government. I also know that what they're stealing are the details of some sort of nerve agent that we're developing. Even though, according to the Chemical Weapons Convention of, let me see now, 1993, that's illegal."

I'd done a bit of research on the whole nerve agent thing the night before. I was feeling quite pleased with myself.

Lambert raised his eyebrows.

"What else do you know?"

"Well, through the judicious use of Google and Wikileaks I know that a Dutch scientist was reported to have developed some super new strain of nerve agent, something more powerful, more toxic, and more scary than has ever existed before. Something that would make sarin look like eau de cologne. Unfortunately that Dutch scientist disappeared. There are quite a lot of theories being put around about what might have happened to him, and there are a lot of people very keen on finding out. It did occur to me that perhaps this whole caper might have something to do with that."

The expression on Lambert's face made me feel very smug. I'd really hit a nerve.

He ran a hand through his hair. He wasn't the same happy soul that he'd been on our previous meetings.

"I can't believe it," he said.

"Can't believe what? It's definitely the Americans."

"No, it is the Americans, you're right. What I find hard to believe is that you managed to find that out."

"You seem surprised."

"Well, I'll be honest with you, Mr Jones, I am surprised. Very surprised. Your carefully researched theory is entirely correct I'm afraid to say. There was a Dutch Scientist and he had developed a new super nerve agent, as you call it. Well, we now have that scientist and, therefore, we now have the capability to manufacture this new strain of his. Which, in actual fact, is exactly what we are doing. You see, in this country we have cut back on our defence budget so much over the years that we really don't have a valid nuclear deterrent or much of a military capability of any sort any more. So we're producing the gas instead."

"But it's illegal. Everybody signed that treaty saying that they wouldn't make it or use it any more. That was years ago."

"Yes indeed, we did. And so did everybody else. But you can bet your life that everybody kept on manufacturing it. Just in case, as it were. Only now, ours is significantly better than everybody else's. Significantly better. Which is really quite a good position for us to be in."

"But all that horrifying stuff that went on in Syria. Everyone was outraged by it."

"Hypocrites, the lot of them. Politicians. Say one thing, do another."

"But it was shocking. The pictures of all those dead kids. Surely we can't really be thinking about using that stuff."

"Hopefully it will never come to that, but needs must I'm afraid."

"That's the most terrifying thing I've ever heard."

Then a thought hit me.

"But if we know how to make it, and we are making it, what's the stuff that the Americans are stealing. Their guy said we hadn't got it right yet. He said it would be better for everyone that we didn't."

"Ah, yes. Perhaps it would be more accurate to describe it as us letting the Americans steal it. And, as you say, what the Americans are stealing, are test results that show we haven't been successful yet. Which isn't true of course."

"You mean you're letting them have false information?"

"Exactly. Via the unwitting efforts of your Mr Darby."

"Good god. But why? I thought we were on the same side?"

"Yes. And we are. In a manner of speaking. But our relationship with the Americans is a strange one. They're very happy for us to have our "special relationship", but only if they're in charge. They have to be the one calling the shots, making the decisions, telling us what to do. They rather like it that we have to rely on them for our defence for instance. So, now that we've decided to take responsibility for our own welfare for once, it's become absolutely vital that they never find out. Hence the leaking of false information. This way everyone's happy."

All I could do was stare at him. I let everything he'd told me sink in.

"But," I said eventually, a realisation gradually dawning on me. "Why did you need me to find out who was behind it all if you were running the whole thing?"

Lambert pursed his lips.

"Ah," he said eventually. "Well, I suppose you do deserve the truth after all you've been through. The thing is, when we said we wanted you to find out what was going on, that wasn't entirely true. Your purpose for being there was to take the spotlight away from what we were doing. We inserted our agent into Tomassetti's gang to make sure that the exchange of information went smoothly, to ensure that the Americans didn't get wind of what was really happening. By putting you in as well, and you asking a lot of dumb questions, we hoped that Tomassetti and his gang would be so suspicious of you that whatever we got up to would go unnoticed."

"Why you bastard, that's...." Lambert put his hands up and cut across me.

"I know, I know, you're right to feel the way you do. It wasn't very sporting of us."

"Not very sporting?" I exploded. "Not very sporting? I should come round there and kick your bloody head in." In truth, my head and face were hurting so much that I didn't have the energy to get out of my chair, let alone go round and do him some damage. Nevertheless, it felt good to let off some steam and I let loose at him. I got a good deal of the pent-up anger inside me off my chest. I hadn't realised I'd known so many swear words or that I could use them so imaginatively. I wore myself out eventually, leaving him looking at me with a half surprised, half admiring look on his face.

"I think I deserved that," he said ruefully. "But look on the positive side of things. You did a remarkable job. You should be very proud of what you managed to achieve."

He glanced up at me.

"But achieved not entirely painlessly, by the look of it."

I gingerly put a finger up to my nose which was throbbing furiously after my rant. I'd taken a handful of painkillers when I'd woken up, but they were wearing off.

"But I still don't understand why you had to give me all that guff about Integrated Electronics and all that research and development malarkey," I said.

"Purely to lead you up the garden path, to confuse everything, hopefully get you asking some stupid questions that would throw the spotlight on you."

"Christ. You really are a lot of bastards. You sent me in there knowing that I'd probably never get out alive."

Lambert didn't say anything.

"You bastards."

He nodded.

"You're right to say that. We are. But this is a nasty business. Decisions are sometimes made because of the greater good, even if it means that innocent individuals might have to be sacrificed along the way. It's when you're sitting face to face with that individual that it doesn't always seem such a good idea."

It was as I was pondering the fact that just about everything that Lambert had ever told me had turned out to be a lie, another thought hit me.

"What about Paradine?" I asked.

"What about him?"

"Was it Tomassetti who had him killed?"

Lambert looked sheepish once more.

"Ah. No. Again, the Americans must take the blame there, I'm afraid. They picked up on the fact that the test sheets were being circulated and traced them back to Paradine. The rest was all their own work, nothing to do with Tomassetti. Think about it. Why would Tomassetti's thugs torture Paradine to death to find out his source without putting two and two together and realising that you had something to do with it? That would make no sense. The Americans had no idea you were involved of course. I must say though, you had a very loyal friend there, he never revealed it was you. And let me tell you he suffered."

I was silent for a while. I was feeling very stupid. And very guilty.

I just looked at Lambert. I had nothing left now, I was empty. All I wanted was to get out of this place and forget the whole thing had ever happened.

He asked me to wait for a moment and left the office. I thought about what he'd just told me. Jesus Christ they'd stitched me up good and proper. And when he said he was surprised, the biggest surprise for him was that I was still alive. The bastard.

After about ten minutes he came back in, carrying a small holdall.

"Our Lord and Master sends her apologies. She would have liked to give you this in person, but she's a bit tied up at the moment. She didn't think you would be too unduly upset at that."

I snorted. It hurt.

"But anyway, here's our side of the bargain."

With that, he hefted the holdall onto the desk and pushed it towards me.

"Five hundred thousand pounds in used notes. You can count it if you like."

I shook my head.

"That's okay," I said. "If I can't trust you, who can I trust?"

He had the good grace to look slightly embarrassed at that.

We shook hands as I left. It wasn't what I felt like doing to him.

"Thank you Mr Jones," Lambert said. "I'd like to say it was a pleasure working with you, but I don't suppose you'd believe me."

Outside, grateful to be free and feeling soiled and dirty, I caught a cab to Neasden. In the middle of a very non-descript, dull-looking terraced street, I knocked on the door of number twenty-nine. A non-descript, dull-looking woman answered the door. She looked like a shrew.

"Mrs Paradine?"

"Yes?"

"I was a friend of your husband."

"So?"

"I wanted to give you this."

I dropped the holdall at her feet and got back into the waiting cab. I hadn't even looked inside the bag, and as the cab drove off, I hoped that those faceless men in their grey suits hadn't screwed me over again.

✳✳✳

"Oh Jonesy, thank god you're safe, I was so worried. Oh my goodness, just look at the state of you, dear, are you okay?"

Mimi gave me an almighty bear hug. I looked down at the top of her hair net fondly.

"Make me a cup of tea, I said."

I sat in my little room cradling my mug of extra strong tea contemplating what had happened to me over the last few months. It had been extraordinary.

But no matter what I thought about, and how hard I tried not to, my mind kept going back to just one thing. You see, in our meeting earlier, Lambert had told me about the agent that they'd planted in Tomassetti's gang.

It wasn't Winslow after all. It was Carrot.

I knew I'd be seeing those staring, helpless eyes for the rest of my life.

Printed in Great Britain
by Amazon